CHASING THE DRAGON

CHASING THE DRAGON

MARK WIGHTMAN

This edition produced in Great Britain in 2023

by Hobeck Books Limited, 24 Brookside Business Park, Stone, Staffordshire
ST15 0RZ

www.hobeck.net

A CIP catalogue for this book is available from the British Library.

ISBN 978-1-915-817-17-4 (ebook)

ISBN 978-1-915-817-18-1 (pbk)

Cover design by Jem Butcher

www.jembutcherdesign.co.uk

Printed and bound in Great Britain by Clays Ltd, Elcograf S.p.A.

For Alma

perfunctory coroner's hearing, and move quickly on to more important things. Those would have been his orders. But a dead European would mean all hands on deck.

Betancourt wondered if he'd just made a pun, and decided that if he had, it wasn't a funny one.

'Give me half an hour.'

He returned to his room and felt about under the bed until he located the lost watch, a scuffed old Elgin, and fastened it to his wrist. When he was young – eleven or twelve, perhaps – his Aunt Theresa, the woman who'd raised him after his mother left him at her door, presented him with it. She'd kept it wrapped in a square of silk at the bottom of her jewellery box. It belonged to his father, she'd told him. It was the only thing that Julius, an itinerant jazz pianist and serial womaniser, left behind when he abandoned his young family, silently, in the middle of the night. Theresa considered it important that fathers passed things on to their sons. Betancourt thanked her, because she meant well, but he knew Julius left the watch behind by accident and not as part of any rite of passage. At school, the wearing of any timepiece, even a modest example like his, was a small badge of honour, but nowadays he wondered why he bothered with it, as the events that made up his life were too uncertain to permit fixed and accurate timekeeping. At least, that's what he told people when they asked why he was late again.

A voice came from down the hall.

'You swear too much.'

His daughter, Lucia, stood in the hallway, one hand pulling sleep-mussed hair from her eyes, the other stifling a yawn.

'I don't swear. And anyway, you shouldn't be listening.'

'Sister Mary Michael says swearing is the product of a limited vocabulary.'

Betancourt had met the Mother Superior of Lucia's school and he could imagine her saying that.

'Where are you going?' Lucia continued.

'Out. It's work. Someone has found a body.'

'Is it a murder?' Lucia's previously dimmed eyes brightened. 'Can I come?'

She'd recently taken an interest in American detective novels and had been pestering him to take her on a case.

'It's probably just an accident, and no, you can't come. Go back to bed.'

'Will Evelyn be there?' Lucia studied him, waiting for his reaction.

Evelyn was Dr Evelyn Trevose. It was six months since they'd worked together. Since they'd become close. And since he'd pushed her away. She'd taken a posting up country, and he'd tried to put her out of his mind. He realised, with a pang of regret, how much he missed her.

'What on earth makes you ask that? She's in Penang. You know that.'

'Oh, no reason.' A Delphic smile danced at the edges of his daughter's mouth as she retreated into her bedroom.

It was a little before seven o'clock when he arrived at Jardine Steps, and the sun was gaining the upper hand in the current round of its eternal battle with the darkness.

Though it was still early, he spotted activity out in the harbour. In the middle reaches, towards Pulau Bukom, amongst the patchwork of navy vessels that now decorated the Singapore Strait, an eager little tugboat pulled first one way and then the other as it strained to bring a great grey slug of a gunboat neatly alongside its sister ship. Barely a day went by without the newspapers reminding the good folk of Singapore that, even if the Japanese were to have the unthinkable temerity to attempt an invasion of Singapore (which, apparently, they wouldn't), the island fortress was unassailable, and there was nothing at all for anyone to worry about. They should all just carry on about their business, specifically that of enriching their colonial overlords. If there really was nothing to worry about, he wondered, why did a new ship arrive every week?

His wasn't to question why.

Beyond the ships, a bank of thunderclouds amassed over the South China Sea to the east. The threat of storms gave Betancourt the shivers, and he hurried along the quayside, eager to get the formalities over with.

A mob had gathered around the steps, like a wake of vultures around a stricken beast. There was no need for him to brandish his warrant card; enough of the crowd recognised him, and the mass parted, allowing him space to pass through.

The singular smell of durian filled the air, an aroma so pungent many of the better class hotels in the city barred their clientele from bringing it inside. Between the boats that buffeted the seaweed-covered steps below and the wharf above, a line of coolies had formed a human chain, expertly tossing the fruits from one to another. Though seemingly effortless to the inexperienced eye, their activity was carefully orchestrated, and the men took great care not to bruise the fruit. The season was short, and each fruit commanded a high price at the market. Any damage would lead to a severe tongue-lashing from the owner of the consignment, and if the damage was especially egregious – say a handler dropped a fruit into the sea and could not recover it – or if the owner happened to be in a particularly foul mood that day, the errant coolie might find himself on the wrong end of a stinging cuff around the ear.

The exorbitant price of the durian, coupled with the

desire of the sellers to be first to market, led to inevitable squabbles. Squabbles amongst the boatmen ferrying the durians from the lighters moored just offshore, all aiming to grab the best spot nearest the quay, and squabbles amongst the merchants, eager to claim first pick of the new crop, and so guarantee themselves a premium price at the stalls in the city. What he hadn't foreseen when he ordered Quek to stand guard against any trouble, was a fisherman turning up with a dead body in tow.

He found Quek leaning against the jetty wall, talking to Yung, the perpetually glum police photographer, who appeared, as usual, to be wishing he was anywhere but where his services were required.

Below them, a single *tongkang* yawed and pitched in the foaming surf. Unlike the other boats milling around the steps, this one was bereft of durians. Indeed, it seemed empty of anything, save for a fishing net bundled untidily into the rear of the craft. A Malay man, whipcord-thin and baked teak-brown by sea and salt, wrestled with the tiller, trying to keep the craft alongside the steps.

'That him?'

Quek nodded. 'Yes, boss.'

Betancourt leant over the seawall and shouted to make himself heard over the din of the durian sellers.

'Tie up.'

The man acknowledged the order with a wave of his hand, and Betancourt turned back to Quek. 'I need the body up here so I can have a look. Go down and give our friend a hand. And take a couple of this lot with you.'

He called to the two coolies standing nearest and told them to accompany Quek. They shrank back. The wharf coolies were a superstitious bunch, and this pair had seen enough to work out the contents of the net. Betancourt dropped his tone half an octave and gave the command again. This time, the voice of authority worked.

Quek descended the algae-covered steps gingerly until he reached the boat. Leaving the craft to the mercy of the waves for a moment, the fisherman coiled a rope and threw it. Quek caught the sodden sisal and, holding it at arm's length, wound it around a bollard.

Eventually, the coolies hauled the body, wrapped in its cotton cocoon, up the steps and onto the jetty, and Betancourt peered into the parcel. From what he could see, the man's skin was fair, if tanned, and even in its sodden state, his hair was no darker than a medium brown. Quek had warned him the body was that of a European, but he still cursed quietly under his breath.

He stooped and examined the net more carefully. Lifting the free end, he pulled, but it caught fast. He squinted under the body and saw that the net went all the way around.

'If this man had fallen into the sea and became caught in the net, how would you expect it to have looked?'

'Tangled up?' said Quek.

'Exactly. But this net is smooth.'

'What are you thinking?'

'I'm thinking he wasn't caught in the net: someone wrapped him in it. We'll let Yung take a few pictures, and then we'll have a better look.'

Rousing Yung from his gloomy reverie, he set the photographer to work capturing the situation for posterity. When Yung finished, Betancourt took the head and Quek the feet, and together they rolled the body until it lay uncovered on the stone surface of the quay.

Betancourt put a hand to his mouth and waited for the nausea to subside. The man's eyes were missing, as were his ears, his nose, and his lips, leaving his teeth exposed in a rictus grimace. Crabs. They always started with the soft bits. A pair of thousand-bird pattern trousers, fashionably cut, covered the man's legs. Lucky for him, Betancourt thought, or there might have been more of him missing than was already the case. But then again, the man was well past being able to thank his luck.

He took in the rest of the dead man's appearance. His stature was similar to his own – about five feet eight inches, and thin. Wiry thin, not scrawny – muscles taut and well defined. Even after being submerged in the sea for who knew how long, it was obvious he had been heavily tanned. Used to physical work, outside, in the tropical sun.

The man wore no wristwatch, nor any other ornamentation that might have given a clue to who he was, so Betancourt checked his pockets. He hated this bit. Even though he knew the dead were past caring what he did to them, it always felt like a violation. The front pockets offered up fifty-five cents in assorted coins; a handkerchief, now drenched but ironed and apparently unused when it was placed in the pocket; and a token – the sort used in gambling halls – comprising alternating red and yellow circles, with a black centre. Chinese characters, worn so smooth they were almost illegible, were engraved in the centrepiece.

He held up the token so Quek could see it.

Quek squinted. 'Lucky Seven.'

Betancourt nodded. The Lucky Seven gang dabbled in all the vices – prostitution, gambling, protection rackets, and opium – anything illegal that could turn a dollar. By itself, the token indicated nothing too sinister. The man could have picked it up anywhere. Or been given it. Or, of course, he could have acquired it in one of the many Lucky Seven gambling dens.

'Give me a hand.'

With Quek's help, he eased the body onto its side, and he felt in the back pockets. The first was empty, but the second yielded a slim brown leather wallet – one of the fold-over types with internal compartments and the owner's initials embossed in gilt in the corner: RHF. Betancourt examined the contents. From the outermost compartment, he withdrew a thin sheaf of sodden banknotes – thirty-odd dollars in total. He laid the notes down next to the coins and the gambling token and checked the rest of the wallet.

Finding nothing else of interest, he scooped up the man's belongings and handed them to Quek, giving him instructions to bag them and file them when he returned to the station.

Having dealt with the evidence, such as it was, he summoned the fisherman. The man shuffled over and stood before them, hands together in front of his body, an anxious look on his face, like a schoolboy expecting a reprimand from the headmaster. Like many of his sort, the man had a natural desire to avoid the police. No good ever came of an encounter with the authorities for him and his kind.

'How did you come to find him?' Betancourt asked.

'The net caught on the leg of my *kelong*.' The man glanced down at the body and gave a small shiver. Betancourt supposed men like him must deal with the effects of nature all the time, and yet the sight of the disfigured body disturbed him. 'He probably got drunk and fell overboard and got caught up in the net. You know what they're like.' He gave an impression of someone pouring liquid down their throat. Apparently, all Europeans spent their lives in a state of inebriation.

'Fell overboard from where? Did you see a boat?'

The fisherman shook his head. 'No. But where else would he have come from?'

'Where else, indeed,' said Betancourt, half to himself. 'Tell me what happened.'

The man explained how he'd gone to answer a call of nature and discovered the net-bound body staring up at him.

It hadn't been there the previous evening when he'd used the long drop before retiring. He would have noticed. It must have been drifting and became snarled on the *kelong* during the night.

'What time do you go to sleep?'

'Ten o'clock. I need to wake early, so I never stay up late. Besides, what is there to do on a *kelong* at night, other than burn kerosene? The lamps attract the insects and who needs that?'

Betancourt nodded at the logic of this. 'Did you hear anything during the night?'

'Nothing. It's like a graveyard out there.'

'And you found him at what time?'

'Around four o'clock.'

'This morning?'

The man nodded.

'All right. One more thing. Where is your *kelong*?'

The man pointed along the coast, towards the east. 'Pasir Panjang.' He waited for a response, and when none was forthcoming, he asked, 'Can I go now? I have work to do.'

It would have been easy for the man to have cut the net loose from his *kelong* and left nature to dispose of the body as she saw fit, but he'd done the decent thing and brought it in. And he'd asked for the police when he arrived at the wharf. It was more than many of his fellows would have done. Betancourt shook his hand and thanked him for his civic mindedness.

'Give the sergeant here your details, and then you can go.'

By this time, the wagon had arrived, and two porters waited patiently, stretcher at the ready. Betancourt gave them the signal, and they removed the body. After they'd gone, he briefly considered calling the Crypt, as the police morgue was known colloquially, to let them know there was a body on the way, but decided instead it would be good experience for Quek.

'Tell whoever is on duty I need the post-mortem results as soon as possible. When they see the colour of his skin, they'll understand why. And make sure Yung brings the photos to the station today.'

He was about to remind Quek to call the fingerprint bureau and have them send someone round to the morgue when he noticed the state of what remained of the man's fingers. He'd need to find another way of putting a name to the body.

Quek's face was a picture of concentration, tongue edging out of the corner of his mouth, pencil flying across the page of his notebook, as he transcribed his instructions.

'On it, boss.'

On it? Quek, too, must have taken up American detective novels.

Having breakfasted at a *roti paratha* stall on Market Street, Betancourt arrived back at the Marine Police offices on Empress Place at the same time as a dishevelled-looking Quek. He waited on the steps until the young sergeant caught up, and then immediately took a step backwards, clamping an involuntary hand to his nose.

'What happened to you? That smell would bring down an elephant.'

Quek explained that the trouble Betancourt had warned him to watch for had come later in the morning. After accompanying the body to the Crypt, he returned to the jetty where he found two wholesalers engaged in an argument over a patch of ground both considered to be lucky, and which both insisted they'd occupied every year since they started in the

13

durian trade. The heated discussion might have resolved itself without further rancour had one man not cast aspersions on the moral character of the other man's wife, leading to an exchange of blows. Quek, eager to bring the hostilities to a swift close, attempted to separate the men by stepping between them and, for his trouble, found himself lifted off his feet and deposited onto a pile of discarded durian husks.

He sniffed at the sleeve of his uniform. 'It stinks. I'm going to smell for a week.'

Betancourt didn't disagree. 'Get yourself along to the carpool. Ask them to hose you down. You're not coming into the station like that. When you smell better, find Constable Aroozoo. I want the pair of you to work your way around the ship's chandlers. See if anyone has recently purchased a net like the one the body was wrapped in.'

'How recently?'

'Stick to the last month for now and see how you get on.'

Quek trotted off to get himself deodorised, but Betancourt called him back.

'How did you get on at the Crypt?'

'I said you wanted it treated as a priority.'

'And? What did they say?'

'She said, "Oh, he does, does he?" But then she said she would have the results later today.'

She? The last Betancourt had heard, the acting Police Surgeon was a Scot from Malacca named McKiltie, who was rumoured to be more dedicated to the drinking of whisky and the smiting of golf balls than he was to attending to dead bodies.

A broad smile broke out across Quek's face, as though he'd remembered something pleasing. 'I forgot. Good news.' His smile beamed ever brighter. 'Your lady doctor is back.' Having dropped his bombshell, he turned on his heel.

'Wait! You saw Evelyn? I mean, Dr Trevose?'

Quek nodded over his shoulder, increasingly pleased with himself.

'What did she say?'

'She said I was very smelly.'

'Apart from the obvious. Did she say anything else?'

'She said to say hello.'

'Is that it?' Betancourt was hunting for something personal, and right then, he didn't particularly care if Quek knew.

'No time. Got to go. Very smelly.' Quek ran off down the steps, still grinning.

'And I've told you before: she's not *my* lady doctor,' Betancourt called after the disappearing figure, knowing it was futile.

He unlocked the door of his small office overlooking the river. Evelyn? Back in Singapore? The news had tilted his world on its axis. He'd known that the previous Police Surgeon, Hugo Gemmill, had moved upstairs to take up a position as the new coroner – he'd even attended his leaving do and contributed to the customary decanter the department bought for him as a gift – but he hadn't been near the Crypt since the Sleeping Tigers case.

A recollection of an inter-departmental missive stirred in the outermost recesses of his memory. Where had he put it?

The piles of paper obscuring the surface of the old table that served as his desk never seemed to shrink, mostly because he rarely touched them, and as he pushed them away to create a bit of space, the documents reminded him of his prolonged lack of activity by releasing a swirling cloud of dust.

When he'd stopped coughing, he sifted through the papers until he found what he was looking for. It was a memo announcing Gemmill's promotion.

Gemmill's job as Police Surgeon had always seemed to

Betancourt to interfere with his principal interests: attending to his private practice, ministering to the great and the good of the island, and playing an active part in its social activities. So, when the death of a person who wasn't part of that exalted circle required medical investigation, he passed the task off to his assistant, McKiltie. When McKiltie found himself with a prior engagement on the first tee at the Island Club, a locum, usually Evelyn, picked up the slack. After Gemmill moved upstairs to the Coroner's Office, McKiltie took up a less arduous posting in the sleepy beachside town of Port Dickson, in the Federated Malay State of Negeri Sembilan, where hardly anyone died under suspicious circumstances, leaving the post of Police Surgeon to be filled with a succession of substitutes.

He read on. There was an addendum to the news about Gemmill.

New Police Surgeon... Assistant Commissioner Bonham is delighted to announce... Permanent appointment...

Permanent? There it was, in black and white: Dr Evelyn Trevose was the new Police Surgeon.

He recalled Lucia's knowing smile when she'd mentioned Evelyn's name earlier that morning. She must have known somehow. And then Quek. Was he the last person in town to hear about everything? It might be an idea to read his post occasionally, he ruefully admitted to himself.

Chapter Three

Home was a flat above a *kopi tiam* on Duxton Hill, in Chinatown. Betancourt had leased the space when his finances were precarious, and when Mr Tan, the owner, was attracting the wrong sort of attention from members of the local chapter of the Lucky Seven triad. The gang members were doing their best to convince the shopkeeper he should pay them an insurance premium, to ensure nothing untoward happened to his business or, heaven forbid, his family. Tan was quick to spot that having a police inspector as a tenant would provide a welcome deterrent and leased the space to Betancourt at a fraction of the going rate. The gang never saw the need to trouble him again.

Later, after Betancourt's part in the now infamous Victory Parade betting coup, which banished his money woes forever, he convinced Tan to sell him the flat. Tan agreed on one condition: that Betancourt carried on living there. The deal was done, and Betancourt hired a carpenter to refurbish the place. His parents-in-law, the Cléments, had wanted to buy him and Lucia a house near them, so their granddaughter would be closer. He'd thanked them, grateful for the healing of the rift between them that followed Anna's disappearance, but said he preferred his independence. When Lucia decided that as her *very best friends* (as distinct from the vast throng of girls who deserved only the simpler appellation of *best friends*) were all weekly boarders at St Seraphima's School, it would suit her to board, too, the decision was made. Betancourt had the carpenter convert a boxroom Tan had once used to store provisions into a bedroom, so Lucia had her own space. She shared her weekends between him and her grandparents, and the arrangements, now they'd all settled into them, seemed to suit everyone.

He'd taken out the old rattan furniture he'd purchased as a job lot at a house clearance sale when he'd first moved in and burned it, replacing it with what he hoped were more modern, substantial, and permanent items. When the carpenter finished with the flat, he brought out of storage the pictures, mirrors, ornaments, crockery and cutlery, glassware, and all the other domestic impedimenta with which Anna had created their home in the police quarters in Pearl's Hill, during the early days of their marriage.

Of the items of furniture that he'd chosen himself, the one that gave him the most satisfaction was a carved rosewood Malacca bookcase, which reached almost to the ceiling. Enough room, though only just, to house the collection of books he'd inherited from Stanley, his Aunt Theresa's elder brother, the nearest thing he'd had to a proper father. It was Stanley who, as well as showing him the power of books when he'd felt his time would have been better spent playing with his friends on a construction site or going to the cinema, had introduced him to horse racing, and he was profoundly grateful for both those introductions.

He looked around. It wasn't a bad facsimile of the home Anna had created, and for that he was happy.

On the credenza, leaning against the telephone that

Bonham insisted he install and keep switched on, and which had so rudely awakened him earlier that morning, was a neatly stacked pile of letters. He checked that none of the missives bore red stamps and returned them to the sideboard without opening them, safe in the knowledge they'd keep for another day. That the letters were here and not stacked behind Mr Tan's till downstairs meant that Mr Tan's wife had been in to clean. He'd told her there was no need, that he could manage himself, but she wouldn't hear of it. She had, she said, seen the results of a man claiming he could keep a place habitable. Her expression made it clear she'd found the results disappointing. He'd offered to pay her, but she'd refused, so each month he made a donation to a nearby orphanage in her name, and when she found out about it, she beamed with pride.

He hadn't eaten since early that morning, and he was ravenous. Another benefit of his tenancy was a regular supply of freshly made hot food from the *kopi tiam* below. He unwrapped the waxed brown paper package Mr Tan had pressed into his hand when he'd arrived home. Hokien *mee*: thick yellow Hokien egg noodles, marinated pork belly, white fish balls, and pieces of sliced cabbage, slathered in oyster sauce and sesame oil. He devoured the lot.

After he'd finished eating, he went to the bookcase. His fingers trailed along the spines before stopping at *The Call of the Wild*. He hadn't picked it up for a while, and it was overdue another read. He settled in front of the open verandah, the winking neon advertising signs from the bar across the road casting a kaleidoscope of polychromatic shadows on his living room wall. He read a few pages of Jack London, but his mind kept wandering back to the image of the man in the net.

· · ·

He was about to abandon the book altogether when the telephone bell, always unwelcome, interrupted his thoughts.

'Betancourt.'

'Hello, stranger.'

The breath caught in his throat. Since he'd heard from Quek that Evelyn was back in town, he'd been both dreading this encounter and relishing it. They'd met during the Sleeping Tigers investigation. It was Betancourt's first proper case with the Marine Branch. The body of a young woman named Akiko Sakai had been found on the dockside. Evelyn did the autopsy and showed how the young woman hadn't committed suicide, as everyone else involved, Betancourt's superiors included, wished the world to believe, and had, in fact, been murdered. Later, she helped him find some justice for Akiko. During the investigation, they became close – too close, he thought at the time – and he pushed her away. And now it was too late. He'd heard through the grapevine she'd accompanied her suitor, Alistair Grey – his surname matching perfectly his personality, in Betancourt's estimation – to Georgetown on the island of Penang, where she was, according to the popular view, happy and settled.

'You're supposed to be in Penang.'

'I was in Penang. And now I'm back. I'm the new Police Surgeon. Don't you ever read your memos?'

'Not if I can avoid it. I file everything bearing an official letterhead in the wastebasket.'

There was a pause in the conversation. Instinct told him the next move was his.

'Congratulations on the promotion.'

'Technically, it wasn't a promotion. I was only a stand-in for Gemmill before; I didn't actually work for the government. Now I do. But thank you anyway. Had you really not heard?'

'Quek said he'd spoken to you. Then I read the memo.'

'Ah,' she said, and he'd no idea what *ah* meant. 'Well, if

you insist on finding dead bodies around the docks, we're going to be seeing more of each other.'

'I'd like that.' Then, realising she might take his response as meaning he considered more deaths as something he'd look forward to, he added hurriedly, 'Not the dead bodies, I mean...'

She laughed. He'd missed that laugh.

'What about the Hospital?' he asked. Evelyn ran a free clinic serving the women and girls who worked in the *Suteretsu* – the Japanese red-light district surrounding Bugis Street. The women who availed themselves of its services referred to it as the Hospital. It was an in-joke: they could tell those to whom they were indentured that the doctor said they had to go to hospital, thus gaining a respite from their quota of servicing nine or ten men a night.

'It's fine. Martha kept things ticking along while I was up country.' Martha was Evelyn's nurse and general factotum. 'I'm enjoying being back, though. There's something very satisfying about the work.'

There was silence. He wasn't sure if she expected him to say something in response. She took the decision out of his hands.

'How's Lucia?'

'She's good.' He explained about his new domestic arrangements: how Lucia had joined the world of the weekly boarders, how she stayed with him at weekends in the apartment in Duxton Lane and how it seemed to suit them both. 'I bought the place. Did you know that?'

'I remember you saying your father-in-law offered to buy somewhere close to them, but that's the last I heard.'

He wondered if there was a hint of accusation in her tone, as if he'd disappointed her by not getting in touch to update her on his domestic arrangements.

'It's funny,' he said.

'What is?'

'When I was leaving to attend to the body this morning, Lucia asked me if I'd be seeing you. Odd, don't you think? I didn't even know you were in town at that point.'

Evelyn had cared for Lucia during the Akiko case, and Lucia had told him how much she enjoyed her time helping in the clinic in Holloway Lane. But that morning was the first time in a while she'd mentioned Evelyn's name.

'Ah.' There it was again. Apparently, *ah* served a multitude of uses in the right hands.

'Ah what?'

'Lucia and I may have stayed more closely in touch than you and I have.'

'You've been writing to each other?'

'And maybe the odd telephone call.'

'So, all this time, she knew you were in town, and I had to find out from Quek.'

Evelyn laughed. 'She's a lovely girl. You're very lucky.'

He wasn't sure how to proceed. Or if he should.

'If you're free any time…'

'Yes?'

'If you'd like to, you could come round and see her. I know she'd like that.'

'I would like that very much.' She sounded almost grateful, as if an invitation was overdue. He was confused. She'd gone to Penang to join Alistair Grey. How could he have invited her before? Not for the first time, Betancourt reflected on how, no matter how much effort he put into the exercise, he just didn't understand women.

'I'm sorry for calling you at home,' she continued, 'but I thought you'd want to hear this. It's about your dead body — the one Sergeant Quek brought in. Have you identified him yet?'

'Not yet. I'll try Missing Persons in the morning.'

'I'm afraid there isn't much I can do to help you. No fingerprints and precious little else.'

'I take it he drowned?'

'Hmm… That's why I'm calling. There was water in his lungs, but there's more to it.'

'What do you mean?'

'He'd been in the water quite a while – well, you'd know, you saw him when you fished him out – but I believe he may have been dead before he went in. I examined the contents of his stomach and I found two balls of opium. Big ones. About three ounces worth, by the time I weighed them. And that's having had twenty-four hours for him to digest them.'

'Is that how long he was in the water?'

'Since he died. At least. Could be as much as forty-eight. Exactly how long he was in the water for is hard to gauge.'

Betancourt made a note on the back of one of the envelopes.

'Suicide, do you think?' He was sceptical. Swallowing opium was a popular way of committing suicide in the poor areas of the town: Chinatown, and the red-light districts of the *Suteretsu*, but Europeans, especially European men, were more likely to opt for a pistol to the head.

There was a pause before she answered. 'I can't rule it out, not completely, but I found abrasions on the back of his throat that would be consistent with someone having forced the opium down his throat using some sort of instrument.'

'What sort of instrument?'

'Who knows?' He heard the shrug in her voice. 'A pair of long-handled forceps? Something like that.'

'Like the ones a doctor would use?'

'Well, yes, but they're not exactly difficult to get hold of. There's something else odd. This was poor quality opium, not the government-issue stuff. Even if he decided to use opium to end it all, he'd surely have laid his hands on the real McCoy.'

Betancourt grunted. Since the colonial government monopolised the production and distribution of opium in 1930, it had used only Bengal's finest product in the manufacturing process. Bengali opium was purer and had the quickest and strongest effect. It also produced the most revenue.

'Have you sent it off for analysis?'

'Of course.' She sounded vaguely offended. 'I'll wait and see what the lab comes back with, but I've seen enough opium in enough stomachs to know the difference. The drug this poor chap swallowed was rough – full of adulterants. I'd bet it was smuggled in. I'm seeing more and more of it these days.'

Betancourt rubbed his eyes with his free hand, trying to make sense of everything Evelyn had said.

'Would it have been enough to kill him?'

'It depends on how pure it was, and how potent, but I'd say yes. And if it wasn't enough to kill him, it certainly would have been enough to knock him out cold for a good few hours.'

Betancourt thought for a moment.

'When we found the body this morning, it was wrapped in a net. And I mean wrapped, not entangled. What if the man was force-fed the opium, wrapped in the net, and dumped in the sea? Would that work with what you've found?'

'Yes, it would. If he was in a deep stupor, his breathing would have been shallow. The water he inhaled would have been enough to drown him. Is that what you think? That he was murdered?' He thought he detected a vein of excitement in her voice.

'It's looking that way.' He paused for a moment. Something she'd said wriggled out of his subconscious. 'You said you'd seen a few deaths due to adulterated opium?'

'More than a few. I reckon there must have been about a dozen since I came back. More than I'd seen in the entire time before I left.'

So, no coincidence then. 'Could you let me have a list of the names of the other deaths?'

'It might take a day or two, but I'll get it for you. Sorry I can't give you more on our mystery man.' She sounded genuinely apologetic. 'I'll send you a copy of the post-mortem report as soon as I've typed it up. When you have a name for our man, could you let me know, so I can arrange the official identification?'

He said he would and thanked her. He was about to ring off when she spoke.

'Max? It really is good to hear your voice again.'

She hung up before he had the chance to respond that it was good to hear hers. Very good.

Thunder rumbled, and through the window he saw clouds like black balls of cotton amassing in the night sky. The beginnings of a headache pulsed across his forehead, and he rubbed his temples as he considered his next move. As if it wasn't enough that the dead man was a European, it now looked as though he'd been murdered.

He picked up his book again and tried to read, but he soon felt his eyelids sinking, and before his hands relinquished their hold and sent Jack London and his dog, Buck, crashing to the floor, he was sound asleep.

Chapter Four

F rom the outside, the Crypt was an unassuming place. To the uninitiated, it looked for all the world like some sort of storeroom, the contents of which had been protected from prying eyes and thieving hands by a pair of wooden doors. Leading to these was a short colonnade forming a portico, which itinerant river-dwellers used by day as shade from the sun, and by night as a place to sleep, sheltered from the monsoon rain.

When he arrived, Betancourt found his entry blocked by an old coolie sitting on the ground with his back to the stout teak portals, sucking his teeth and watching the world pass. Seeing the policeman, the old man shuffled to one side, bowing his head slightly, allowing Betancourt entrance.

Closing the door behind him, he was, for once, relieved to enter, if only for the coolth of the cavernous tunnel that connected the world of the living with the netherworld of the police mortuary below.

He knocked at the door of the post-mortem room and entered without waiting to be admitted. It never failed to surprise him that, although ample electric lighting illuminated the room, it had to for Evelyn to perform the procedures she did – the tableau before him seemed bathed in an unsettling gloom.

Nothing had changed since his last visit, several months previously. Martha, the stout Indian woman who was Evelyn's nurse, was collecting instruments, dropping them into a kidney dish ready for cleaning while, in the centre of the room, Evelyn, her copper hair now tied back in a loose knot, and with wire-rimmed spectacles perched on the end of her aquiline nose, applied the finishing touches to the final examination of some poor soul.

He stood and watched her for a few moments, and she regarded him quizzically, almost with an air of amusement, he thought. He wondered if she would give him some sort of sign that she was pleased to see him, but he was disappointed.

'Inspector,' was all she said.

'Doctor. I was wondering if you found anything else on my drowned man? Other than the opium.'

'Just the clothes he was wearing.' Evelyn called to Martha, who left the room briefly before returning carrying a galvanised steel pail, which she placed on the floor, half-hidden in the semi-gloom beneath the steel bench. He peered in.

'Do you have a pair of gloves I could use?'

'In the cupboard.'

He strained to pull a cotton glove over his entire hand. He'd never thought of himself as having large hands before now, but whoever had purchased the gloves had intended them for hands more delicate than his.

'And something to…' He pointed at the pail.

Evelyn exhaled audibly. It was a sigh of mild annoyance. The sort of sigh he could imagine her using tending to a demanding child, when she had better things to be doing.

'Here.'

She handed him a pair of long-handled forceps and he picked through the contents of the pail. Brown checked trousers, the pockets of which he'd searched the previous morning, white cotton shirt, underwear. The clothes smelled of the harbour: seaweed and sewage and sulphurous gas.

He picked up the trousers and rolled the waistband over, so the inside faced out. A red-lettered label described the name and address of the tailor who had made the garment.

Sam Fong
No 1 Exclusive Tailoring
"Tailor to the Stars"
176 Katong Road

Tailor to the Stars? Sam had gone up in the world, even if it was only in his own estimation. Sam was popular with expatriates and had catered to the sartorial needs of the Clément family for years. Whenever Anna had felt he needed new clothing, she dragged him to Sam's shop to be measured and prodded and pinned. Sam was an enthusiastic, if not very capable punter, and Betancourt occasionally passed him a tip for the races.

'Can I take these?' He held up the trousers.

'Not yet,' Evelyn replied. 'I've not finished my report.'

'A sample, then?'

'As long as it's only a small one.'

He held out his hand. 'Pass me a pair of scissors, would you?'

'These are surgical scissors. If you want to perform surgery on a pair of trousers, I suggest you find a tailor to do it for you.'

He continued to hold out his hand, palm flat, until she placed a pair of scissors into his hand, with more force than was strictly warranted, he thought. It stung, but he said nothing.

Holding the waistband of the trousers with the forceps, he

snipped around the label until it was free, and placed it in his jacket pocket. Then, for good measure, he cut a square of fabric from the trousers and placed that, too, into his pocket.

He handed the instruments to Martha to be autoclaved, and then peeled off the gloves and dropped them into the basket reserved for the purpose.

Evelyn ceased her needlework. 'What do you propose to do with that?'

'I'm going to do as you suggest and find myself a tailor.'

She shook her head, good naturedly, and once again he had the inescapable feeling that he was a child being tolerated by a grown-up.

The drone of aircraft arriving at and departing the nearby Kallang Airport filtered through the steel of his helmet as he steered Alex onto Mountbatten Road. Alex was a 1926 Scott Flying Squirrel motorcycle, his most prized possession. He'd confiscated her from an antiquities smuggler who had tried to bring her in with a load of illegally exported Egyptian arte-facts. After he purchased her from the police pound, he restored her, and then restored her again following a crash during the investigation into Akiko Sakai's death.

He pulled up outside Sam's shop. He hadn't visited the self-styled 'tailor to the stars' since Anna's disappearance and hadn't expected to be seeing him again under the current circumstances.

Whenever Sam took an order for a new suit from one of his clients, he'd snip a piece of the chosen pattern and pin it into his order book, alongside the client's measurements. As Betancourt's first task was to identify the dead man, the tailor's shop seemed as good a place as any to start.

Sam had installed air conditioning since his last visit and

Betancourt stood for a moment, enjoying the respite from the morning sun.

In the corner, an old man sat cross-legged on the floor, his mouth full of pins. He was pulling long tacking threads from what looked like the makings of a pair of trousers. Acknowledging Betancourt's entrance, the man rocked forward and grinned, and when he did so he looked for all the world like a porcupine.

'Sam in?' Betancourt asked.

As if he'd been standing in the wings, awaiting his cue, Sam emerged from the rear of the shop.

'Inspector. Long time.' He shook Betancourt's hand warmly. 'I heard the news about *mem* Anna. I'm sorry.' The tailor really was sorry, and not just for the loss of business. His eyes confirmed his sincerity. Betancourt had learned to tell the difference.

Social necessities completed, Sam stood back and appraised his erstwhile client. He clicked his tongue and shook his head, apparently not liking what he saw.

'*Aiyah*. Is that one of mine?' A look of disbelief clouded Sam's face, as though he was willing Betancourt to answer in the negative.

'Yes. Why?'

'What have you done to it?'

Betancourt looked down and examined himself again. He was a policeman. His suits – well, strictly speaking, his suit, given the one he was wearing was the only one that was serviceable any more – saw a bit of action now and again. It went with the territory. 'It just needs a bit of a clean.' He brushed at a patch of red laterite dust but only succeeded in rubbing it in further.

'Never mind that.' Betancourt withdrew the still-damp square of cloth he'd removed from the dead man's garment at the Crypt. 'You made a pair of trousers.'

'I make lots of trousers.' Sam took the cutting and examined it. 'Why is it wet?'

'Don't ask. Can you tell from the material who you made the trousers for?'

'Maybe.' Sam passed the scrap of material to the cross-legged man on the floor and fired a staccato request in a dialect that was beyond Betancourt's limited ken. The old man held the swatch up close to his eyes and made a pronouncement.

'He says it was an American. About a month ago.'

'An American? He can tell that just by looking at it?'

'He never forgets. He's my uncle on my mother's side. They're all like that.'

The old man said something else and pointed to the top of a teetering stack of bales of material on the far side of the shop. Sam mounted a ladder and pulled out a skein of cloth. He held Betancourt's fragment against the skein. 'Same. See?'

Betancourt nodded. 'And you're sure no one else ordered anything using this material?'

Sam barked another question at his uncle 'No one. He's sure, too.'

'All right. Would this American have a name?'

'I need to check my order book. Wait a minute.' Sam disappeared into the back of the shop. When he returned, he carried a large journal filled with pages of orders. As Betancourt had remembered, Sam had pinned snippets of the material from which the order was to be made onto each page. He matched Betancourt's sample with the one on the page. They were the same material. Sam read from the order.

'Dr Fulbright. Yes, American. I remember him now.'

'How did he spell his name?' Betancourt squinted across at the order and made a note. The man had given his address as Mount Emily Road, and he noted that, too.

He knew the street. It wasn't far from Kandang Kerbau,

the maternity hospital where Lucia was born. Hers was a difficult birth, and the hospital staff kept Anna in while she recovered. He had passed Mount Emily on his nightly visits to the hospital.

Sam disturbed his reverie. 'What's all this about?'

'A man wearing these trousers you made was found dead yesterday.'

'Drowned?'

'What makes you say that?'

Sam pointed to Betancourt's swatch. 'It's wet.'

Betancourt pocketed the sample, feeling a little foolish. 'Maybe. We'll see. Thanks for the information.' He turned to go.

Sam called after him. 'Wait. Let me measure you up. You can't go around looking like that. It's bad for my business. I'll give you a good price. Old customer.'

Betancourt waved over his shoulder. 'Maybe next time, Sam.'

Betancourt knew he should alert Bonham before the jungle drums started beating and the Assistant Commissioner heard about it for himself. But before he did, he wanted to at least confirm the man's identity, to show he was making progress in resolving how he died. Armed with a name, and with fingerprints out of the question, his next stop was the Missing Persons Bureau on Hill Street.

A round-faced, red-cheeked constable of twenty-one or two greeted him.

'Morning. Lost someone, have we?' The man's countenance appeared cheerier than this job merited.

Betancourt identified himself. 'I'm looking for reports of a missing man. Possibly American. Possibly named Fulbright.'

'When are we talking about?'

'In the last week or two.'

The constable screwed up his face as he considered the request, as though the very act of thinking was a painful process.

'Don't remember nothing. Hang on, let me have a shufty.'

He lifted the covers of several large leather-bound ledgers, closing each one in turn with a forlorn sigh. He continued to search until, eventually, he gave a long, slow shake of his pudding-shaped head.

'A Yank, you say? Fraid not. Plenty of their lot, but none of ours.' By *their lot*, he meant Asians. As a *Serani* – a Eurasian – Betancourt was unsure which pot he'd fall into. Nor did he care. 'If you want to leave your name, I'll let the sergeant know. He might have heard something.'

He gave the constable his details and told him someone was to call him the minute any report came in.

Leaving the building, he turned up Hill Street, towards the river. Thinking about the exchange, he shook his head, as much in resignation at the young policeman's incompetence as in annoyance. If this was what it was like when a European went missing, God knows what it was like for the local people, who disappeared in their dozens every week. Murders. Suicides. Debtors absconding from their creditors. People who'd just had enough of it all and taken themselves off somewhere to wait for death to take them away. None of them were as high on the list of priorities as a missing *mat salleh*, and even one of those didn't seem to arouse much interest.

Back at the station, Betancourt asked Djulkifli, the duty sergeant, if there had been any sightings of Quek that morning. Djulkifli replied in the negative and made a note and underlined it when Betancourt told him he wanted to see Quek as soon as he arrived.

Standing at the window of his small office, Betancourt looked out at the lattice of criss-crossing bumboats as they plied their trade along the river. He was debating again whether to alert Bonham about the dead man before he'd confirmed Sam's identification when the phone rang. A crackle on the line was followed by the sound of the operator completing her part of the transaction.

'Putting you through now.'

'Is that...' There was a pause. The voice seemed to need to check who it was he'd just called. '... Betting-cot? Sergeant Hobbes here from Missing Persons.'

It was a different voice from the one he'd spoken with earlier at Hill Street – older, gruffer, and a good deal less respectful. The man had used a common mispronunciation. There was no reason he should expect Hobbes to know how to pronounce his name, but the man's insolence annoyed him, so he gave the man the correct pronunciation, slowly, and stressed that his rank was inspector. Not that he expected it to make much difference; Hobbes sounded like the type who wouldn't be much impressed by anything. Betancourt had known a lot of men of like Hobbes. Men for whom race trumped rank every time.

'I beg your pardon, I'm sure, *Inspector*.' Hobbes's voice oozed disrespect. 'My constable tells me you were in looking for a missing gentleman.'

Betancourt confirmed that the constable was correct.

'Well, as it happens, I took a call last week. Some woman phoned in saying her bloke had scarpered. A Yank, she said he was. The pair of them probably had a barney, and the Yank decided he'd had enough. Took himself off to find a billet somewhere else, I shouldn't wonder. I told her we'd look into it, but we don't get involved in domestic arguments, so I forgot about it.'

'Are you saying you didn't record the report?'

'We've got a lot on here, you know. We can't be expected to find every boyfriend who gets fed up with having his ear nipped by his missus.'

Betancourt gave a silent prayer, calling on some unnamed deity to protect him from idiots.

'I suppose you were too busy to ask for any names?'

The man sounded decidedly peevish now. 'The boyfriend's name was Fullerton or Fulton. Something like that.'

'Fulbright?'

'Might have been. Yes, now I think about it, Fulbright sounds about right.'

'And the name of the woman?'

'Can't say I remember.'

Can't remember or didn't ask.

'Speaking of names, Sergeant, what did you say yours was again? Hobbes, was it? And who do you report to?'

He wouldn't report the man. There was no point. Nothing would be done about his incompetence. But there was no harm in letting the fool stew for a few days.

He hung up. So, it seemed the only European reported missing in the last week might be an American named Fulbright. Or Fullerton, or Fulton, or something like that, if Hobbes was to be believed. With Sam's identification of the material taken from the dead man's trousers, it felt like progress.

He summoned the operator and asked her to put him through to Immigration. An adenoidal voice identified itself as belonging to a man named Purvis. Betancourt had dealt with Purvis before and knew how to get him to cooperate. He adopted his clubbiest voice and launched into it.

'Looking for a bit of info. Fellow named Fulbright. Might be Fulton or Fullerton – line was a bit muffled. Thought you'd be able to help. I know how you Immigration chaps always have your finger on the pulse. If anyone can track him down, it will be Purvis, I thought to myself.'

'We do our best.' Betancourt could almost hear the man preening. 'Let's have a look, shall we? Fulbright, you say?'

'Might be Fulton.'

'Right, Fulbright or Fulton.'

'Or Fullerton.'

The line went silent, and only the hum of a distant background let Betancourt know they were still connected.

Purvis picked up the receiver again. The sound of cards being flicked through echoed down the line. 'Fun... Fum... Here we are: Ful.' Apparently, his card system worked in reverse. 'We've got three Fullers, two Fullertons, four Fultons, a Fulwell, a Fulwick, and a Fullybeloved.' The immigration man chuckled. 'Fullybeloved. What kind of name is that? Engineer... Ship's engineer... Engineer... Doctor... Civil engineer... How many bloody engineers does Singapore need?'

Perhaps his Aunt Theresa had been right after all. She'd wanted him to become an engineer and work for the Public Works Department. 'A respectable job,' she used to say. She never actually said she considered that being a policeman was unrespectable: she was silent on the subject.

Something on his desk caught Betancourt's eye. It was the corner of the wallet he'd taken from the man's pocket, poking out from under a sheet of paper.

Initials.

'Do any of them have the initials RH?'

'Doesn't look like it... Robert St John... Roy Neville... Ralph Cartwright... Roger Donald... No, can't see any RHs.'

Damn. He was sure he'd been onto something. Worst case, he'd have to ask Purvis to send him all the records, and he'd get Quek to wade through them.

'Hang on a minute,' said the nasal voice. 'Here's one. Filed in the wrong place. RHF. Dr Richard Hiram Fulbright. A Yank. Point of embarkation: San Francisco. That the one you're looking for?'

'Sounds like our man.' He made a note of Fulbright's full name on his desk blotter.

'Do you want the address he gave us? Everyone who comes in must give a contact address. They usually give the name of a hotel or some such, so I'm not saying it's current.' There was another pause. 'Hmm. Says here his address was care of the Raffles Library and Museum. What would a doctor be doing staying at a museum?'

Betancourt made another scribble. Richard Hiram Fulbright. RHF. Doctor. Raffles Museum. He doubted Fulbright was the sort of doctor that Purvis seemed to think he was, and he was sure he wasn't camping out at the museum.

'Do you have anything else?'

'Not much. Aged thirty-two – at least he was when he arrived.'

'Which was when?'

'25 June 1938. Two years ago.'

'Travel record?'

'Let's see. Since he arrived here... three re-entries. Two from Medan, the first year he was here, and one from Batavia during the last year. That's it. At least he's not another bloody engineer.'

Betancourt wondered what grievous harm an engineer had inflicted on Purvis. He thanked the man for his time before promising to buy him a drink the next time they saw each other at the club. As he'd no idea which club Purvis frequented, and as he patronised none himself, he was pretty sure he wouldn't need to follow through on his offer.

Chapter Five

H e had a name and a couple of addresses: the Raffles Museum and a street address. That gave him enough to investigate what he was increasingly convinced was a murder. If he'd learned anything at all in his years as a detective, it was that one thing led inevitably to another. All he needed to do was to poke at the problem and see what came scuttling out. Then he would follow wherever the clues led him.

A knock at the door interrupted his thoughts.

'Busy, boss?'

Betancourt sniffed. The odour of durian hung over Quek like a rain cloud hovers over a mountain. He wondered if the sergeant would ever be free of it.

'Do you have any after-shave?'

Quek looked puzzled. 'No, boss. Do you need it now? I can go and buy you some.'

On reflection, Betancourt questioned whether a blend of durian and cheap cologne would be a harmonious one.

'Never mind. It looks as if we may have our man. His

name is Fulbright.' He shared what he'd learned from Purvis at Immigration.

'An American?' Quek's eyes filled with wonder.

What difference did it make that the dead man was an American? Betancourt still felt irritable, and at first he put it down to the attitude of the Missing Persons sergeant, Hobbes. Then he realised he was choosing to ignore the fact that he'd felt that way before speaking to Hobbes, and the real reason was that seeing Evelyn again had unsettled him more than he cared to admit, even to himself.

'Never mind that for now. What did you find out?'

Quek, notebook at the ready, as always, reeled off the ship's chandlers he and Constable Aroozoo had visited. Aroozoo had taken the stores west to east along Keppel Road and Tanjong Pagar Road, and he, Quek, had started at the southern end of Beach Road, turned westward along Arab Street, returning southward down North Bridge Road.

'Thanks for the geography lesson. Did either of you learn anything?'

'A few sales, but only one net the size of the one we found yesterday.' Quek flipped a few pages until he found what he was looking for. 'Sharif & Sons, Baghdad Street. The owner remembers it because he received a delivery of nets from the shipping agent the same day. He'd only ordered one that size.'

'And did the good Mr Sharif remember who he sold the net to?'

Quek looked pleased with himself. 'A squaddie.'

'A squaddie?'

'It's what they call the British soldiers. I think it's because—'

Betancourt rubbed his eyes. This wasn't going well. 'I know what a squaddie is. I'm surprised to hear a member of the British Armed Forces purchased a fishing net that was—' He corrected himself. 'That *may* have been used in the murder of an American subject. Did you ask Mr Sharif if he had a record of the sale? A copy of the invoice? Something like that?'

'I did, boss.' Quek looked pleased with himself again.

'And?'

'Oh, I see. No, boss. The squaddie paid cash.'

Of course, he did. No records – nothing for the authorities to pry into later. Cash was king in Singapore.

'How about a description? Did they remember what he looked like?' He was going through the motions now, and he knew it. European. In uniform. If Quek had got any more, he'd have been amazed.

'*Mat salleh*. Army uniform. Nothing special.'

'And Sharif sold this net when?'

'Last week. Tuesday.'

That meant the squaddie would have purchased it two or three days before Fulbright met his creator. Of course, it was conceivable the purchase was an innocent one. A soldier wanted to do a bit of fishing on his day off. Hired a boat and headed out to one of the islands. A picnic, a few bottles of beer. Had no idea how to go about it and bought the wrong type of net. Told the shopkeeper he wanted the biggest net in the shop. Big net, big fish, right? So, the shopkeeper sold him exactly the same type of net a dead man was discovered tied up in less than a week later. Coincidence? It was possible, but Betancourt didn't like coincidences.

'The post-mortem results came back,' he said.

'Drowned?'

'Maybe, but unlikely.' He told Quek what Evelyn had discovered. 'It's possible he was dead before he hit the water. Either way, our man didn't die of natural causes. So, that leaves accident, suicide, or murder. We can rule out accident. Dr Trevose said she found three ounces of opium in his stomach, and that was after it was partly digested. People eat opium, but not in those sorts of quantities. Not even by accident. Not unless they're trying to do away with themselves. Which brings us to suicide—'

'It can't have been suicide.'

'Why not?'

'Because of the net. You said yourself he was wrapped up. If he killed himself, he couldn't have wrapped himself in the net.'

Betancourt liked how Quek was trying to work things out – cause and effect, even if he was drawing specious conclusions.

'It's not impossible he could have swallowed the opium, wrapped himself in the net before it took effect, and thrown himself into the sea. Or he swallowed the opium, died, and then someone found him, wrapped him in the net, and disposed of the body. But neither idea sounds likely, I'll grant you. Which leaves us with murder.'

Quek's eyes lit up again with the relish of the neophyte. He wears his heart on his sleeve, Betancourt thought. And, as an afterthought, he hoped the boy didn't play cards. While he understood Quek's zeal, he didn't concur with it. He'd seen too many deaths for another one to raise his mood.

'Why does one person kill another?' He listed the reasons. 'Lust? This doesn't feel like a crime of passion. A letter opener to the heart? Sure. A shot from a pistol? Certainly. But two balls of opium inserted into his oesophagus? No. Jealousy, then? Our man was having an affair with someone's wife. Husband finds out. Does away with his rival. Possible, but the opium still feels wrong. What else?'

Quek's brow furrowed in concentration. 'Revenge?'

Betancourt nodded in approval. 'Good. Revenge for what, though? If we're right, and this is a murder, then it's a wicked one.' Betancourt stopped himself and shook his head. The idea of qualifying a murder as wicked implied there must be other murders that were merely a bit unethical. It was absurd. He shook his head again, more vigorously this time, as though the agitation would free his mind of such preposterous thoughts. 'So, what does that leave us with?' Betancourt's musings on the relative flagitiousness of murders had caused him to descend into a reverie, and he was now speaking to himself as much as his sergeant. He answered his own question. 'Profit. The dead man had something that someone wanted. Or he knew something that someone didn't want known and he was killed to secure his silence.'

He snapped himself out of his abstraction. 'Right. Those are our working hypotheses. For now, at least. I'm not saying they're right, but we have to start somewhere. You go and write up the business with the net. I'll let the Assistant Commissioner know what we've got so far.'

Quek had been furiously scribbling down everything Betancourt said. He stuffed his notebook into the pocket of his uniform shirt and, for some unexplained reason, snapped off a hasty salute, before disappearing out of the door as if Cerberus, the three-headed hound of Hades, was on his tail.

Betancourt wondered how many notebooks the sergeant went through in a month. Quek had potential; he just needed a bit of polishing.

The Special Investigations Unit of the Marine Police was the idea of the then Inspector-General, René Onraet. No one, except for Onraet himself, saw the need for such a department, no matter how small a staff it entailed, given the rest of the Marine Branch dealt with on-the-water crime, and the other large tranche of activity – smuggling and its deterrence – was the province of the Customs Service. But, like so many senior colonial servants, Onraet carried a deep mistrust of his fellow administrators and saw a great deal of value in having someone he could trust on the ground, keeping an eye on goings on within Customs. When it was suggested to Onraet that Betancourt might be a suitable candidate for the new post, Onraet approached him. Betancourt was grateful for the opportunity, his previous career as a detective in the CID having skidded off the tracks and landed in a twisted, steaming pile of wreckage.

Although Onraet sponsored the new position, there was never any question of Betancourt reporting to him directly. At least not officially. For one thing, the position, at least on the face of it, lacked the requisite seniority to merit such a relationship, and for another, Onraet knew his time in the Straits Settlements was drawing to a close, and while he could advise the man chosen to succeed him, he hadn't felt it was fair to lump him with an additional report.

So, with the original suggestion to Onraet of appointing Betancourt coming from Marjorie French, a long-time friend of both the Onraet family and Anna, and there being no natural reporting line, Onraet decided Betancourt might as well report to Anthony Bonham, the Assistant Commissioner, who believed himself to be Marjorie's boss, although never had the description *power behind the throne* been more apt than in the relationship between Marjorie and Bonham.

For the most part, Betancourt and Bonham kept a wary distance from each other, and Betancourt sidestepped contact until it proved absolutely unavoidable. Now that the dead man had turned out to be an American, the US Consul would have to be involved. The Americans would, of course, expect their British counterparts to drop everything else and concentrate on Fulbright's death. Worse still, they might try to insist on pursuing the case themselves. Bonham would view managing the Americans as an opportunity to add a feather to his cap. *Not* having to deal with the Americans would allow Betancourt to get on with the job at hand. So, as far as he was concerned, everyone was a winner.

He picked up the phone and gave the operator Marjorie's number.

'I need to speak to your lord and master,' he said, when she answered. 'We have a delicate situation.'

'Serendipity. I was just about to call you. I take it this is about your dead man. His Nibs wants an update as soon as possible so he can show the I-G he's in full control of the situation.'

The jungle drums had indeed been beating. Betancourt had to credit Bonham with one thing: he possessed a remarkably sensitive set of antennae for identifying events that held the possibility of painting him in either a good or a bad light. He told Marjorie what little he'd found out: the man's name, how he came to be found, and a sketchy outline of the post-mortem findings.

'What shall I tell him? That you're treating the death as suicide?'

Betancourt thought for a moment. 'Don't say anything yet. Be as evasive as you can. Blame me, if he gives you any grief. Fulbright gave his address as care of the museum when he arrived here. I'll go there this afternoon to see what I can find out.'

'All right, I'll stall him. But the American consul has been onto the Inspector-General and the I-G has been onto Himself, and you know what he's like when he thinks the spotlight is on him.' There was a sound of pages being turned. 'His diary is pretty full.' She hummed and hawed for a few moments. 'He's due to meet with Callan from Customs at four. I could move that.' Betancourt tried to object, but Marjorie ignored his remonstrations. 'Plenty of time for you to make yourself presentable. Look smart, Max, or you'll be ten points down from the start. He has a bee in his bonnet about standards at the moment. Listen.' Judging by the promptness with which she read out the relevant passage from the regulations concerning compliance with standards regarding the wearing of uniform, and general neatness of presentation, she must have had it open and underlined, waiting for his call. 'So don't say I haven't warned you.'

Betancourt grunted noncommittally and rang off.

What was it about people and his attire? First Sam the tailor and now Marjorie. He looked down and examined himself. Black linen suit, admittedly a little crumpled – well, quite a lot crumpled, but that was linen for you; white shirt, clean on that day – if Marjorie was being picky, which she would be, it could have done with an iron; black tie – there was nothing to be said about his tie, it was the same one he wore every day; plain black leather lace-up shoes, although you'd be hard pushed to recognise them as black given the liberal coating of red dust that enshrouded them. This had been his uniform for as long as he'd been working the water-front, and he wasn't going to change it now, regulatory diktats from Bonham notwithstanding. Marjorie knew it. Even Bonham knew it.

He checked the time. If he was to question whoever it was that inhabited a museum and be back at Bonham's office on Hill Street by four o'clock, he wouldn't have a lot of time to spare.

He lifted first one foot and then the other, polishing the dusty shoes on the back of his trouser legs. Or, as he reflected having completed the exercise, transferring red dust from leather to linen. He looked down again. On balance, much better, he decided.

Chapter Six

Betancourt drove along North Boat Quay and up Hill Street, thinking about what he'd discovered that morning. Over the years, he'd learned to trust his instincts, and those instincts informed him there was more to the death of Dr Fulbright than the bare facts told. He still didn't know what the man's connection with the museum was, but if he gave the institution as his contact address when he arrived, there must have been some sort of association.

Who worked in a museum? His own experience was limited to a school outing when he and his classmates were packed into a bus and dragged round a succession of musty exhibits by Mr Han, the history teacher, who had sounded barely more enthusiastic about the exercise than his charges. The only workers he remembered seeing were a man at the front desk who greeted Mr Han and checked off their attendance in a register, and attendants in each of the large rooms who stood expectantly, waiting to be asked questions about the exhibits. Questions that never came. He wondered if Lucia came here with her school. He didn't know, and with that realisation he was forced to acknowledge how much there remained to know about his daughter's life.

At the junction of Stamford Road and Bencoolen Street, just beyond the canal, stood an ancient banyan tree, its aerial roots forming a series of pillars dense enough to keep out all but the most persistent ray of sunlight. Betancourt had discovered the tree several years previously, and it regularly provided the perfect parking spot. He wheeled Alex into the cool void and left her there with two ancient bicycles and a small boy for company. He tipped the boy above the going rate and, warning him to remain extra vigilant, crossed the road to the museum.

Standing at the foot of the steps leading to the entranceway, he admired the building before him. A small plaque informed him the Raffles Library and Museum had stood on its present site since 1887. It was older than he was. Its columned windows looked out onto both Stamford and Fort Canning Roads from the front, and, he recalled from his previous, long-ago excursion, onto Fort Canning Hill itself to the rear. By any measure, it was a striking building.

Inside a wood-panelled foyer that smelled of beeswax, a Malay man wearing a brass-buttoned tunic and a black velvet *songkok* greeted him. A brightly polished badge adorning the man's breast declared him to be named Mohammed. Betancourt showed Mohammed his warrant card.

'I'm looking for the offices.'

Mohammed pursed his lips and shook his head, a little sadly, as though sorry he couldn't provide the answer his questioner sought.

'Many offices, *tuan*. Which office are you looking for?'

'Dr Fulbright's office.' It was worth a stab. 'I believe he works here.' He nearly said *worked* but caught himself in time.

The sad look returned. 'Dr Fulbright is gone,'

Mohammed said, and Betancourt wondered if
American's death had circulated quicker than he'd

'Gone? Gone where?'

The man gave an exaggerated shrug. 'Gone awa
knows.'

'But before he went away, he worked here, correct

The man inclined his head, a tentative sign of asse
but now he has gone away,' he repeated, as if that t
Betancourt's conditional enquiry.

Betancourt frowned, unsure where to take this con
tion. The man wasn't exactly being uncooperative, but
seemed unwilling to over-commit himself.

'I have a few questions about Dr Fulbright's work. Is t
someone I could speak to? Does he have an assist
perhaps?'

'No assistant.' Then Mohammed raised his eyebrow
apparently having had a welcome thought. 'Maybe *Me*
Ridpath can help you.'

'Perhaps. Where would I find her?'

'Wait here.'

The man went back behind the reception counter and
lifted a telephone receiver. He informed *Mem* Ridpath there
was a policeman here who sought information about Dr
Fulbright. This development must have met with *Mem*
Ridpath's approval, and Mohammed pointed to a grand
central staircase.

'Upstairs. Take the third corridor on the right. When you
reach the end, you'll see another flight of stairs going up.
Follow the sign for Research. You will find *Mem* Ridpath
there.' The man brightened considerably, and added, incongruously, 'A very nice lady.'

Betancourt thanked him and set off up the stairs, feeling
as if he was on some sort of scientific expedition himself.
Every inch of the museum walls was clad in wood: skirting

ards, wainscotting, picture rails, elaborate corbels and rnices. When he reached the second landing, the sweet ell of alcohol assaulted his nostrils. It was strong enough to ritate his sinuses, and he took a handkerchief from his ocket and held it to his nose. Turning the corner, he came ce to face with the source of the irritation. A workman, dressed in a pair of dark cotton shorts and a sleeveless singlet, was filling a paint bucket from a gallon can of shellac. The shorts were too large for his narrow frame and, despite being tied around his waist with a length of binder twine, he had to tug at them repeatedly to prevent them from falling to the floor. He picked up the shellac in one hand and what looked like half a dozen bamboo and horsehair calligraphy brushes glued together to make one big brush in the other and surveyed his task. He wasn't a tall man, and the walls were at least ten feet high. He wouldn't have been able to reach the topmost parts on his own, so, necessity being the mother of invention, he'd tied two empty paint tins to a pair of wooden slippers with rattan twine. Atop his makeshift stilts, he was touching up all the yellow streaks that told where the fine varnish that should have protected the wood had bubbled and peeled.

When the man noticed Betancourt's presence, he either mistook him for a member of the museum staff, or, with the unerring sixth sense Singapore's labouring classes seemed to possess, guessed he was police. Stepping out of the slippers and down from the paint tins, he gave a gap-toothed smile and a small bow. Betancourt nodded back and pointed to a lighter patch on the cornicing.

'You've missed a bit.'

The man hastily remounted and set his brush to work, keen that Betancourt should see him take action. Betancourt, enjoying himself, nodded his approval, and said, 'Very good,'

and 'Carry on,' before setting off again in search of the elusive *Mem* Ridpath.

After a couple of wrong turns, one of which involved a storeroom containing the bones of what, judging by the size of its teeth, must have been a fully grown tiger, Betancourt found a door to which an index card was pinned. The card stated, simply, *History*, inscribed in mauve ink by someone in the habit of using a ruler to perfect the alignment of their handwriting. He knocked, and a woman's voice invited him to enter.

The room was little bigger than his own office. The mahogany shelving lining the walls was overdue for a visit from the stilt-walking shellacker. The lack of square footage wasn't the only way in which the room reminded Betancourt of his own; it was similarly untidy. Textbooks, scientific journals, and pile upon random pile of loose-leaf documents filled the shelves, the surface of the desk, and the seats of two wooden chairs that comprised the only other furniture.

A European woman stood amid the jumble. She looked to be in her late twenties. She wore a white laboratory coat, like the one Evelyn wore when working at the Crypt, unbuttoned at the front to reveal a tweed-clad, elfin figure. Pale, wispy, fair hair framed a narrow face, set off by a pair of astonishingly blue eyes, which were currently skewering Betancourt with an inquisitive stare.

'Miss Ridpath?' She didn't correct him, so he continued. 'I'm a detective. My name is—'

'About time too.'

'I beg your pardon?'

'You're here about Dr Fulbright, aren't you? I reported him missing. This is the first I've heard. Have you found him?'

'That's what I'm here to speak to you about.' He handed her his warrant card, and she peered at it.

'It says here Marine Police. What on earth does the Marine Police want with an archaeologist gone walkabout?'

'Walkabout? What do you mean, exactly?'

'My colleague, Dr Fulbright. He's missing. Isn't that why you're here? No one has seen hide nor hair of him for days. Typical man. Doesn't even have the courtesy to call in.'

Betancourt decided it wasn't politic to rise to this gibe about his sex. 'Do you mind if we sit?'

She made a show of looking at her wristwatch before sighing and waving a hand towards one of the chairs. Betancourt lifted the pile of documents from the chair and, not seeing any obvious piece of space to move it to, deposited it on top of another pile, where it teetered briefly before settling, stable for now. Miss Ridpath, unable or unwilling to free up the other chair, leant against the desk.

Taking out his notebook, Betancourt said, 'When did you make the report?'

She thought for a moment. 'Saturday.'

Betancourt made a note. 'And what first made you think Dr Fulbright might be missing?'

'He didn't turn up for work on – let me see – Thursday. Look, I told your colleague all this when I reported him missing.' She sounded exasperated.

'I understand, but if you wouldn't mind running through it again. We police – well, we're not always the best at sharing information.' He smiled, hoping to convince her to lower her hackles, but there was no immediate sign of the tactic having worked.

'Oh, very well. At first, I thought nothing of it. I assumed he'd been out at some party or other and he'd show up, eventually. He usually does. When he didn't turn up again on Friday, I began to think something was up. When there was no sign of him again on Saturday, I called you people. I take it all these questions mean you haven't found him yet?'

One of the first things they'd taught him when he joined the Detective Branch was to always keep control of an interview. He avoided her direct question.

'Could you describe Dr Fulbright to me?'

She frowned. 'Don't you lot write anything down?' He thought it best not to tell her that, in this case, the answer to her question was no. She turned her head to one side, as though appraising him. 'About the same height as you, I suppose. Same build, too. Brown hair – shorter than yours. And neater.'

Betancourt passed an involuntary hand over his head. Tonsorial elegance had never been one of his strong points.

'His skin was tanned, healthy looking. He spent a good deal of time outdoors – digging, cataloguing, that sort of thing.'

Betancourt cast his mind back to the unveiling of the corpse at Jardine Steps the previous morning. 'Did he have any distinguishing marks?'

'Nothing I'm aware of.' Something must have clicked into place for her, and the look in her eyes moved quickly from impatience to concern. 'Wait, why would you want to know that? Has something happened to Richard?'

So, it was Richard now. No more Dr Fulbright.

Betancourt had a decision to make. Fulbright's death wasn't common knowledge yet, and he was keen to stop the spread of gossip before he'd investigated his death. In fact, until someone formally identified the body, he wouldn't even know for certain the man found tied to the *kelong* was Fulbright, although all the evidence was pointing that way.

'I'm afraid we've found a man's body. The description you gave me of Dr Fulbright fits that of the man we found.'

'Oh, God. What do you mean, *found*? Found where?'

'In the sea, off Pasir Panjang.'

She appeared to relax.

'That's impossible. It can't be Richard. You must have found some other poor soul. Richard hates the sea. A few weeks back, friends of mine chartered a boat for a picnic to one of the islands. I asked him if he'd liked to join us, but he said he couldn't imagine anything worse. He said he couldn't swim, and even though I told him the boat was a ketch and perfectly safe, he was adamant.'

Betancourt took a parcel containing the wallet from his pocket and unwrapped it. He showed it to her, initials uppermost. 'Do you recognise this?'

It was obvious she did. She gave an involuntary sob and put a hand to her mouth. Instinctively, he wanted to reach out a hand and comfort her but stayed himself.

'Forgive me, Miss Ridpath, but I have to ask a few questions.'

She didn't answer at first, and Betancourt wondered if she was in a state of shock.

'Would you like me to see if I can find someone to bring some tea?'

She rejected his offer with a dismissive wave of her hand. 'I'm fine. What did you say? Not about the tea, before that?'

'I need to know what you can tell me about Dr Fulbright.' He looked around the room. 'What did he do here, for instance?'

'Do? He's an archaeologist.' She stared at the wall opposite – at nothing in particular that Betancourt could see – and her voice took on a faraway, dreamlike quality. She didn't sound upset exactly, but the news of her erstwhile colleague had clearly affected her deeply.

'How well did you know him?'

She turned back to face him. 'I've known Richard for ages, on and off. Since I was a girl, I suppose. He's American.

Did you know that?' She was still using the present tense. Not yet accepting the idea of her colleague being dead, Betancourt thought, rather than not believing the fact of his death. 'I first met him when he came to Cambridge to complete his doctorate. My father was his supervisor.'

'Your father? Is he also an archaeologist?'

'Was. My father is dead.'

She'd tensed when he posed the question, and when she answered, her voice contained a barely concealed antipathy. He'd clearly touched a raw nerve, but somehow he hadn't got the impression she'd aimed her animosity at him.

'I'm sorry.'

'Yes, Inspector. So am I. First my father and now Richard.'

'How had Dr Fulbright seemed recently? Had his behaviour changed at all?'

She thought for a moment and shrugged. 'I hadn't really thought about it. We're both busy and we no longer see – *saw* – much of each other, apart from at work. Although, now you mention it, he'd been less talkative than he used to be, I suppose. A bit, oh, I don't know, distracted.'

No longer saw much of each other? Betancourt considered pressing her, but if his instincts were right and someone had killed Fulbright, he would be speaking with Miss Ridpath again in the coming days, possibly several times. Poking that particular anthill could wait.

'Do you know of anyone who might have wanted to cause him harm?'

'We're archaeologists, Inspector, not Chicago mobsters. There are professional jealousies, of course. You know what men are like. Rivals might go up against each other for awards, or dispute each other's findings in journals, but actual harm? People don't harm archaeologists. Although...'

'Yes?'

She shook her head. 'I'm sure it's nothing, but there's a man named Lenehan. I wouldn't call him a rival – he isn't talented enough for that, but he and Richard were both nominated for a prize. They were adversaries, professionally speaking, but I'm sure there was nothing more in it.'

'Where would I find Mr Lenehan?'

'Here, I would imagine. Or, at least, next door. He does all his research in the library. Doesn't enjoy getting his hands dirty.' She stopped and stared at him, eyes wide. 'Wait, why are you asking these questions? You said it was an accident. You said Richard drowned.'

'I said we found Dr Fulbright's body in the sea. We are still investigating the cause of death.'

'Oh, my God. Are you saying—'

'I'm saying nothing at the moment, Miss Ridpath. But I have to ask these questions.'

'Yes, of course. I understand.'

'You mentioned professional jealousies. Did Dr Fulbright hold a grudge against anyone in particular?'

She shook her head emphatically. 'Richard was a brilliant man. He had no reason to envy anyone.'

'What about drugs?'

'What about them?'

'Did you ever see Dr Fulbright using anything?'

'You mean like medicines? The only thing I ever saw him take was salt tablets when he was out in the field. It's hot work. It's easy to get dehydrated.'

'I mean narcotics. Opium, for instance.'

'Opium? No. Of course not. That's ridiculous.' Then, with a good deal less vehemence, she said, quietly, 'I'm sure it's ridiculous. What on earth makes you ask that?'

'The police doctor found evidence of opium ingestion.'

'Oh, God. This is becoming a nightmare.'

Her composure was crumbling. He raised a placatory hand.

'Just a few more questions, Miss Ridpath, then we can leave it for now. I understand Dr Fulbright lives at Mount Emily Road.'

'He used to. The flat on Mount Emily Road is owned by the museum. He stayed there when he first arrived. He mentioned he'd moved out. Something about wanting to move to somewhere quieter.'

Betancourt remembered Mount Emily as being a sedate area, bordering on the genteel. He wondered what Fulbright considered quieter.

'Did he say where he moved to?'

'I don't recall. As I said, we didn't socialise, so it's not as though I visited him.'

'Who would know?'

She shrugged. 'I'm sorry.'

'One last thing, for now. Do you have a picture of Dr Fulbright?'

Her head turned to a gilt-framed photograph, half-hidden by scientific journals. Betancourt stood and lifted the picture, placing it on a pile of magazines where they could both see it. It showed three people. To the left of the trio was Miss Ridpath herself, though he had to look twice as her appearance was quite different from the academic who sat before him. Like the other two, she wore khakis, similar to those he'd seen worn by army sappers digging gun emplacements or erecting Nissen huts. She looked relaxed, smiling. Happy. Flanking her was an older man, heavy-set, with a weather-beaten face and a shock of grey hair sticking out from under his sunhat. Her father? He guessed the last man was Fulbright. So, this is what he would have looked like in life. Lean-faced, clean-shaven, clear-eyed, hair fashionably cut. Betancourt considered himself far from expert in the machinations of the minds of women, but it wouldn't have surprised him to learn Fulbright had set a few hearts aflutter. The photographer had caught him in a serious pose, unsmiling, his gaze almost one of defiance.

'Do you mind if I borrow this?'

'No. I'm sorry. That's not possible. My father…'

She didn't need to finish. 'I understand it's important to you, but I need a picture of Dr Fulbright if I'm to investigate his death. I'll take care of it, I promise.'

She hesitated; her hand half-stretched towards the frame. Then, seized by some sudden resolution, she grasped the picture and handed it to Betancourt.

'All right. Take it. But I'll need a receipt.'

Betancourt scribbled a note on a blank page in his notebook, signed it, and handed it to her. 'I'll have it copied and returned to you tomorrow.' She nodded, her concerns assuaged for now.

'I'm sorry to hear about Richard, Inspector, truly I am, but if there's nothing else, I have plenty to be getting on with.' She looked around, as though a little lost and not sure where to start. 'And now twice as much, it seems, starting with a visit to the bank.'

She discarded the white coat and offered to accompany him to the front door. With an experienced guide showing the way, Betancourt found the return journey considerably more straightforward than his earlier peregrination. On the way down, they came across the shellacker and Betancourt re-enacted his role as supervisor of the varnishing, pointing out spots the man had missed. His performance seemed to amuse Miss Ridpath, and for the first time he saw for himself a glint of the warmth he'd seen in her eyes in the photograph.

Once they reached the foyer, she offered her hand and he shook it, and she wished him luck in finding out what had happened to her colleague.

'You'll let me know, won't you? And if there's anything else, Inspector, anything at all…'

He paused. 'There is one thing. I realise this may be difficult for you—'

'You want me to identify the body?' She'd read his mind. 'Now?'

'No. Not now. It's still being… attended to. The police doctor will call you to let you know.'

She agreed, and he gave her directions for the Crypt. She was midway through the door when she called back to him.

'Inspector?'

'Yes, Miss Ridpath?'

'For a start, you can stop calling me Miss Ridpath. It makes me sound as if I'm my maiden aunt. My name is Molly.'

He wasn't sure what to say, so he said nothing.

'And Inspector…'

'Yes.'

'Thank you.'

'What for?'

'Do you know, I'm not really sure. But thank you, anyway.'

Betancourt was unsure what to make of this parting exchange and was pondering the thought when he noticed Mohammed standing motionless behind his counter, waiting for someone to assist. In his starched white uniform, he reminded Betancourt of a white heron, hovering in the margins of the river. Betancourt cast an eye across the expanse of the foyer and realised Mohammed must have seen, and possibly heard, his exchange with Molly Ridpath, while giving a very good impression of not having done so. He wondered how many conversations the serene concierge overheard.

He approached the desk.

'As you can see, I found *Mem* Ridpath.'

Mohammed gave an almost imperceptible bow of acknowledgment. 'Is there anything else I can help you with?'

'You could point me in the right direction for the accounts office.'

Mohammed replied that indeed he could but cautioned there would be little point in the inspector going there as Mrs Rosario had just left for her tea break and wasn't due to return for at least another twenty minutes. It seemed Mrs Rosario was the mistress of all things accounting. Could he, Mohammed, assist the inspector with his query?

'Thank you, but I doubt it. I need a home address for Dr Fulbright. Miss Ridpath said he'd moved from his old lodgings, but she didn't know where to. I thought that whoever does the payroll might know. It can wait; I'll telephone Mrs Rosario later.'

Mohammed frowned, as though trying to nail down some slippery thought. 'The Excelsior Hotel,' he said finally.

'What about it?'

'That's where Dr Fulbright moved to: the Excelsior Hotel. I have a gazette, if you'd like to look up the address.'

'There's no need.' Betancourt knew exactly where it was. The Excelsior was a converted godown at the seafront end of Shaik Madersah Lane that now served as a sort of private hotel. It was aimed at long-term guests, usually appealing to those in straitened circumstances. Betancourt had no idea how much American archaeologists earned, but he suspected it was more than he did. What was Fulbright doing staying in a place like the Excelsior? And of more immediate interest, how did Mohammed know what Fulbright's colleague hadn't? He asked the question.

Mohammed frowned again, as if stricken by a crisis of confidence. 'Dr Fulbright, is he all right? I mean, has something happened to him?'

Given he'd already broken the news to Molly, and assuming Mohammed was bound to ask her what was going on anyway, it would only delay the inevitable to keep the concierge in the dark.

'No, I'm afraid he's not all right, and anything you can help me with would be most helpful.'

Mohammed greeted this with one of his saddest nods. But there was also an air of resignation that suggested the news hadn't entirely surprised him.

'A few weeks ago, two men came here asking for Dr Fulbright. I told them he wasn't here, and they asked me where they could find him. Before he left, Dr Fulbright told me he was going to Bukit Chandu – he'd been digging out there – and afterwards he was going home, but I didn't want to tell them, so I just said I didn't know. They asked if there was anyone else who they could speak to, just as you did, and so I called *Mem* Ridpath, just as I did when you asked.'

Betancourt wondered if the coincidences between his own enquiries and those of the strangers might have led to Mohammed holding him at least partially responsible for whatever fate had befallen Fulbright.

'Did *Mem* Ridpath speak to the men?'

Mohammed nodded. 'She came down and spoke to them here. They asked her the same thing: did she know where they could find Dr Fulbright? She asked them who they were and why they were looking for him. They said it was a money matter. They said they'd looked for the doctor at his home, on Mount Emily Road, but he wasn't there.'

'They knew he'd lived on Mount Emily?'

'Yes. Definitely. I remember what they said. My bones are old, Inspector, and a little weary sometimes, but my memory is still good.'

Betancourt smiled. 'I'm sure it is. What happened next?'

'*Mem* Ridpath thought for a moment and then said they

might try the Excelsior Hotel. That was how I knew where he'd moved to.'

There was no obvious reason to mistrust the man's memory, nor any justification for thinking he might have had any dishonest motive. So why had Molly Ridpath told him she didn't know where Fulbright had moved to, when it was clear she did?

'These men, were they chettiars?' Mohammed had said the men wanted to speak to Dr Fulbright about money. Most of the money lending in Singapore was still in the hands of the chettiars, a Tamil-speaking business caste who'd migrated here from southern India during the nineteenth century. Chettiars were easily recognisable, dressed simply in a white dhoti and sandals, their foreheads smeared with lines of *vibhuti*.

Mohammed chuckled. 'No, *tuan*, not chettiars. They were British soldiers.'

'Soldiers? Are you sure?'

'They were British, and they wore uniforms like soldiers.'

Betancourt was rarely dumbfounded, but this information went a long way towards rendering him so. Increasingly, he wanted to know why, given she'd just been told the police had retrieved the body of her erstwhile colleague from the sea, and his death was being treated as suspicious, Molly Ridpath had omitted mentioning a meeting with two British soldiers, presumably strangers, to whom Fulbright owed money, and to whom she had given instructions where he might be found.

Chapter Seven

'You're late.' Marjorie was in her usual place at her desk, barring the entrance to Bonham's inner sanctum or, as Betancourt preferred to think of it, keeping Bonham *in*. He peered at his wristwatch, shook it, put it to his ear, and shrugged.

Although they spoke semi-regularly on the phone, he'd seen little of Marjorie since the Sleeping Tigers affair six months earlier. He'd always thought of her as a handsome woman, and he was concerned to see how thin and pale she looked.

Despite many offers from eminently eligible males, Marjorie had remained staunchly unmarried until the previous summer when she'd surprised everyone by returning from leave in England with a husband, Raymond French, in tow. When it turned out that French had wooed and then married Marjorie not out of love but because of who she was – one of the most well-connected women in the colony – she was, unsurprisingly, devastated. Since then, she'd placed herself in self-imposed social seclusion.

'I thought I told you to look your best.' Marjorie had never been one for mincing her words.

He adopted an aggrieved look. 'This is my best. Isn't it obvious?'

Marjorie shook her head resignedly. 'Anna would be mortified.'

Anna and Marjorie had been best friends growing up, and he knew Marjorie still felt his wife's loss as keenly as he did.

'How is my goddaughter?'

'She's well. She seems to grow taller every passing week. And more impertinent.'

Marjorie smiled. 'It would be good to see her again.'

'I'll bring her round. Next weekend suit?'

She gave a satisfied nod. 'I ran into Evelyn the other day. I take it you know she's back in town.

'I heard it first from my sergeant. Then we spoke on the phone last night.'

She eyed him expectantly. 'And?'

'And nothing. I stopped in at the Crypt this morning. She found two balls of opium in a dead American's stomach, and that's all there is. Besides, the Grey Man is still on the premises.'

'Oh, for God's sake, grow up, Max.' *The Grey Man* was the childish sobriquet Betancourt used when referring to Evelyn's suitor, Alistair Grey. Even he didn't find it funny. 'Did you expect her to wait about like a love-struck schoolgirl while you decide whether to move on with your life?'

She was about to say something else when a Bakelite device occupying a large part of her desk erupted into life with a loud crackle. A reedy voice emanated from it's wire-gauze speaker.

'Is he here yet?'

The voice sounded annoyed, but then, Bonham usually sounded annoyed.

His desk was only ten feet from the door outside which Marjorie sat, but the ostentatious display of proprietorial power that the intercom represented was as much a part of his character as his fastidious attention to the trappings of office Marjorie had warned Betancourt about on the phone earlier.

She regarded the squawking box incuriously. 'He has an American with him, from the Consulate, so he'll be keen to show off. Remember, best behaviour.' And then, flicking a white lever on the box, she said, 'Just sending him in now.'

Nothing remained confidential for long in the overgrown village that was Singapore, and Betancourt hadn't been surprised when Marjorie had informed him earlier that news of Fulbright's death had seeped out. He knew how seriously Evelyn took her responsibilities and he was confident nothing would have leaked from the Crypt. In any case, all Evelyn's staff would have known was that the body of a dead European had been brought in. The incompetent Hobbes at Missing Persons knew Betancourt had been asking about a European. Hobbes had received a call about a missing American, but Betancourt hadn't mentioned a death. He hadn't even told Purvis at Immigration the whole story, only that he was looking for information. So, he was curious how much this American from the Consulate already knew.

It was uncanny how little Bonham's appearance varied, Betancourt thought. Same perfectly pressed uniform, same perfectly trimmed moustache, same perfectly coiffed hair. His trademark pigskin-covered swagger stick lay at rest on the surface of an oversized desk bearing just enough paperwork to make it clear to any visitor that the man who sat behind this desk had important things to do.

In what Betancourt knew to be the more comfortable of the visitor's chairs sat a narrow-framed, languid-looking man dressed in a double-breasted blue suit, a blue button-down shirt, a tie whose purple and yellow stripes doubtless signified membership of some exclusive club or society, and black wingtip shoes polished to such a shine they could have provided service as a pair of mirrors.

Bonham didn't rise when Betancourt entered the room. To do so would represent some sort of concession; ceding some imaginary piece of territory he wasn't prepared to let go. His guest appeared to have no such reservations. The man rose from his chair, giving the impression more of unfolding than merely standing up. Having satisfied himself his host wasn't about to provide introductions, he took a step forward and extended a long, narrow, manicured hand to Betancourt.

'Theodore Garfield. I'm with the US Consulate. Assistant Commissioner Bonham was kind enough to invite me along to this…' He paused, as if momentarily unsure how he should refer to his involvement. 'To this briefing. The Consul-General expressed to me his deep regrets about what happened to Dr Fulbright, and he gave me *carte blanche* to provide the Singapore Police with whatever assistance you might require.'

Unseen by Garfield, who was facing away, but not by Betancourt, who wasn't, Bonham gave a petulant frown at this summary. Betancourt knew Bonham would much rather deal with the organ-grinder himself, and not with the organ-grinder's monkey.

Betancourt shook Garfield's hand and introduced himself. Sherry had been dispensed. It didn't appear he was to be included in the ritual imbibing, so he sat in the remaining, uncomfortable, seat.

'Can I ask what line you are in at the Consulate, Mr Garfield?'

Garfield, who had steepled his long fingers while he listened to Betancourt speak, untangled them again and gave a languid wave. There was a considered pause before he spoke. He seemed to enjoy choosing his words.

'I'm what you might call… a generalist.'

He smiled, but his expression was, thought Betancourt, entirely humourless.

A generalist. Betancourt knew about men like Garfield. The British called them caretakers. The term carried no derogatory intent, quite the opposite, in fact. Caretakers followed in close attendance of those in power, fixing things when the need arose. That the Americans had sent Garfield to investigate the circumstances of Fulbright's death suggested they held the dead archaeologist in some esteem. Why? he wondered.

'I understand Dr Fulbright was an archaeologist, working with the museum here. Can I ask why the Consul-General is taking a personal interest?'

'The Japanese are no friends of my country, Inspector, and, given events to the north, there is always a possibility it may prove necessary to evacuate our people at short notice. So, we keep a record of all our citizens who are resident on the island.'

Bonham interrupted, apparently put out at the implied slur on the ability of the British colony to defend itself.

'I can assure you, Mr Garfield, and be sure to pass on my assurance to His Excellency the Consul-General, Singapore is completely safe. The Japanese wouldn't dare invade. And if they were foolish enough to try, we'd send them away with their tails between their legs.'

Bonham's conceit was commonplace amongst the British expatriate community, but Garfield didn't appear to share the sentiment any more than Betancourt himself did. He gave Bonham a small pacific smile.

'Let's hope what you say proves to be correct, Assistant Commissioner, but in the meantime, forewarned is fore-armed.' He turned back to face Betancourt. 'Dr Fulbright was highly regarded in his field. An eminent scholar, even though he chose to study at one of your British universities.' He seemed to consider Betancourt to be British, which none of the British themselves would ever do.

Garfield leant forward, his brow furrowed with intent. Whatever message he'd been sent here with, it was about to be delivered.

'The Consul-General is an old friend of the Fulbrights. A fine old Providence family. He intends to call Dr Fulbright's father later today. Naturally, the family will be distraught when they hear of their son's death.' Garfield paused again. When he resumed, it was with a perplexed how-do-I-put-this-delicately look. 'I believe there may have been a suggestion that certain *items* were found about Dr Fulbright's person.'

'Can I ask how you came to be in possession of this information?'

Garfield gave another languorous wave. 'Singapore,' he said, as if the word was an ample explanation of how things worked in the strata of society in which Garfield and his like moved.

'If you're referring to the two large balls of opium that were recovered, then, yes, you're correct.'

Garfield's face tightened into an inchoate wince, as though Betancourt, by giving name to the *items*, had introduced an unnecessarily distasteful element into the conversation. He spread his hands, as if presenting an offering to the gods of reason.

'Perhaps Dr Fulbright was carrying these... items, on behalf of someone else. Young men get up to things they shouldn't when they're in the tropics. A foolish thing to do, but nothing more.'

The American was making it clear he intended to frame the narrative surrounding Fulbright's death, and Betancourt was growing tired of it. He nodded soberly, as though giving Garfield's idea deserved consideration.

'Perhaps. But if Dr Fulbright was, as you suggest, carrying

the opium on behalf of someone else, it would be an odd place to carry it, don't you think? In his stomach, I mean. Would his pockets not have served better?'

Garfield's demeanour changed in an instant. He sat upright and turned to face Bonham, any attempt to appeal to Betancourt's reasonableness forgotten. Bonham responded as expected.

'That's enough, Betancourt! You'll show some respect.' And then, to Garfield, 'My apologies, Mr Garfield.'

Garfield regarded him coldly. 'Assistant Commissioner, the Consul-General's wishes are clear. When he speaks with the family, it will be to tell them their son was involved in a misadventure. He fully expects that any inquest into Dr Fulbright's death will happen quickly and will bear out the conclusion that this was nothing more than a regrettable accident. No extenuating circumstances. I trust I've made myself clear.'

'As crystal, Mr Garfield. I will ask the coroner to schedule the inquest immediately.'

'Ask?'

'Tell. I will *tell* the coroner.'

Garfield rose to his feet, buttoned his jacket, and gave Bonham a cursory nod of the head and Betancourt a stare laden with intent. 'Good day, gentlemen.'

Betancourt waited until Garfield had left before saying anything.

'What was that about? Schedule the inquest immediately? Tell the coroner? Who's running this case, the Americans or me?' Betancourt regretted his outburst the second the words left his mouth. It was best not to tempt fate.

When Bonham spoke, it was in a voice like distant thunder, rumbling and ominous. 'Tidy this up, Betancourt. And if you know what's good for you, you'll keep a bloody lid on this opium thing. The last thing I need is the Americans bleating to the Governor-General that we – *you* – have been making scurrilous accusations.'

Betancourt departed without another word. There was no point. He was so focussed on his own anger he even forgot to say goodbye to Marjorie.

'Charming,' he heard, as he swept out of the office.

Chapter Eight

At his desk the following morning, Betancourt pondered again Mohammed's account of the two men who had gone to the museum, looking for information on Fulbright's whereabouts, and Molly Ridpath's subsequent disclosure of his move to the Excelsior. Then he thought about Garfield's insistence that the inquiry into the death find nothing untoward, and Bonham's sycophantic assurance that the American Consul's wish was his command. He knew the more time that elapsed, the harder it would be for him to investigate the circumstances surrounding Fulbright's death, and examining the archaeologist's room was a priority.

A knock at the door interrupted his thoughts. Sergeant Djulkifli stuck his head in and held out a sheaf of pink slips.

'Messages, boss.'

Unsurprisingly, despite the earliness of the hour, there was one from Bonham, demanding an immediate progress update. He looked at his watch. Eight-thirty. He'd left Bonham's office exactly fifteen hours previously. He shook his head and consigned the slip to the resting place of ignored requests in the rattan wastepaper basket next to his desk.

He riffled through the rest of the pile, separating the messages into those deserving of action and those he could safely file alongside Bonham's.

An invitation to purchase a book of raffle tickets for the Policemen's Provident Fund. Bin.

A reminder he was overdue for his annual medical check-up. He wondered idly who performed the physicals these days; it was so long since he'd attended one, he genuinely did not know. Was it the Police Surgeon? He entertained himself for a moment or two with the thought of Evelyn taking his temperature and telling him to bend over and touch his toes, before consigning that one, too, to the bin.

A request from the British Women's Guild, asking if someone could come and give the ladies a talk about safety at sea. What? Bin.

The final message piqued his attention. It was from George Elias, a reporter at the *Straits Tribune*. The message read:

Check the paper. Something about your American.

That was quick, even by George's standards. Betancourt and George had established what George described as 'a productive symbiotic relationship'. In other words, if Betancourt scratched George's back, George would return the favour. George had an excellent ear for news, and if something out of the ordinary came across Betancourt's desk, it wouldn't be long before George was on the phone, sniffing around for information. It wasn't all one way. Betancourt had his own network of contacts, but there were some places his tentacles just didn't reach, and that was where George came in useful.

In the beginning, there had been an inevitable caginess between the two men, but they'd come to trust each other, and had become allies. When George had mentioned some particularly fruitful collaboration to his wife, Mrs Elias (what was her name again?) insisted he and Lucia join them for Sunday lunch at their home in Katong. The couple had a daughter (Rosa? Rosie?) about the same age as Lucia, and the two girls had got on well together, sharing an interest in the latest musicals and the stars who played in them. Betancourt reflected that, weekly dinners with his parents-in-law aside, his visit to the Eliases was probably the most domesticated activity he'd taken part in since Anna disappeared.

The American in question would be Fulbright, though quite how George not only knew about the man's death, but had managed to dig up something juicy already, was beyond Betancourt. He'd often thought the reporter would have made an excellent detective had he not been lured down the murky path that led to the pressroom.

He rang the *Straits Tribune*. The receptionist said George wasn't in. He hadn't come in yesterday either. No, she'd no idea when he could be expected.

Betancourt opened the door and shouted to Djulkifli.

'This message. The one from George Elias. When did he call?'

'First thing, boss.'

'Did he say anything else?'

'Don't know, boss. I was on a coffee break. Aroozoo was covering for me.'

Often, when George wanted him to call, it was because he'd just broken a story and either he wanted Betancourt's take on things or he needed help to develop the story.

'Do you have a copy of the *Straits Tribune*?'

Sergeant Djulkifli rummaged around under the reception counter. 'Sorry, boss. Got the Malay papers, if you want them.' Betancourt shook his head and walked to the front door.

There was a gang of street urchins who hung around the entrance, ready to run any errands anyone in the station might need. Errands like fetching coffee or tea from the *kopi tiam*, or something to eat from one of the street stalls that set up each morning at the entrance to Cavenagh Bridge, or buying cigarettes or lottery tickets from the kiosks dotting the riverside. Or picking up copies of newspapers.

Only the smallest of the boys was there, patiently awaiting a commission, the others presumably already occupied. Betancourt handed him a dollar note and told him to find a copy of the *Tribune*. Betancourt made a play of looking pointedly at his watch. If he was back inside five minutes, he could keep the change. The boy's eyes lit up, and he scampered off. The tip was too much, but Betancourt knew the lad lost out to the bigger kids on most of the errands.

The boy returned a few minutes later with a rumpled copy of the newspaper, obviously used. Betancourt considered asking for a partial refund, but as he hadn't specified that the boy was to bring a fresh copy, he sent him on his way, coins jangling in the pocket of his shorts and a large grin on his face.

Closing the door of his office behind him, he leafed through the pages of the paper. There was nothing in the news section, but buried away in the journalistic depths, between the cinema schedules and the sports news, deemed by the editor to be a lower priority than the news from London, the prices of commodities, the shipping news, and the engagement of a locally based Brigadier, he found an obituary. It was a brief piece, only a couple of column inches, and contained only the bare facts of Fulbright's short life. Funeral details were to be announced. The article concluded with a reminder to all members to attend a talk to be given by the undersigned that evening at the Raffles Museum and Library, 7pm, during which Fulbright's life and work would be celebrated. The entry bore the name T.J. Lenehan, Hon Sec, SAS.

SAS? It meant nothing to him.

He shouted again for Djulkifli and asked him to bring in the telephone directory. He leafed through the listings beginning with S. There were pages and pages of them. It shouldn't have surprised him. Most of the entries began with the word Singapore.

Picking up the receiver, he asked the operator to connect him with the museum. An English voice answered. Betancourt introduced himself, giving his full title to pre-empt any objections.

'I believe there's an event taking place this evening.'

'That is correct. Mr Lenehan, from the Society, is giving the monthly lecture.'

'Which society would that be?'

'The Straits Asiatic Society. They meet here every month. May I ask what this is in connection with?'

'It's in connection with a murder investigation.' That ought to ruffle a few feathers. 'Leave a message for Mr Lenehan, will you? Tell him I called, and tell him I'd like a word with him, after the talk. I understand it starts at seven o'clock. Is that right?'

'That is correct, Inspector. Seven till eight. There will be drinks following the lecture, of course. I'll make sure your message is passed to Mr Lenehan. Good morning, Inspector.'

He couldn't fault the man for manners.

The faces in the photograph he'd borrowed from Molly Ridpath stared up at him. He'd promised to return it promptly. There was a place he knew near the Excelsior Hotel that did copies. He'd stop in there on the way to examining Fulbright's accommodation. But first, he wanted to visit the docks. Evelyn said the body had been in the water for over twenty-four hours, but less than forty-eight. He knew how the tides had been running, but he needed more detail, the kind only the harbourmaster could provide. Detail that might help him narrow down where the body was dumped in the water. Whether that knowledge proved to be of any help remained to be seen, but anything was better than nothing.

The harbourmaster's office overlooked the Victoria Dock. It stood, as did the rest of the dockyard, on reclaimed land, a few yards from where the shoreline would have been in Raffles's time. It was an odd-looking building, comprising a wooden box elevated from the yard below by a set of legs, which were strapped to each other by cross-members that gave the thing – so its designer had claimed – structural strength. It reminded Betancourt of a giant insect. Looking at it again, he wasn't sure he believed in the claims of structural integrity.

He climbed the steel stairs leading to the upper tier and stopped, half in and half out of the open doorway. He rapped on the door and called out.

'Anybody home?'

The harbourmaster, a burly Scot named Ramsay, appeared from behind a pillar.

'Inspector. It's yourself. You'll be taking a cup of tea?' Without waiting for an answer, Ramsay lit a flame beneath a soot-blackened kettle. Ramsay had introduced him to navy tea: tar-thick and overly sweet, and it had surprised Betancourt how much he enjoyed it.

With his grizzled beard and shock of untameable white hair, Ramsay looked every inch the old sea dog he was. The first thing he'd done when taking over as harbourmaster was to quit his assigned office in the head office building up the road and have the carpenters and fitters build this eyrie for him. The habitable part of the building – the part Betancourt now found himself half in and half out of – comprised a single room. Along three sides stood doorless cabinets, each divided into compartments containing a motley collection of rolled up charts, weather maps and shipping forecasts, and, on the tops of the cabinets, all manner of cartographical equipment. A long table that hadn't been there the last time Betancourt called in filled the centre of the room. On the table were more charts, weighed down with offcuts of cold-rolled steel. The front of the building consisted of a panoramic wall-to-wall window allowing Ramsay a wide vista of the docks below and the harbour beyond. Master of all he surveyed.

Taking a chipped enamel mug from the harbourmaster's great paw, Betancourt stood silent for a moment, sipping and watching the fevered activity on the wharf below, until Ramsay broke his reverie.

'What brings you down here? Wouldn't have anything to do with a body tied up in a net, by any chance?'

'You heard about that?'

'Nothing happens in this harbour without me hearing about it. Have you figured out who it is yet?'

'He's a man named Fulbright. An archaeologist. Works for the museum. None of this is official; not yet – his colleague has agreed to identify the body – but it looks as though he's our man.'

'Accident?'

'Doubt it. Our man had enough opium in his stomach to kill him, and there was next to no water in his lungs, so he may have been already dead when he hit the water. We – that is, Dr Trevose, the police doctor, thinks he'd been dead for over twenty-four hours but less than forty-eight. He was found around four o'clock on Sunday morning. So, if someone killed him, it would have happened sometime between Thursday and Saturday morning. What were the tides like last week?'

Ramsay was now all action, pleased at receiving a challenge that required his expert knowledge of the local waters. He picked up a roll of charts and crossed to the table.

A problem posed by the large glass window was that the room heated up in no time. It was barely nine o'clock and Ramsay's shirt was already a patchwork of damp spots. He laid out the charts before switching on an industrial fan, which swept the room, stirring up the tepid air as it went.

Ramsay patted the surface of the table.

'Got the boys down in the carpenter's shop to make this for me. A Dutch East Indiaman called the *Oranjee* foundered on the rocks off Pulau Hantu, back in the days before Raffles had even heard of this place. There was always a rumour she was carrying a load of silver dollars from the United Amsterdam Company in Batavia when she went down. They pulled her up last year. Nothing but spice chests, and even they were empty. The fish had got there first. Say one thing for the Dutch: they built their ships from beautiful timber.'

As the fan did another pass, the charts fluttered in its breeze, and Ramsay weighed them down with the steel offcuts. He rummaged through a tin of wax crayons until he found one that met his satisfaction.

'Where did you find your man?'

'A fisherman found him. The net snarled on the leg of his *kelong*. Off Pasir Panjang.'

'How far out?'

Betancourt hadn't asked. There was a time when he was known as the master of the probing question. He was becoming slack, and it irked him. He shrugged. '*Kelong* distance? How far out are they usually?'

Ramsay gave him a sidelong glance, as if to say, *you're not helping*. 'About a quarter of a mile, if it's a decent sized one. Let's go with that.' He licked the point of the crayon and drew a series of lines on the chart. 'This time of year, we get high night-time tides. On top of that, we're at the end of a spring tide. Third thing is, we've had tide and current in the same direction since the start of last week.'

Betancourt understood each of the individual words, but the whole might as well have been gibberish.

'What does all that mean?'

'It means we've had a fair amount of water flowing through the Straits this past week, mostly from the east. If he ended up at Pasir Panjang, I'd reckon…' Ramsay stood back, staring at the map. He scribbled some figures in the margin of his chart and tapped his front teeth with the crayon as he thought. 'If he'd been in the water twenty-four hours, I reckon your man would have come from somewhere near here.' He pointed out of the window. 'If it was nearer forty-eight, it could have been as far along the coast as Bedok. Mind you, if he started that far along, he'd have been lucky not to hit Blakang Mati, or one of the other islands.'

There it was again: the idea of a dead man being lucky. Betancourt made a mental note to ponder the concept further.

'Of course, that's assuming he travelled at all,' Ramsay said.

'How do you mean?'

'Big tides travel faster. It's possible he could have drifted straight offshore from Pasir Panjang on an outgoing tide and become caught fast.'

'If that was the case, the body would have been in the water for no more than an hour before it became trapped. The fisherman would surely have noticed him.'

Ramsay shook his head. 'Not necessarily. It can get pretty deep out there, even a few hundred feet offshore. The net could have become snagged on the foot of the *kelong* for a couple of days before tearing free.'

It wouldn't have made any difference to Evelyn's estimate

of the time of death, but it widened the list of areas where the man might have entered the sea. Betancourt made a few notes and finished his tea. The harbourmaster looked disappointed the exercise was over and, having bade his visitor farewell, took his place once again in front of the long pane of glass and gazed out over his fiefdom.

Chapter Nine

The view from Betancourt's own office of the river and all its activities was a special one, and he guarded his possession of the small room jealously, but he'd always thought the men and women assigned to the Beach Road Station overlooking the seafront had the best vista of all. He stuck his head through the station door and let the desk sergeant know he intended leaving his motorcycle outside for an hour or so. The man waved a hand. No problem.

Parking sorted, he scanned the shops across the road. His eyes alighted on a narrow-fronted building on the corner of Rochor Road, outside which a billboard with a painted image of a roll of film proclaimed:

Kang's Speedy Photographs
Wedding
Funeral
Passport
Opium Licence
Discretion Guaranteed!

He wondered what sort of photographs the speedy Mr Kang was required to be discreet about. The mind boggled. He crossed the road and placed the Ridpath photograph on the counter.

'I need a copy of this. Urgently.'

'No problem. Urgent is four dollars.' It was an extortionate price, but Betancourt didn't want to trail around every chemist in town trying to save a dollar.

'All right. But for four dollars I want it now. I'll wait.'

'OK. Fifteen minutes. You got the negative?'

Betancourt could see where this was going. 'No. Do you need it?'

The man shrugged. 'No negative, I take a picture of the picture. Take longer. Thirty minutes.'

'Thirty minutes, but no longer.'

'No problem. Eight dollars.'

'You just said four!'

'Four dollars for negative. Fifteen minutes. No negative, thirty minutes. Eight dollars.'

Merdra.

Betancourt waved the man away. 'Get on with it, then.'

The chemist eyed him thoughtfully. 'I see you before. You policeman.'

Betancourt wondered if his status might buy him a discount. 'That's right.'

'Huh. Policeman never pay. Money first. Eight dollars.'

'You'll get your money when I get the picture.'

The man shook his head emphatically. 'You pay first. Eight dollars. No money, no picture.'

Betancourt sighed, counted out the money, and handed it over. 'Thirty minutes. I'm counting.' He tapped his wrist for emphasis.

The man picked up the photograph and studied it. Then he held it up to the light and nodded to himself. He waved

Betancourt towards the entrance. 'Go get coffee. Thirty minutes. No problem.' He pointed to the billboard outside his shop. 'Speedy Kang, that's me!' He chuckled to himself, much amused, as he disappeared through a bamboo chick to the rear of the shop.

From the entrance to the photographer's shop, Betancourt could see the sign for the Excelsior Hotel a few streets away. He thought briefly about going straight there but decided the photographer's suggestion of coffee was a good one. It was proper Nanyang coffee he needed, thick and black, made from beans that had been roasted in sugar, the way the Portuguese did it. There was a place he knew on Bugis Street, just a stone's throw from where he stood, that used to do a good brew.

The stallholder, a tiny, ancient Chinese woman, ladled two heaped spoons of coffee into a small metal pot and added shaved palm sugar, a pinch of nutmeg, and water before setting the pot onto the burner. The flames licked up the side of the pot and soon the coffee was bubbling away. When the woman decided the coffee had had its allotted time, she poured the steaming liquid through a net into a waiting glass, lifting the pot all the time so the coffee spewed out in an ever-lengthening arc, cooling it so it could be enjoyed straight away. Betancourt perched astride a rickety stool, watching this piece of street theatre and inhaling the intoxicating smells of burnt caramel and spices. The coffee was as good as he remembered, and he swallowed another glass before it was time to head back to Rochor Road.

Kang was as good as his word. The photographer laid the two pictures side by side on the countertop – the Ridpath original and the copy. Had he not been able to view the date stamps on the back of the two pictures, Betancourt would have been hard pushed to tell which was which. He returned the original to its frame and folded the copy so that it only showed Fulbright's image. Kang wished him a good day and told him to return any time, especially if he needed any more rush jobs.

As well as a name change, the Excelsior had been given a lick of paint and a general spruce up. Betancourt remembered the place as the Strand. In his previous life in CID, he had reason to investigate goings on within its walls. There were several theatres in the surrounding area, and the Strand had become popular as a flophouse for itinerant musicians and actors down on their luck. It was the sort of place that hadn't asked too many questions of its guests, and as long as the visitor could stump up the cost of a bed – cash in advance, no exceptions – the owner found a space for them. Whether their stays were temporary or longer term depended on how far their fortunes had descended.

A new sign outside advertised the building as *A Gentleman's Home from Home*. Given its location, only a few minutes' gentle stroll from the fleshpots of Malay Street and Hylam Street, it would ill suit the requirements of someone wishing to distance themself from the beguiling inveiglements of this wicked world. If, as Molly Ridpath had suggested, Fulbright had moved here as he'd considered it quieter than his previous accommodation, Betancourt dreaded to think what Fulbright had managed to find in Mount Emily Road.

Hotels like the Excelsior didn't care for their inhabitants hanging around in their rooms all day, and it was common for the management to chase the residents out of the building in the morning and not allow them back in until the evening.

Those performers who had employment tended to work in the evening, and those who were between jobs had even more time on their hands. Such appeared to be the case here, and a small group had gathered outside the entrance to the hotel, smoking and putting the world to rights. Betancourt's impending presence in their midst raised their suspicions and the volume of conversation dropped a little, although none of them went so far as breaking for cover at the sight of him. He greeted the little group with a friendly 'Good morning' and made a point of walking between them as he approached the entrance, so that they would have to step backwards. It never hurt to remind them who was in charge.

A rickshaw-puller had parked his contraption in the shade of the hotel's portico, where he would find refuge from the heat of the day and would be in prime position for any fares that might come from the hotel. The man put down the newspaper he was reading and grinned at Betancourt, gesturing towards his machine. Blackened, stubby teeth betrayed him as a long-time opium user. Addicts didn't have the energy or stamina of their brethren who hadn't succumbed to the allure of the drug, which meant they had to spend more time resting. Which meant they earned less money. Which meant they could afford less food. Which meant they had less energy to devote to pulling fee-paying passengers. It was the appurtenant effects of opium addiction that ended up killing the addicts, not the drug itself.

In the small reception area, a tabletop electric fan struggled to stir the hot, humid air. On the counter, a wooden box contained business cards printed in red ink. A representational view of the hotel made the place look much grander than it actually was. In the stylised version, the building appeared to be surrounded by nothing but trees, under one of which a courting couple stared into one another's eyes. Above this Elysian image was the name of the hotel and a telephone number, and to its side, the words *Chee* and *Proprietor*. He took a card.

Next to the box of cards sat a brass bell, which Betancourt tested. It worked fine, and the peal of its chime brought forth the sounds of a flurry of activity from a rear room. Shortly, a small bandy-legged Chinese man appeared. The man wore the standard issue: a short-sleeved white rayon shirt over a faded singlet, black trousers, open-toed wooden clogs. He carried a much-creased issue of the *Nanyang Siang Pau*, folded open at the racing page. Betancourt must have interrupted his deliberations on how to lose his money that weekend. The man brightened at the possibility of custom.

'You want room? Very cheap for you. Twenty dollars. Long time, short time, also can.' The man spoke serviceable, if somewhat ungrammatical, English.

Betancourt pretended to read from the card. 'Are you Chee? The proprietor?'

'Who wants to know?'

Betancourt took out his wallet and showed his warrant card. The man lifted a pair of reading glasses hanging from a chain around his neck and peered at the card. He was unfazed by Betancourt's interest and seemed more curious than concerned as to why a *Serani* policeman was standing in the foyer of his hotel.

'Marine Police? You go the wrong way.' He pointed towards Beach Road. 'You should have turned right at the bottom. That's where the sea is.' He laughed at his own joke, revealing several gold teeth. Clearly a man who believed in keeping his savings close. Again, there was no note of anxiety; Mr Chee seemed to be enjoying himself.

Betancourt made a show of gazing around the small foyer. 'You've done the place up. Changed the name, too. The Excelsior?'

'Better class of customer. *Mat salleh*. Pay more.' Chee

rubbed his thumb and fingertips together to emphasise his motivation for renovating the place.

'Is it working?'

The man gave an expansive shrug, as if to say, 'You win some, you lose some.'

'How about this man? Does he stay here?' Betancourt showed the photograph of Fulbright.

Chee nodded enthusiastically. 'Fulbright.' He pronounced it *Foo-blight*. 'Yes, yes. He stay here. But not paid long time.' An idea seemed to descend and settle into the hotelier's consciousness. He regarded Betancourt with renewed interest. 'You pay his bill?'

Betancourt admired the man's enterprise. If you don't ask, and all that.

'When did Dr Fulbright move in?'

'Doctor.' The man laughed again. 'Fulbright no doctor. Fulbright dig stones.'

'When?' Betancourt repeated more firmly, determined to keep the upper hand in the conversation.

Chee thought. 'Maybe three months.'

'And how long since he paid his bill?'

'Three months.'

'He never paid?'

'Little bit only.'

'Why didn't you ask him to leave?'

Chee frowned, as though the idea hadn't occurred to him before.

'Fulbright very nice man. No problem.'

'I'd like to see his room. Can you show me?'

'You have...' Chee seemed to scratch around in his head for the right word.

'A warrant? I don't need one. Not if you offer to show me the room.'

Chee thought about this. Probably, thought Betancourt,

considering how he might turn the situation to his advantage. He was correct.

'OK. I show you Fulbright room. And you tell all policemen about my hotel. Very clean, very cheap. Long time, short time, also can. You tell everybody.'

His sales pitch completed, Chee snatched a key from a hook on the wall and beckoned Betancourt to follow him up the stairs.

Chapter Ten

T he hotelier unlocked a door at the end of a dark corridor and stood back, allowing Betancourt to enter. The air inside the room was stale. No one had opened the door in quite some time. Judging by the decor, any investment by Chee in the newly styled Excelsior hadn't reached the habitable part of the building. At least not Fulbright's room. What on earth, Betancourt asked himself again, was an American archaeologist employed by the Raffles Museum doing staying in a place like this? He opened the single dust-smeared window and the sounds and smells of the street rushed in, accompanied by a waft of welcome air. He stuck his head through the window-frame to orientate himself with the geography outside. The wall of the room that housed the window opened out onto Shaikh Madersah Lane. He looked down. A few feet away, the rickshaw puller sat, his emaciated legs crossed, like two bamboo poles intertwined. He'd nodded off.

Withdrawing from the window opening, Betancourt took in the contents of the small room. As well as the window, the wall he faced held a dilapidated air conditioning unit. He placed a hand on it and felt it move.

'Is that safe?'

'Very powerful. Very cold,' Chee answered, skirting the question.

Betancourt pressed a button on the front of the ancient machine, and it rattled into life. The noise it made was more akin to a piece of earth-moving equipment than a domestic appliance. No one could have slept with that racket going on. He peered out of the window. Sure enough, the racket had woken the rickshaw puller, who rubbed his eyes and looked around, as if unsure how he'd come to be where he found himself. He switched the air conditioner off again.

'Never mind noise,' said Chee. 'Noise OK. Very powerful. Very cold.'

Next to the air conditioner was a small, narrow wooden table. On top of the table sat a single gas burner connected to a bottle of Calor gas on the floor beneath it. A touch of modernity in an otherwise aged setting. There were no cooking utensils, and the burner appeared to be unused.

The other three walls held a single item of furniture each. Immediately to his right, next to the door they had entered through, was a wardrobe, made from what looked like rosewood. Portuguese colonial style. It had probably cost a few dollars in its past, before the woodworm and dry rot had got to it. He swung open the door. Suspended from unmatched wire coat hangers hung a couple of suits. Next to the suits were several sweat-stained khaki shirts – Fulbright's working gear. '*Digging and cataloguing, that sort of thing*,' Molly Ridpath had said. On the shelves, half a dozen white cotton shirts, laundered and pressed. Khaki shorts to match the work shirts. Socks, garters, underwear. He moved the items aside and felt behind. Nothing. On the floor of the wardrobe was a pair of leather boots, unpolished. He picked one up. It had seen plenty of service and had been re-soled, possibly several times. When he replaced the boot beside its partner, his hand was covered in red dust. The boots must have been Fulbright's working footwear. He lifted down a suitcase from the top of the wardrobe. It felt empty, and, when he opened it, he discovered that it was. He ran a hand along the top of the wardrobe, in case Fulbright had secreted anything there, but found nothing but a thick layer of dust and the corpses of several bluebottles.

'Having trouble finding chambermaids?'

'Malay people. Very lazy.'

Chee's throwaway remark was typical of the casual lack of esteem in which each of the groups of people that made up Singapore's population held each other. To the Chinese, the Malays were lackadaisical and shiftless; to the Malays, the Indians were factious and quarrelsome; to the Indians, the Chinese were rapacious and selfish. To the Europeans, they were all simply not to be trusted, and were to be watched like hawks. About Betancourt's people, the *Serani*, there seemed to be no unifying stereotype about which anyone could agree.

Against the far wall lay an unmade divan bed, enshrouded by a mosquito net that hung from a hook in the ceiling. Betancourt lifted the edge of the horsehair mattress to check whether Fulbright had hidden anything underneath. There was nothing he could see, and the smell of stale sweat discouraged him from investigating further.

'When did you last see Dr Fulbright?'

'Why you ask so many questions? Fulbright dead?'

Betancourt turned sharply and stared at the hotelier. 'Why do you ask that? What do you know?'

'Fulbright not come home. Policeman ask lots of questions. I think maybe Fulbright dead. Very bad. Dead man not pay bill.' Chee shook his head. He appeared disconsolate.

'Never mind his bill. I need you to think. Exactly when did you last see him?'

'I go check.' Chee scuttled off to check whatever it was he was going to check.

Betancourt had saved the desk until last. Propped up against the wall were some well-thumbed books. On the desk lay a small pile of papers, mostly handwritten, and mostly scientific in origin. On a sheet of drafting paper were rows of symbols that seemed at first glance to be little more than random squiggles. Some sort of script or language, Betancourt guessed. Next to some of the marks were notes made in indigo ink: *Plural? Wrong case? Countable?* Some were crossed out and further commentary added in red. *No, too simple!!* and, further down the page, *Proto-Sanskrit? Maybe.*

There were no photographs, he noticed. No parents, no brothers and sisters, no female friends, no pictures of home. However much his family might be about to miss him, he, it seems, had not needed to be reminded of them.

He moved to the single drawer, which contained a bank-book, a passport, a pocket diary, a manila folder containing a folded sheet of paper, and, somewhat incongruously, a programme from the races at the Bukit Timah Turf Club.

He flicked through the bankbook. The most recent with-drawal was dated ten days previously. The transactions appeared to be the usual sort of thing. A cheque deposit once a month, presumably his salary, and then, usually on the same day, a withdrawal of all the funds save for a few dollars. The balance on Fulbright's account was perilously low for a man of his position, but there was no crime in that. The crest on the cover identified the bankbook as having been issued by the Royal Edinburgh & Imperial Bank. If it turned out he needed to know more about the dead man's financial affairs, he could rely on his old ally, Sir John Cluny, the owner of the bank, to fill in any gaps.

He opened the passport at the personal details page. Fulbright's face stared up at him. The picture couldn't have been taken long before the one he'd borrowed from Molly Ridpath, but this Fulbright was a softer, paler version of the one he thought of as the original. He leafed through the rest of the document, flipping backwards and forwards, putting the stamps into chronological order. Why was it, he wondered, that immigration officers insisted on stamping pages at random? The passport was issued in Boston. Since its issue Fulbright had sailed into Southampton on three occasions, roughly two years apart, the most recent three years ago. The latter two stamps had a corresponding entry for New York, a few weeks prior. So, he'd travelled to England from America, presumably to take up the posting with Molly Ridpath's father at Cambridge, and had returned home a couple of times. The entry stamps for New York were both made in December, so visits home for the festive season would make sense. The entries since then matched what Purvis had told him.

Placing the passport with the bankbook, he turned his attention to the diary. It was a page-a-day affair – the sort with an outer cover into which the owner could insert a blank diary. Come the end of the year, the diary part could be discarded, and a replacement inserted. The cover was expensive-looking – fine-grained ox-blood morocco leather, decorated with the initials *RHF* in gold leaf across the corner of the outside, a match for the wallet. The inside of the cover contained a series of small pockets inside which the owner of the pocketbook could secrete business cards or the like. He tipped the diary up and gave it a shake. Two cards dropped out and fluttered to the floor. The first was one of Chee's hotel cards. Written on the rear was *Suite 6 – $40/mo.* A crude contract for the rental of the room. The other was the standard sort of thing seen everywhere: a name printed in bold script in the centre of the card with columns of smaller characters he took to be an address in the lower corner. An address for what, he'd no idea. Although he could speak a little Hokien – enough to prevent the denizens of the docks attempting to take too much advantage of him, he couldn't read Chinese, and that was what the card was written in. It might be nothing, but it was curious that, however he'd come by the card, Fulbright had seen fit to keep it safe. When he returned to Empress Place, he'd have Quek translate it and the mystery would be solved. He flicked through the pages of the diary insert. There were precious few entries. Either Fulbright had led an uneventful life, or he'd kept the details of his appointments elsewhere. Betancourt stopped at one entry dated the previous month. It simply read *8pm MR.* M for Molly? A dinner date? She had said they were nothing more than colleagues. If it was her the initials referred to, of course. He emptied the contents of the manila folder onto the desk. When he unfolded the sheet of paper, he saw it was decorated with rows of free-form concentric lines, marked in gradations of 50'. He didn't need to be an archaeologist to know the rings were height marks. Someone had marked crosses in red ink at various points on the map. The first cross was outside the outermost ring, near the bottom margin of the page, and the last one near the smallest of the concentric rings, at the top of the hill, whichever hill it was. Written next to the crosses were inscriptions, which, to Betancourt's uneducated eye, appeared to be coordinates:

01.29.16N, 103.84.77E, 01.27.97N, 103.79.46E …

If Fulbright had made the marks, and it seemed a reasonable assumption, then what did they represent? Coordinates for a dig site? He'd ask Molly Ridpath.

He placed the map with Fulbright's other belongings and picked up the race programme. It was dated six weeks previously. Betancourt recognised the line-ups; he'd been there that day. His friend, the trainer Bill Allenby, had a runner and he'd made a few dollars when the horse won. He turned the pages until he found what he was looking for. There it was: No 4 – Fast Crowd, trained by W. Allenby. The horse was known previously as Bintang Emas. It was sold to new owners who changed its name to Fast Crowd. There was an old saying in racing circles: change your name, change your luck. It had worked for Fast Crowd and the horse won first time up for his new owners. It looks like he wasn't the only one who'd won money that day. The horse's name was ringed in red ink, and next to it was written *50/50*. In betting parlance, the fifties would have referred to totalisator tickets, and for the serious punter, those would have been five-dollar tickets. So, the 50/50 would have meant two hundred and fifty dollars to win and the same to place. Five hundred dollars seemed a lot of money for a man with less than twenty dollars in his bank account. Betancourt turned the page, looking for evidence of other bets, and came across a small badge made of pink card, attached to a short loop of cord with a tiny gold safety pin. An owner's badge, allowing entrance to the area of the grandstand reserved for the owners of horses running that day. Usually, a clerk at the Turf Club office handwrote the name of the owner to which the badge was assigned, to stop them being passed along or sold. Betancourt turned the badge over. Inner Circle Stable. He checked the entry in the programme for Fast Crowd. Sure enough, the horse was registered as being owned by Inner Circle Stable. It was common for horses owned in partnership to run under a stable name. He'd ask Allenby who'd bought Fast Crowd.

He gathered his finds together and stuffed them back into the manila folder before going to see what was keeping Chee.

. . .

He found the hotelier out the back, playing cards with a fat, bald man wearing an apron stained with who knew what. Presumably the chef from the restaurant next door. Betancourt made a mental note to avoid frequenting the place.

'Finished.' He handed Chee the key. 'Did you check when Dr Fulbright was last here?'

'I check. Fulbright here on Wednesday. He ask to use telephone. I write it on his bill. Use phone, must pay. Thursday.'

'Who was he calling?'

Chee shrugged. 'I don't listen. Not my business.'

Betancourt doubted that very much. He could well imagine Chee listening into every conversation within earshot, just out of nosiness, if nothing else.

He smiled. 'Are you sure? If I find out there's something you haven't told me...'

Chee gave him a sidelong look. 'OK. Maybe I hear, but I don't listen. Maybe he talk about dragon. I don't remember.'

'A dragon? What did he say?'

'I don't know. I don't listen. I only hear dragon.'

Archaeologists dealt in fact, not fantasy, didn't they? Maybe the dragon was some sort of artefact? Another one for Molly Ridpath.

'What time was this?'

'Night-time. Maybe six o'clock.'

'Did he make any more calls that day? Or did anyone call him?'

"No one.' Chee was emphatic.

'What about visitors? Did anyone come here asking for him?'

'Fulbright very quiet man. No visitors. No hanky-panky. Not like some.' At this, Chee rolled his eyes upward as if inviting Betancourt to engage some superpower that would allow him to see up through the ceiling and into the rooms above.

'All right. That's all for now, but I may need to return, so don't rent the room out in the meantime. And tell the maid not to clean it.' Given that the room had shown no signs of being dusted in weeks, Betancourt felt safe with that one, and Chee readily agreed.

He was walking to the door when the hotel proprietor called him back.

'Wait. I forget. Fulbright have a lady visitor. Very nice lady. Very polite. No hanky-panky. I tell her Fulbright not here.'

'What did she look like?'

'English lady.'

'Come on, you can do better than that.'

'I don't know. All look the same to me.'

'How old?'

'Young, I think. Maybe twenty. Maybe thirty.'

'What colour was her hair?'

Chee scowled and pondered the question, as if he wasn't sure how to answer. Then he brightened. 'Like *fen si*.'

Like glass noodles. Pale and fine.

'Long,' Chee went on. He turned sideways and pointed to the small of his back. Long and very—' He stopped, searching for the right word.

'Curly?' Betancourt suggested.

'Curly,' Chee agreed. 'Like corkscrew.' He seemed pleased with his analogy.

'Did she give a name?'

'Maybe. English name.'

'An English name like Ridpath?'

Chee shrugged again. 'Maybe.' He wasn't being evasive. Betancourt was sure of that. It just hadn't been important and there was no reason he should have consigned the name to memory.

'When I tell her Fulbright not here, she ask me for his key.

She said she work with Fulbright at the museum. Very important she collect some papers.'

'Did you let her have the key?'

'Sure. Why not? Very nice lady.'

'You wouldn't let me have the key before.'

'That's because you policeman. She was very nice lady. I trust her.'

Chapter Eleven

With that endorsement of the lack of trust in which the Police Force appeared to be held by the hotel-keeping community ringing in his ears, Betancourt left Chee to his card game.

Outside, the sun was dropping towards the west and the shadows thrown by the awning of the Excelsior's portico had lengthened. So much so that the rickshaw-puller, still reading his newspaper, was now enveloped in shade, and at first Betancourt failed to notice he was still there. The old man called out, pointing at his machine. Betancourt shook his head and made a hand signal that imitated turning the handle of a motorcycle throttle. The old man raised a hand in recognition and returned to his news.

Betancourt turned to head back towards the Beach Road station when a thought struck him. Between his few sketchy words of Hokien and the coolie's similarly limited Malay, they fashioned a conversation. Betancourt took out the business card he'd found in Fulbright's diary and showed it to him.

'Do you know this place?'

The man nodded enthusiastically. '*Sinseh.*'

Betancourt frowned. A *sinseh* was a Chinese herbalist. What would Fulbright have wanted with one of those?

'Did you ever take the American *tuan* to this place?'

The man nodded again. '*Sinseh*,' he insisted. He pulled at Betancourt's sleeve, urging him to climb into the rickshaw.

'Where?' Betancourt asked, but by way of reply the man took up the shafts of the rickshaw and stood waiting for his passenger to get in. Betancourt shrugged. He'd asked, after all.

Checking his fare was ready, the man turned the rickshaw through 180 degrees and set off along Shaikh Madersah Lane, westward, towards Victoria Street and, beyond that, the Rochor Canal. Betancourt found himself gripping the frame of the rickshaw as the puller, seemingly oblivious to the threat of the streams of snarling traffic, deftly steered his way onto Jalan Besar. As they turned northward, and with no more major crossings in sight, Betancourt relaxed a little and began to enjoy his mystery tour. They reached the shops and restaurants of Little India. Preparations were underway for a festival of some sort and the buildings were ablaze with colour. Betancourt admired the Indians; they required very little convincing to celebrate, and even the most minor of festivals would find some group or other eager to mark its coming.

The rickshaw puller showed no signs of stopping until they neared Kitchener Road, where he slowed slightly and turned off to his left. The sounds of Singapore at play blared out from the New World Amusement Park across the road. A billboard foretold of a much-anticipated heavyweight match between two Filipino boxers. Judging by their caricatures, Betancourt decided he wouldn't like to have to separate them. A crowd had already gathered outside.

They came to a halt. Not at the entrance to the amusement park, but outside a shophouse opposite, which, judging by the rows of jars containing dried roots, leaves, animal parts, and who knew what else, was the premises of a practitioner of traditional Chinese medicine.

Betancourt pointed to the business card, which the rickshaw puller still held tight in his fist.

'Here?'

The man nodded vigorously and handed back the card. Betancourt gave him a dollar note, and the man beamed and set off again. Betancourt's dollar would mean he could retire for the evening.

He parted the chicks that shielded the entrance to the shop, and a melodious chime rang out. Inside, the full pungency of the medicines assaulted his nose. It didn't matter how many times he entered one of these places; he'd never get used to the smell.

The shop was clearly open for business, as evidenced by the unshuttered doorway, but it had an odd sense of disuse, as though the glass countertop and the cabinets that flanked it were covered with a layer of invisible dust.

A man appeared from the rear of the shop, his wooden slippers click-clacking on the floor of the shophouse. He was one of those people that Betancourt found impossible to age. The skin on his face was taut and almost wrinkle-free, and on that basis alone, Betancourt would have placed him around forty. But he walked with a slight stoop, and his shuffling gait and bowed posture suggested he might be older.

Betancourt was about to identify himself when the man gave a warm smile of recognition.

'Inspector Betancourt. It is good to finally meet you in person.'

Betancourt was taken aback. He'd no recollection of

having visited the shop before, nor, indeed, any shop in this or any neighbouring streets, and yet the *sinseh* claimed to know him. His confusion must have been apparent.

'Forgive me, but have we met?'

'Alas, no,' said the man. 'My name is Loong. Dr Trevose and I have crossed paths. Medical matters. She mentioned you. How is she, by the way?'

Loong had thrown him. Evelyn and a Chinese herbalist?

'She's well.'

'I'm glad to hear that.'

Betancourt had been unsure how this interview might go without Quek there to translate for him, but he needn't have worried; the man spoke perfect English.

'I should hope so,' said Loong, when Betancourt mentioned it. 'Six years at Raffles Institution. Three at Cambridge. I studied medicine there. Western medicine. It would be a shame if my English wasn't "up to scratch", as they would say.'

From another pair of lips, this might have sounded defensive, or even aggressive, but the apothecary spoke softly and with a gentle smile. He seemed amused at Betancourt's interest in his linguistic abilities.

'But I'm sure you didn't come here to discuss my education. What is that I can do to help you, Inspector?'

Betancourt showed Loong the business card he had found in Fulbright's room.

'Is this one of yours?'

'It is. Do you read Chinese?'

'Unfortunately, no. Perhaps I should learn. My rickshaw puller knew where you were.'

'Yes, I saw him when he dropped you off. I recognised him, too. I've treated him once or twice. Sadly, he hasn't been here for a while, but it's good that he brought you here. Perhaps he will consider coming by himself next time.'

The man had a talent for turning the conversation, and Betancourt was surprised to find himself enjoying being gently steered this way and that.

'I see. Sick, is he? He seems to prefer resting to working.'

'Sick.' Loong considered the word for a moment. 'Yes, he is sick. He comes here and asks me to cure him, but the only one who can make him better is himself.'

Betancourt remembered the rickshaw puller's lethargy and his nubby blackened teeth. He had an inkling of what was going on here.

'He came to you to seek your help to rid him of his addiction. This is an addiction clinic?' Betancourt looked over the doctor's shoulder. The shophouse didn't appear large enough to house a hospital, even a small one, and he'd already seen signs of domestic habitation on the upper floors.

'Not a clinic. At least, not in the sense I believe you mean it. I used to work at the Anti-Opium Society clinic until it closed. Now I do what I can from these modest premises.' Loong cocked his head to one side and regarded Betancourt inquisitively. 'May I ask, Inspector, is your interest in me and my establishment professional?'

Betancourt wasn't sure if he should take offence or not. Marjorie was always on at him to pay more attention to his appearance, but had things got so bad that he could really look like he might be someone with an opium habit?

Loong, perhaps realising his question might be misconstrued, smiled. 'What I mean is, someone must have given you my card. Perhaps a patient? How we proceed depends on whether you are seeking my professional advice as a *sinseh*, or whether you are making your own professional enquiries as a detective.'

'My interest is strictly professional. My profession.'

'Very well.' Loong raised a flap set into the counter and beckoned to Betancourt to follow him into what looked like a consulting room. 'Perhaps you would care for some tea.' Betancourt imagined some herbal concoction that tasted as bad as the shop smelled and was at the point of demurring when Loong allayed his fears. 'I have Darjeeling, that's my favourite. Or there may be some Assam left, although I'm afraid it may no longer be in its first flush of youth.'

Betancourt had his provisions delivered by a store a few doors away from his flat, and it was Lucia, on her weekend visits, who placed the orders. All he knew was that the tea she ordered came in a cheerful-looking red packet. He had a feeling it might be *Boh* brand, but then again, he might just have noticed one of that company's ubiquitous advertising hoardings. Either way, he'd no idea about tea origins.

'Darjeeling would be fine. Thank you.'

Loong disappeared off down the corridor to arrange beverages, and Betancourt took in the room in his absence. It was much like any consulting room that any practitioner of western medicine might have. There was a desk placed against the wall, and upon it was a bust marked with lines and dots. Acupuncture points, he presumed. On the far side of the room was an examination table, sheets neatly tucked in, ready for its next patient. A glass-fronted cabinet contained what he guessed were medical textbooks, and illustrations of the human figure adorned the walls. Above the desk was a framed picture of a flowering plant, beautifully drawn, with the fiery-red petals of the flower tightly circling an ink-black anther. The flower looked infinitely fragile, as if the gentlest breeze would blow it apart, its parts to be dispersed forever. Underneath, in fine calligraphic script, was the name of the plant. *Papaver bracteatum*. The flower was clearly a poppy, and he wondered if Loong had an ironic sense of humour.

'My hobby.' Betancourt hadn't noticed the doctor re-enter the room. 'Watercolours. It's something I picked up during my time in England. I loved to paint the meadow flowers. There was something so innocent about them.'

The doctor placed a tray on the desk and poured tea.

'The opium poppy is hardly innocent, though, is it?'

'Well, that is something we could debate, Inspector, if we had the time. A flower is a flower. What mankind does with it… In any case, a small detail, but that is not the opium poppy; it is its cousin, the Great Scarlet Poppy. From Persia. But enough about botany; I know you must be busy.'

Betancourt sipped his tea and made a mental note of the name Darjeeling. He showed Loong Fulbright's photograph.

'Do you recognise this man?'

'Yes. That is Mr Smith. He was my patient.'

'Is that what he called himself?'

'I assume, then, that Smith was not his real name. I did wonder.'

'His name is Dr Richard Fulbright. He worked at the Raffles Library and Museum. Why would an American archaeologist wish to consult you?'

'Why does anyone come to see me?'

'So, Fulbright was an addict?'

'Inspector, you realise that any conversation between a patient and his doctor is sacrosanct.'

'Dr Loong, I appreciate your loyalty to your patients, but Dr Fulbright may have been murdered. The man is dead, and you would do far more good by helping me find whoever it was who killed him than by honouring some abstract principle.'

Loong sat quietly for a moment, considering Betancourt's words.

'Very well. I'll tell you what I know, although it isn't a great deal. He came to see me about three months ago. Someone gave him my name – I don't know who – and he asked me to give him *kratom*. It's a plant, grown up-country. It used to be popular as a cure, but it doesn't work. *Kratom* leaves themselves contain a psychoactive drug. It's like drinking toddy to cure an addiction to whisky. I asked him why he wanted *kratom*, but he wouldn't say. I thought he seemed nervous – anxious – so I prescribed him a sedative.'

Molly Ridpath said she was sure Fulbright wasn't taking drugs. But then she studied rocks and bones and pieces of porcelain teacups, not human frailties. Would she even have recognised the signs?

'Tell me, Dr Loong, if a person is an addict, would it always be obvious to those close to him?'

'It depends, really, on what the patient is addicted to, and to what lengths they are prepared to go to hide their addiction. Take your rickshaw puller, for instance. I could spot him as an opium addict from fifty feet away. But then, I don't suppose he cares if anyone knows. A European, in a position of trust, of authority even – he may take more care to cover the signs. But it's never possible to mask addiction completely. Someone who knew him well would spot the differences.'

'What sort of differences?'

'Well, there are the physical differences, of course. Weight loss, clammy skin, constricted pupils. But sometimes the signs are more subtle: changes in mood, irrational or out of character behaviour, risk taking…'

'And did you observe any of that in Dr Fulbright?'

Loong shook his head slowly. 'Nothing that I recall.'

Betancourt thanked the doctor for his time and left his card. The description of Fulbright given by Loong was markedly at odds with that given by Molly Ridpath. It made no sense. He checked his watch. It was getting late, and he hoped Chee stayed on the premises, or, at the very least, worked late. He wanted to have another look round Fulbright's room. If what Loong had said was correct, and Fulbright had enough of a drug problem to warrant visiting a doctor, there should be evidence of drug paraphernalia in his room. That he had found nothing earlier wasn't conclusive; he'd expect a drug user to keep the paraphernalia of his addiction hidden from casual view. He'd just need to look harder.

Chapter Twelve

I t was only a twenty-minute walk from Kitchener Road to Shaikh Madersah Lane, but he wanted to get this last task of the day over with. It was past six o'clock, and the dusk had started to descend over the city. He squinted at the cars that rushed past, hoping that one of them might display a *For Hire* sign behind its windscreen. He started as a rickshaw appeared, seemingly from nowhere.

'Hotel, *tuan?*'

It was the rickshaw puller from the hotel. He must have remained in the vicinity, no doubt encouraged by the prospect of another dollar fare. The Excelsior was probably the locus of his world and perhaps he assumed it was Betancourt's, too. He settled in and allowed himself to be carried back.

The traffic was worse on the return journey than it was on the way up. Still, the puller took risks that no fare, no matter how generous, merited, and on one or two occasions Betancourt called out to the man to take it easy. No hurry.

The Gods were with them, and they arrived back at the Excelsior in one piece. Betancourt paid the man another dollar and watched as he pulled his contraption close to the wall underneath Fulbright's window. He thought the man would have had enough for the day and would head off home. In a flash of realisation, he wondered if this was his home. His suspicions were confirmed when the puller unfolded a piece of hessian he'd stowed under the seat of the rickshaw and lay down between the rickshaw and the wall of the hotel. Where he ate, where he washed, Betancourt did not know. But the sheer, pathetic aloneness of the man's life struck him most of all. What hopes did he have when he first ventured to the Lion City? What lies had he been told? He left him to his slumbers.

Inside, a quartet of elderly women sat at a table mixing a set of mahjong tiles. One of the women, who bore a passing resemblance to Chee, regarded him quizzically.

'Hello, Aunty. I'm looking for Chee.'

'*Chee! Customer!*' She shouted the hotel proprietor's name in a voice so loud Betancourt felt himself wince. Her friends seemed to be accustomed to the amplitude of her voice, and they carried on mixing tiles as though they hadn't heard a thing.

Chee shuffled through from the rear of the building and brightened when he saw Betancourt. He looked over Betancourt's shoulder, as if to see whether he'd brought a companion with him.

'You want room? Long time, short time, also can.' Betancourt decided this must be the standard advertising mantra of the Excelsior.

'Not this time. But I would like to have another look around Dr Fulbright's room. Could you let me in?'

'Fulbright, Fulbright,' Chee muttered to himself, as if he'd had nothing all day but a steady stream of enquirers wanting to view Fulbright's room. He found the key and beckoned resignedly to Betancourt to follow him.

Chee squinted as he inserted the key into the lock, and Betancourt stood back to give him more light. Eventually, the

MARK WIGHTMAN

coupling of lock and key was achieved, and Chee pushed at the door. He appeared to be meeting with some resistance and pushed harder. The door remained resolutely shut, and Chee breathed a quiet expletive. Placing his shoulder against the frame of the door, he gave it one almighty push, and whatever was holding the door shut gave up its grip.

Betancourt felt the explosion before he heard it.

A rush of wind picked him up and smashed him against the far wall. Fragments of plaster and wood large enough to brain a man rained down on top of him and the unmistakable odour of singed flesh perfumed the air. There was a momentary quiet during which he was only aware of the thick, billowing cloud of dust that enfolded him, and then the screaming started.

A man in a singlet pulled at his arm. He'd no idea who. Two of the women from the mahjong table sobbed and chattered in a dialect he didn't understand. A third stood behind them, peering round mouselike and frightened. The one he'd thought bore a resemblance to Chee was on her knees, wailing and scrabbling at the pile of rubble.

Betancourt steadied himself against the wall. Everything felt as though it was in one piece. He wiped a hand over his face. A crimson smear across his dusty palm told its own story. Whatever it was, it couldn't have been too serious. The worst thing was the thunderous ringing in his ears. He staggered over to where Chee lay and pushed the kneeling woman aside with a curt '*Get out of the way.*' He felt for a pulse. It was faint, but it was there.

The fat cook he remembered from earlier in the day appeared at his shoulder. Betancourt shouted at him to call for an ambulance.

'What about police?'

'I'm police,' Betancourt replied, spitting out a thick lump of plaster, saliva, and blood.

. . .

He waited with Chee until the stretcher bearers arrived. When he reached the ground floor, what looked like the entire population of the neighbourhood had joined the occupants of the hotel, and Betancourt had to push his way through the crowded foyer to reach the ambulance. A fire engine had arrived, too, along with a van bearing military markings.

'How is he?' he asked a man with a stethoscope hanging from his neck, pointing towards Chee's blanketed form lying inside the ambulance.

'Could be worse. Broken bones: ribs, one arm, collarbone. Maybe a punctured lung. We won't know until we get him to the hospital.'

'Is he awake?'

'Barely.'

Can I speak to him?'

'Best not to. I've given him morphine. I'm just waiting for it to take effect before I send him to the hospital.'

'I'll be quick.' Betancourt climbed into the back of ambulance and perched on the wheel arch. Chee could barely open his eyes and Betancourt wasn't sure if the hotelier recognised him.

'You're in good hands now. You'll be all right,' he said, conscious he had no right to give such reassurances.

Chee gave a faint nod of acknowledgment.

'Chee, did anyone ask to see Fulbright's room after I left?'

Chee tried to speak but only succeeded in bringing up bloody sputum.

'It's OK. Just rest. We can speak later, when you're feeling better.'

Betancourt turned to leave, but he felt a weak grip on his arm. Chee whispered something unintelligible, and then broke into another paroxysm of coughing. Betancourt held the man's hand until he recovered.

'I don't understand. What did you say?'

He bent down so that his ear was close to Chee's mouth.

'*Amoy*,' Chee murmured. 'Fulbright, *Amoy*.'

He closed his eyes, and a faint smile replaced the grimace of pain as the morphine began to work its magic.

Amoy? It made no sense. Not in the context of what had happened. He left Chee with the hospital orderlies and returned to the foyer.

A British soldier emerged from the innards of the hotel. His khaki fatigues weren't dissimilar to the working clothes Betancourt had seen in Fulbright's wardrobe. He'd tied an olive-green neckerchief across his face. The kerchief was now covered in fine plaster dust. He came over and stood beside Betancourt.

'You the policeman?'

Betancourt agreed he was.

'Lieutenant Reeves. Bomb squad. Much damage?'

'I've felt better. I can't get rid of this confounded noise in my ears.'

'You should get that checked. Might have perforated an eardrum.'

'Was that what it was then, a bomb?'

'Not explosives, if that's what you mean. Booby trap. Someone rigged up an ignition switch to the gas burner. Ran a wire to the door. Next person who walked into the room: *Boom*. I take it that wasn't you.'

Betancourt shook his head. 'The hotel proprietor.'

'You were lucky. The explosion tore a ruddy great hole in the wall. Anyway, I'm done here. No bomb, so it's somebody else's problem.'

Betancourt stopped him. 'Wait. Which wall?'

'Round the corner there. In the lane.'

Jezus. No. Betancourt pushed his way through the milling throng of humanity until he reached the side of the hotel where the crowd stood ogling the rubble from the collapsed wall. The explosion had taken down enough of the masonry to free the air conditioning unit from the brackets that had held it in place, and the unit had fallen, corner-first directly into the skull of the sleeping rickshaw puller. When they'd returned to the hotel earlier, he'd wondered why the man had wheeled his rickshaw back into position. The two dollars Betancourt had paid him were more than he'd earn most days. He was an addict; why hadn't he headed straight for the opium den? Had the *sinseh*'s potion worked? Had he kicked the habit? Betancourt doubted it. He imagined that life as an addict, wretched though it was, would have been preferable to a drugless reality for men like the rickshaw puller. If he'd gone and spent his two dollars on a few *hoons* of opium, he'd still be lying supine in a den somewhere, probably asleep by now, instead of lying on a filthy pavement with his brains bashed in. Judging by what little remained of his head, Betancourt guessed death had been quick. He hoped so. He realised with a stab of shame that he hadn't even known the man's name. He wondered how many had.

Pushing back the ghoulish hordes, he went to look for the medico. He found the man leaning against a wall, smoking. Betancourt informed him he had another passenger, but this one needed to go to the Crypt.

'No problem.' The man looked him up and down. 'Want a lift to the hospital? You can ride in the front with us. There won't be much room in the back.'

Betancourt declined the offer. The man just shrugged and flicked his cigarette end into the drain. He must deal with death all the time, Betancourt thought. God knew, he'd seen enough of it himself, but he'd never reached the stage of dispassionate acceptance the way the medic seemed to have done.

He gave the man his details.

'Call me if you need anything.'

Looking up the street, away from the chaos that had engulfed the Excelsior Hotel, he took his bearings. If he cut through the back lanes, it was a ten-minute walk to Holloway Lane. He hoped Evelyn was at home.

Chapter Thirteen

An hour later, he sat in the living room of Evelyn's flat, nursing a large glass of whisky and an even larger headache. When he'd arrived at her door, she was dressed to go out and was clipping on a pair of expensive-looking earrings. He'd apologised, and she'd insisted he come in and let her have a look at him. She cleaned his wounds – 'scratches', she'd called them – and was stitching the worst of them: a gash just above his hairline.

'A bomb? You can be a bit annoying at times, but a bomb seems extreme.'

'Thank you for your concern. And it wasn't a bomb. Not really. Not according to Reeves.'

'Who's Reeves?'

'Bomb squad. According to him, it was a booby trap. But you're right, it does seem extreme. At first, I thought perhaps someone was trying to kill two birds with one stone: destroy something that was in the room and get rid of whoever entered it. But even that makes no sense. If whoever it was wanted something that was in the room, and they had access, which they clearly did, then why not just take it? And who was it they were trying to kill?'

'Well, you, obviously. Was there anyone else in reception when you asked to see Fulbright's room?'

He cast his mind back to his first visit to the Excelsior. He hadn't recalled seeing anyone when he first spoke to Chee in the hotel's foyer. There had been sounds of activity from the corridor towards the rear of the building, but the conversation had been an amicable one; neither he nor Chee had had any reason to raise their voices and there was no reason to think anyone might have been close enough to have overheard their conversation without being observed.

'No one I noticed.'

'All right. You said the window opened out onto the street. Perhaps there was someone watching the hotel. They saw you enter Fulbright's room, decided you were a threat, and arranged to have you bumped off.'

'Bumped off? Don't say you've been reading detective novels, too.'

She gave him a questioning look. 'Who said anything about detective novels? Are you sure you're all right? Concussion, perhaps.'

'I'm fine. Besides, it can't have been me they were after.'

'Why not?'

'Because whoever it was couldn't have known I would return.'

Evelyn acknowledged the logic. 'Perhaps your hotelier friend has some nasty acquaintances. Perhaps he owes money to one of the secret societies or something?'

He thought back to her earlier question, about someone listening in to his conversation with Chee. If he was sure that no one had heard them, then that left Chee himself. But it couldn't have been the hotelier, could it? It was Chee who pushed open the door, and he who took the full force of the blast. If Chee had alerted someone to Betancourt's interest in Fulbright's room, then he couldn't have known what the intruder planned to do.

'It would be a funny way to get your money back: blowing up the person you're trying to get the money back from. Remind me not to hire you as my personal debt collector.'

He thought about the conversation with Chee in the ambulance.

'Before they took him away, I asked Chee – he's the man who owns the place – if anyone had asked to see the room after I left. I couldn't really make out what he was saying – he was in a bad way – but it sounded like *Amoy*. Any ideas?'

'Other than being a Chinese island and a brand of soy sauce, no.'

'That's all I could come up with, too. Nothing is making much sense at the moment.'

'I'm not surprised. Blasts from explosions dull the senses somewhat.' Evelyn snipped the last piece of catgut and pronounced herself satisfied. 'You'd better get cleaned up. God alone knows what folk must have made of you walking here. You're lucky someone didn't call for a policeman.'

He knew the locals well. Well enough to know that minding your own business was the preferred method of operation in these streets. If it was one of their own, then maybe. But not a stranger, and especially not a *Serani* policeman.

She left the room briefly and returned carrying a fresh shirt on a hanger. 'Have a bath. There's plenty of hot water. It'll stop your muscles from tightening up too much.' She handed him the shirt. He knew who it belonged to and thought briefly about how it came to be there, but even he knew this wasn't the time to bring up that subject.

'There's no point in giving you a suit. It'd be much too much big for you. I'll see what I can do with your things.'

'I thought…' He gave a small wave of the hand, intended to encompass her finery.

'Oh,' she said, as though she'd forgotten there was somewhere else that she was supposed to be. 'I've plenty of time.' She opened the brown leather Gladstone bag that lay on her dining table. 'Is it hurting yet?'

He stretched and gave an exaggerated grimace.

She handed him two round white pills. 'Take these. In fact, here, take the bottle. You can keep them. In case the pain gets too bad. I shouldn't be encouraging you to take painkillers with alcohol, but the whisky should help. Just don't tell anyone I said so.'

Later, when hot water and Epsom salts had performed their alchemy – the whisky and codeine had probably helped, he acknowledged – he sat on Evelyn's couch, pondering the events of the last twenty-four hours.

'You said that nothing is making any sense,' Evelyn said, as she joined him. 'Perhaps…' She paused, as if weighing up the advisability, or possibly the appropriateness, of what she was about to say.

'Yes?' He looked at her questioningly.

'Perhaps it would help to talk things through with someone. If you'd like,' she said tentatively, 'I'd be happy to listen.'

'I would like that, yes. But you've already done enough, and you need to get away.'

'Don't worry about that. I'll be right back.' She went into the next room, and he heard snatches of a telephone conversation. A date being cancelled, an unhappy recipient of the news, a diffident Evelyn. When she returned, there was a lightness about her he hadn't seen earlier. She was enjoying this.

'Right, tell me everything.'

Where to start? The beginning was usually best. He took a moment to marshal his thoughts.

'An American, an archaeologist of all things, studying ancient relics, is dead, probably killed. In his stomach, a large quantity of opium.'

'Speaking of which, the lab boys came back with the analysis. It's amazing what a little flattery from a woman will do to grease the wheels of bureaucracy.' She reached down, pulled a folded sheet of foolscap paper from her handbag, and read.

Visual analysis: Refined, partly digested.
Quality: Inferior. Visible evidence of botanical matter.
Active contents: Morphine, narcotine, codeine, papaverine, narceine, and thebaine (elevated levels).
Trace contents: Sucrose and small amounts of glucose and fructose. Traces of inulin. Flavonoids (various). Phenolic acids: ferulic and synapic.
Source: Near East (likely).

'Could you translate that into terms an ignorant policeman would understand?'

'Certainly. Opium, probably from Persian or Turkish poppies, palm sugar, and lemon juice.'

'*Cacak.*'

'If you're going to be rude, I won't bother trying to help.'

He laughed, and immediately regretted it as a stab of pain shot through his ribcage.

'*Cacak* is cheap opium, cut with all sorts. Sugar, lemon, and *jijing* – the dross from used opium pipes. It comes in mostly from Java and Sumatra. The Dutch are less fussy about where they get their raw materials. I pick up Bugis fishermen for running the stuff all the time. Small amounts, though. Pocket money stuff. So, the question is, did he kill himself, or was he killed by someone else? You said you found lesions in his throat, as though someone had forced the opium down. You also said the balls of opium were large. If the opium was poor quality, full of rubbish, couldn't the act of swallowing it have caused the marks?'

She appeared unconvinced. 'It would be difficult for anyone to do that. The natural thing would be for the gag reflex to kick in and eject the object. My money is on forced entry. Besides, what about the net? You said someone had wrapped him in it; that he hadn't become entangled. And why did someone booby trap his room if he committed suicide?'

It was Betancourt's turn to concede. 'All right. Murder it is. In that case, the question is why would someone want to stuff low-grade opium down the throat of an American archaeologist? Once we know why, we'll be a lot closer to knowing who.'

Evelyn grinned and he realised he'd been using the pronoun *we*, unconsciously. But instead of correcting himself, he smiled back at her. It felt good to be working with her again.

'The net's another odd thing. I sent Quek to question the ship's chandlers, on the off chance one of them might have remembered selling a net like that recently. He found one. A dealer in the Arab Quarter had sold an identical net to the one that Fulbright was wrapped in to a squaddie, just two days before the body showed up.'

'A squaddie?'

'That's what I thought.'

'Fulbright's colleague at the museum, Miss Ridpath, said she'd noticed no sign of addiction. But would she know the signs?' And was she telling the truth? Betancourt had learned the hard way not to take anything anyone said at face value. 'There was something else that was odd. She said Fulbright had moved out of the flat the museum had provided, but she denied knowing where he'd moved to. But when I spoke to

Mohammed, the doorman at the museum, he said that two men dressed as British soldiers had come looking for Fulbright, and Miss Ridpath suggested they try looking for him at the Excelsior Hotel. Chee – he's the owner of the hotel – told me a woman conforming to her description came to the hotel looking for Fulbright, around the time he disappeared. I'll need to speak to her again. Maybe grill her harder this time. She knows more than she's letting on.

'Which brings us to today. I found a business card in Fulbright's room. He'd been seeing a *sinseh*. A rickshaw puller outside the hotel recognised the address.'

He stopped. He'd put the dead rickshaw puller out of his mind, and a wave of guilt washed over him. Was there something he could have done? He gave himself a mental shake and told himself he wasn't responsible for the man's death. He wasn't sure he believed it.

'He took me to the *sinseh*'s clinic. The *sinseh* said he recognised me. Said he'd heard of me from you. He described you as colleagues.'

'That's ridiculous. Strange though it may seem, I don't spend my days discussing the famous Inspector Betancourt with everyone I meet.'

'In that case, something isn't right there, either. He definitely recognised me. But why would he lie about how he knew my name? He must have known there was a good chance I would mention it to you.'

'How did he even know we were acquainted?'

Acquainted. It sounded somehow odd. Impersonal and distant. Is that what they were? Acquaintances?

Evelyn frowned. 'Did he give you his name?'

'Loong. He has a clinic on Kitchener Road.'

'Loong?' She thought for a moment. 'No. Doesn't ring any bells. What does he look like?'

Betancourt shrugged. 'Shorter than me. Forties, maybe

older. It was hard to tell. Not much hair left. Had a mole on his face, with two long hairs growing out of it. Claimed he used to work at the Anti-Opium Society clinic, the one on Kampong Java Road. He said he was a doctor there.'

'How odd of him to say we were colleagues.'

'He also said he was educated in England. Cambridge, he said. Medicine. He's a fully qualified doctor.'

Evelyn frowned again. She looked out of the window at the building across the road where through the window the silhouette of a woman preparing her family's evening meal was visible. 'I thought I remembered something there, but it's gone. It may come back to me. Go on.'

'He said Fulbright consulted him. It started about three months ago. According to Loong, Fulbright asked him for *kratom*. It's supposed to help with drug withdrawal symptoms.'

'It's a folk remedy. It doesn't work. At least, not in my experience. Did he give Fulbright the *kratom*?'

'No. He concurred with you. He said he gave Fulbright something he'd concocted himself. Some traditional Chinese preparation, I suppose.'

'Maybe he was trying to put you off the scent of something?'

'The scent of what?'

Evelyn shrugged. 'I've no idea.'

She finished the last of her whisky and sat back. 'I've enjoyed this. It's been just like the old days. I can help now, officially, I mean. No need for any contrived telephone calls, inviting me to jazz bars, enlisting my "analytical skills".'

Betancourt's face reddened at the memory. When they had first met, he had convinced her to go for a drink with him on the pretext that her professional attributes might prove useful to his investigation. He remembered how much he enjoyed working with her.

'I'm sorry,' she said. 'I didn't mean to embarrass you. It

was a feeble attempt at humour. I have enjoyed talking, though.'

He'd enjoyed it, too, but talking things through hadn't helped much. If anything, he had more questions than he started with.

'I've asked Miss Ridpath if she would identify the body. She agreed. Could you call her at the museum when you're ready and arrange for her to come into the Crypt? I'll meet her there and I'll talk to her again.'

'Of course.' Evelyn picked up a silver cigarette box from the coffee table and offered him one. She flicked at the wheel of a table lighter, but it refused to spark.

'Empty,' she said. 'Do you have a light?'

Betancourt fished around in his jacket pocket until he found his lighter and lit both their cigarettes.

'Oh, I nearly forgot,' Evelyn said. 'Marjorie called. She said she'd left messages for you at the station, but you hadn't replied. She seemed to think I'd have more luck contacting you. Seems she was right. They've scheduled Fulbright's inquest for tomorrow morning. I told her it was far too early. I haven't signed off the post-mortem yet, and no one has formally identified the body.

'What did she say?'

'She said Bonham was adamant.'

'That didn't take long. I suppose I'd better think about what I'm going to say.'

'Just tell the coroner what you know, and I'll do the same. He'll have no option but to adjourn the hearing.'

She glanced at the clock on the mantelpiece. 'Goodness, I hadn't realised it was so late.'

They both stood, as if in response to an unheard command, and in the act of standing they came together. He could smell the sweet, smoky aroma of whisky on her breath. They avoided each other's eyes.

'It's time I left,' he said.

'No. It's late. And you've had a shock. You can stay here. The couch is perfectly comfortable. I've fallen asleep on it many times myself. I'll find you a pillow and a bedsheet.'

As he lay there, the lights of this town that never really slept winked at him through the living room window, and he thought about Evelyn, and about his wife, Anna, and he thought about fate and about what might have been had the cards fallen differently. He'd told Evelyn there could never be anything between them as long as Anna was still out there. Was she, he wondered? Still out there?

Anna had borrowed his car and driver to take Lucia to a dance class. It was his idea: the car was sitting idle in the station yard, the driver, Manniam, filling his morning by polishing the chromework. The suggestion had seemed like a good one at the time. Now he used the memory as another rod to beat himself. Traffic found the wreckage of the car down an embankment, near the docks. Manniam was dead and there was no trace of Anna. He had discovered later that the Sleeping Tigers had engineered her disappearance, but that knowledge proved to be of little help. In the months that followed , he'd exhausted every avenue, and himself, trying to find her. It was now nigh impossible that he would find any new trace of her. The trail had grown cold, as they said in detective stories. And yet, he couldn't abandon his search. He couldn't abandon her.

It was Lucia, as devoted to her mother as any daughter could be, who'd driven a stake through the heart of any remaining hope he might have held. They were sitting at dinner, a few weeks previously, at the home on Nassim Hill of Anna's parents, Louis and Odette. Out of the blue, and with the same blinding clarity of vision that Anna herself would have shown, Lucia turned to him and said, 'She's never coming back. You know that, don't you?'

They all stopped eating, and there was silence. He thought about what she'd just said and wondered why. Why now?

'We don't know that.'

'I know it. You'll understand when you're ready.'

'Why do you say that, Lucia?' Odette's voice was quiet, accepting, as if she'd already come to the same conclusion as her granddaughter, and this conversation was just a cementing of a shared understanding.

'Because if those men still had her, we would have heard something from them – some sort of demand, or ransom, or something. But we haven't. And if they didn't still have her, if she was free, she would have come home.' She paused and looked Betancourt in the eye. 'She wouldn't have left me.'

It was there – faint, yes – but definitely there. She'd stressed the word *me*. He noticed Odette give an almost imperceptible nod as Lucia spoke, and even Louis, who had obdurately refused to stop believing that Anna would be found eventually, was silent. Betancourt realised there was now only him harbouring any illusion. Everyone else had moved on.

And now it was too late. Evelyn had Grey. Was she happy? He wasn't sure, and he wasn't enough of a man to hope that she was.

Despite everything, he slept an uninterrupted, dreamless sleep, and when he woke, it was to the cries of hawkers on the street below Evelyn's living room, and the whistle of a kettle from the kitchen.

Chapter Fourteen

A fter a simple breakfast of coffee and sweet rolls,
Betancourt called the hospital and enquired after Chee.
'Critical but stable,' a distracted-sounding staff nurse told
him. What did that mean, exactly? Not dead, at least. He
asked when he could speak to the hotelier, and the nurse told
him to call again the next day, before hanging up on him.

While Evelyn made more coffee, he pulled out the envelope containing Fulbright's belongings from the pocket of his
now even more tatty jacket and emptied the contents onto the
table.

'I still don't understand what anyone would find so incrim-
inatory in the work of an archaeologist.' He showed her the
document with the concentric rings. 'What do you make of
that?'

'A map?'

Betancourt nodded. 'That would be my guess, too.
Presumably something to do with his work.'

He stopped himself. What was he forever telling Quek?
Presume nothing. And here he was doing exactly that. But
he'd nothing else, and it seemed a reasonable place to start.

'I'll show it to Molly Ridpath and get her to confirm whether there's anything in it.'

Evelyn eyed him, a sly smile on her lips.

'Molly, eh?'

'She objected to me calling her Miss Ridpath. She said it made her feel like her maiden aunt or something. Are you going to pour that coffee?'

As he reached for his cup, an involuntary spasm pulsed through his body.

'Are you all right?' Evelyn said, a note of concern in her voice.

He nodded. 'I'll be fine. I'd better get going. I need to go and collect Alex. Mustn't keep the coroner waiting.'

'Absolutely not. I'll drive. I won't have you riding that infernal contraption. Where is it anyway?'

'Alex isn't a *contraption*; she's a finely tuned racing machine.'

'It's a death-trap.'

'I left her at the hotel.'

'Well, you can send someone to pick it up. As your doctor, I forbid you from riding it until I'm sure the concussion has passed.'

Evelyn went to find her keys. The blast had shaken him more than he'd realised, and he was pleased to have her company. He found her telephone and called the station. He asked Djulkifli, the desk sergeant, to find Quek.

'What are you doing this morning?' he said, when Quek picked up the receiver.

'Inspections. At the docks.'

'Aroozoo can do that. I need you to get a pool car and go to the Excelsior Hotel on Shaikh Madersah Lane. There was an explosion there yesterday. Take an empty box with you. It'll be cordoned off. Are you in uniform?'

'Of course.'

Of course. Silly question. This was Quek he was talking to. He wouldn't be unduly surprised to learn that Quek slept in his uniform.

'Good. Go to room 6. It'll be cordoned off, but tell whoever is on duty that I sent you. Look for a stove and a gas bottle. There may not be much left. Put what you can find in the box and give it to your driver. Tell him to take it back and get it checked over by the maintenance engineers.'

'What are you looking for?'

'I don't know. Anything that might be a clue. A soldier from the bomb squad said it had been booby-trapped. See what the engineers can find out.'

'On it, boss.' He could hear the excitement in Quek's voice. He had an amusing image of the young sergeant furiously scribbling all this down in his notebook, and he had to force himself to keep his tone serious.

'After that, I need you to pick up Alex and drive her back to the station. She's in the lane behind the hotel, next to a noodle shop.'

A thought occurred to him.

'You have ridden a motorcycle before, haven't you?'

'Of course, boss. Many times.'

'Really?'

'Sure. Not one with an engine, but I'll work it out.'

Before Betancourt could recant his request, Quek hung up. He sat, shaking his head.

'What is it?' asked Evelyn. 'You look like you've lost a shilling and found sixpence.'

'I've no idea what that means, but if it means I've just ordered a complete rookie to drive my most prized possession across town at the busiest time of the day, then you're right.'

Evelyn's little red Austin 10 carried them to the Coroner's Court with speed, if not with comfort. Betancourt wasn't a good passenger at the best of times, and especially not when Evelyn drove, and there was a good deal of imaginary braking on his part when they reached junctions or swerved to avoid the occasional bullock occupying the middle of the road.

They were late, it seemed, and Hugo Gemmill, the newly appointed King's Coroner, paused in his opening remarks to direct a quizzical look in their direction.

'Dr Trevose. And Inspector Betancourt, too. How nice of you to join us. You appear to have been in the wars, Inspector. Everything all right?'

'Quite all right, sir. A domestic accident.'

'Very well. If you'd care to take a seat, I'll continue.'

A row of seats next to the coroner's bench and perpendicular to the rest of the room was reserved for witnesses, and Evelyn led the way, *sorry*-ing and *excuse me*-ing until they reached the seats. There was only one other witness: the fisherman who found the body. The clerks kept spare sets of clothes that coolies could use when they were required to appear, and the man looked uncomfortable in the oversized flannel jacket and trousers he'd borrowed.

Evelyn smiled apologetically at Gemmill, while Betancourt sat stony-faced.

The Coroner's Court always reminded him of a church. He and Evelyn sat in the nave, looking up at the coroner at his pulpit (actually a desk on a low raised dais). Behind that was the altar: a picture of His Majesty the King flanked by the symbols of his authority. On one side was the Union Flag, and on the other the standard of the Straits Settlements: a British Blue Ensign defaced with a red diamond containing three gold crowns – one for each settlement – separated by a white inverted pall. Above was the gallery, where the press and others not considered meritorious of a place in the nave sat.

The windows of the clerestory were badly in need of a wash and allowed only a weak sombre light into the room. It even smelled like a church: stale and frowsy.

As Gemmill launched into his opening remarks, Betancourt's gaze wandered around the room, taking in the attendees. Many of the faces were familiar: clerks, court reporters, newspapermen, and a few unattached regulars who attended out of curiosity.

A few rows back sat two Europeans. The first was a gaunt, sharp-featured man in his forties. He was dressed much like Betancourt himself: a dark linen suit and white shirt, but where Betancourt wore a tie, this man wore a maroon cravat made from some sort of shiny material, perhaps silk. He guessed the cravat was an attempt to draw attention away from the man's most striking feature: a port wine mark that ran from under his ear, stretching the width of his neck. His companion was even more interesting. Even though he'd cleaned up and wore a freshly pressed set of military-style flannels, he bore more than a passing resemblance to the bomb squad technician Betancourt had met at the hotel the previous day. He couldn't swear to it, as he hadn't seen the man's face, but he was sure enough. What was he doing at the inquest into Fulbright's death?

Gemmill completed his opening cant and called the first witness. The fisherman sidled over to the small balustraded pen from where he would deliver his evidence.

The coroner began by asking the witness, in English, to state his name and address. The fisherman stared at him blankly, and Betancourt, deciding they might be there for a while if he didn't intervene, called across to Gemmill. 'He doesn't speak English. He'll need an interpreter. Someone who speaks Malay.'

The court interpreter, a rotund individual wearing thick glass spectacles, which he fiddled with constantly, went and stood next to the fisherman, and translated for him. The witness stated that his name was Aziz, and that he lived on a *kelong* off Pasir Panjang. When Gemmill interrupted to ask what a *kelong* was, the translator explained it was a fishing platform, out at sea, where men like the witness worked and slept. He went on to explain how the fisherman came to discover the body tangled up on the leg of the *kelong*.

'Ask him if it's common to come across stray fishing nets,' said Gemmill.

'He says he keeps his nets safe.'

'But in general?'

'Yes, he comes across stray nets from time to time.'

'So, it is entirely possible that the dead man...' Gemmill checked his notes. 'Mr Fulbright... that Mr Fulbright may have gone for a swim and become entangled in one such stray net? That's possible, isn't it?'

Betancourt smiled as he listened to the ensuing exchange between the fisherman and the interpreter, in which the fisherman asked the translator how the hell he was supposed to know if the *mat salleh* had gone swimming or not, and the interpreter suggested that it would be best for everyone if he just agreed.

Gemmill seemed pleased when the interpreter confirmed that his hypothesis was indeed workable. 'Entirely possible the deceased met his death as the result of an accident,' he intoned to no one in particular, as he wrote in his notebook, underlining some part of the text he'd just written.

Betancourt didn't claim to be a legal expert, but wasn't this akin to a judge in a criminal court leading the witness, which, he was fairly sure, wasn't allowed? A sharp hiss from Evelyn confirmed she was of the same mind.

'What's he playing at?'

Betancourt was about to answer when Gemmill called him forward. He gave his name, address, and occupation, and, when reminded he was speaking under oath, gave his assurance he would tell the truth.

After he'd explained the general circumstances of his presence at Jardine Steps, Gemmill called on him to explain what he had observed.

'The body had been wrapped in a net.'

'When you say *wrapped*, Inspector, surely you mean *became entangled*?'

'No, sir, I mean *wrapped*.'

'Why do you take that view?'

'Because, when I removed the net, it was clear someone had wound the net around the body.'

Gemmill looked out and gave a stuffy half-laugh, as if enjoining the congregation to query the witness's analysis of the situation.

'But Inspector, the court has already heard from the previous witness that stray nets are common in these waters, and it is perfectly reasonable to assume that the deceased simply swam into one of these nets and, sadly, drowned.'

The previous witness had said nothing of the sort, but Betancourt realised that either Bonham or the American Consul, or possibly both, had done a job on Gemmill, and there was no point in him arguing.

There were a few more similar exchanges in which Betancourt would give his understanding of what happened, and Gemmill would reinterpret it for the benefit of the audience.

Eventually, Gemmill summed up. 'I'm bound to say, Inspector, that after due consideration, I'm inclined to favour the previous witness's testimony over your own.'

With that, he was dismissed, and it was Evelyn's turn.

After he had dispensed with her preliminary findings, Gemmill seemed keen to get to what he called the nub of her evidence.

'I have here a copy of your preliminary post-mortem report. Would you care to tell the court what you found?'

'Judging by the condition of the body and observing the degree of tissue decomposition, I was able to estimate the body had been in the water for between twenty-four and forty-eight hours. Ignoring the damage inflicted by sea creatures, the subject appeared to have been in good health. I inspected the contents of his stomach and found two balls of rough opium weighing approximately three ounces in total. On closer inspection of the laryngeal tract, I noticed lesions consistent with the opium having been forced down the deceased's throat.'

'Now, Dr Trevose, let's not jump to conclusions. Any manner of things could have caused these so-called lesions: a hastily eaten chipped potato, a piece of dry toast – the possibilities are endless. Isn't it far more likely the deceased died by drowning? An accident? I understand you are new to your job, but every reader of mystery thrillers knows a person can drown in an inch of water. Isn't that right, ladies and gentlemen of the public?' He turned to the gallery again, hoping to milk another laugh, and found reward in a few isolated titters.

Betancourt couldn't take his eyes off Evelyn. New to her job? So-called lesions? Gemmill's questions were nothing less than character assassination. He waited for her to explode, but to her great credit, she kept a lid on her emotions. Apart from a slight colouring to her cheeks, she gave no sign Gemmill had upset her. She took a deep breath and composed herself before she replied.

'In my professional opinion, the amount of water in the lungs was inconsistent with drowning. It is my belief that the deceased was dead before he entered the water.'

'Dr Trevose, are you prepared to tell this court you categorically rule out drowning as a cause of death.'

'No, but—'

'Thank you, Dr Trevose. That will be all.'

Gemmill didn't need long for deliberation or consideration. After a brief summation during which he heaped praise
on the character of Dr Richard Hiram Fulbright and
bemoaned the cruel fates that took him from his family at far
too young an age, he declared a verdict of death by misadventure. With that, he thanked the witnesses, wished the other
attendees a good day, and declared the proceedings closed.
There being no further business for the court to consider that
day, notebooks were closed and knitting put away, and the
audience exited the court in an orderly fashion.

Outside, in the sunshine, the floodgates lifted, and Evelyn gave
full vent to her pent-up feelings for Gemmill.

'What the hell was all that about?' Her face was flushed.
Betancourt, conscious they were still surrounded by people,
put a finger to his lips and pointed towards a quiet spot across
the road.

A cigarette lit, she resumed her analysis of the coroner's
performance. 'His job is to determine the likely causes of
death of the victims, based on the evidence presented before
the court, not steer the witnesses.'

'I know. He'd made his mind up before he went in. He
was nobbled, and I know who by.' He told her about his
summoning to Bonham's office and his subsequent encounter
with the American, Garfield.

'Why the hell didn't you warn me beforehand? You let me
walk right into a trap.'

'I'm sorry. I didn't think it would be that bad.'

'Watch out, Hugo Gemmill, that's all I'm saying. I intend
to repay him with interest for that.' She checked her wristwatch. 'I'd better get back. I left Martha holding the fort.' She

rummaged in her handbag, searching for her car keys, but instead pulled out a buff envelope. 'I forgot. Martha pulled together that list you were looking for.' She handed it to him. 'Forty-six deaths by opium ingestion this year. Twelve of them – not including Fulbright – had swallowed rough opium. All of them in the last two months. That's when I took the job full time; there may have been more before that.'

He tore open the envelope, scanned the contents, and stuffed it into his jacket pocket.

'Thanks.'

'What do you intend to do with it? Surely, there can't be any connection between an otherwise healthy American and some poor people whose lives were so miserable that they decided to end it all.'

'You're probably right, but whatever their differences, they do have at least one thing in common: they all died after ingesting rough opium. Did you attend all the other inquests?'

She shook her head. 'One or two. I don't normally attend unless the coroner needs me to give evidence. I try to put everything I can think of into the post-mortem report, so there are no outstanding questions, and that's normally good enough. Why?'

'Just curious.' He smiled a deprecating smile. 'Looking for connections. It goes with the job, I'm afraid. Seeking cause and effect everywhere, when, really, a lot of life is just a series of random coincidences. I'm probably tilting at windmills, but I'll come back here later, when the crowds have gone, and have a look at the inquest records. See what I can find.'

'I'd better finish this report, now the verdict is official. Good luck with the windmill tilting. Let me know if you find any connections.'

'I will. By the way, did you see yesterday's *Tribune*?'

'I have it delivered, but I don't read it cover to cover. Anything in particular that I should have seen?'

'Fulbright's obituary. Written by a man named Lenehan. Chair of the Straits Asiatic Society. When I spoke to Molly Ridpath at the museum, she said something about archaeology being a rivalrous game. I'm curious to know how much of a rival Lenehan considered Fulbright to be. Lenehan's giving a talk at the library tonight. Thought I'd wander along and have a listen. Try and catch him afterwards.'

'Sound fascinating. Man gives talk on pieces of broken china.'

'Was that irony? Or do I mean sarcasm? I can never remember which is which. I take it your indifference to the subject means there would be no point in asking you if you're interested in attending.'

'Who said anything about indifference? I told you last night that things are always more interesting when you're around. Unfortunately, Alistair has tickets for *La Bohème* at the Victoria Hall. God, I hate opera. Enjoy your talk.'

They said goodbye, and he watched and waved as the little red car wove its way up South Bridge Road, northward, towards the river.

Chapter Fifteen

He wanted to give it at least half an hour for the crowds outside the court to disperse, so he found a coffee shop round the corner on Hokien Street and ordered. The only vacant table was outside. He sat, squinting in the midday sun and waving an occasional hand at the dust being thrown up by the traffic that formed a constant backdrop to his thoughts as he read Evelyn's list.

Martha had done an excellent job. As well as the names of the deceased – twelve in total – there were the dates of death, the dates the post-mortem examinations took place, and the examination findings distilled from Evelyn's official report.

He'd told Evelyn that he was looking for connections, but his confidence in his investigative abilities was ebbing. She was probably right. What possible connection could there be between the death of an American academic and a dozen impoverished locals? Their lives would never have intersected, and they couldn't possibly have had anything in common. And yet, the fact remained they had all ingested the same kind of rough opium. That alone seemed to contradict their differences. There was one way to find out.

When he returned to the police courts on Upper Pickering Street, the crowd had thinned. He approached the reception desk where the clerk was filing away papers. Showing the man his warrant card, he explained he needed access to the archives, to have a look through some old records. The clerk gave his identification a cursory glance, and after watching Betancourt sign a register, he unlocked the door to the archives room and switched on the electric light. Betancourt followed him in. A single bulb cast a weak, tawny light upon rows of shelves stacked with box files. There were no windows and not a breath of air in the room. The smell of old paper and ink – the essence of the stories of the dead – hit him. He hadn't expected there to be so many records.

'How are they filed?'

'Old ones at this end; new ones at the other end.'

It made sense, and Betancourt felt a little foolish for asking.

The clerk showed him to a small writing desk. 'Looking for anything in particular?'

'Just fishing. Where would I find the inquest reports for the last three months?'

The clerk pointed to a far corner of the room. 'Over there.'

When the man had gone, Betancourt laid his notebook and pencil on the desk, as though he was back at school, readying himself for an exam.

He wandered up and down the rows nearest him, pulling out the odd file and squinting at the faded copperplate writing, trying to get a feel for… A feel for what? For many of the souls whose names rested here, this room contained the only record of their lived existence.

He scanned the list of *cacak* victims that Evelyn had given him and hoped the clerk had filed the records in some sort of date order. The task proved less onerous than he'd feared, and he soon had everything he was looking for. Each of the deceased had a separate form dedicated to them, but their lives and deaths merited no more than half a page each. Seven men and five women. The youngest twenty-four, the eldest sixty. Their occupations showed all the ingredients of a slice through Chinatown's population: rickshaw pullers, dock labourers, a domestic servant, *Samsui* women, a laundry worker, a barber, a prostitute.

The law required that the coroner hold an inquest for any death other than those by natural causes, and as Evelyn had marked all the deaths as being due to 'consumption of opium', a hearing had taken place. He read the reports through quickly, to acquaint himself with the salient facts of the lives and deaths of the subjects. The reports followed a standard format. Witnesses were called to testify to the victim's character, circumstances, habits, and state of mind. The number of witnesses was dependent in part on whether the victims had family and how many acquaintances they had. In these reports, the number of attesters varied from as few as two, in the case of one of the rickshaw pullers, to five, for the prostitute.

Nothing leapt out at him during his first pass. Unsurprisingly, all the victims were known to be habitual opium users. The court had noted that some were also heavy drinkers. Several were heavily indebted to traffickers for their passage to Singapore, even though their passage might have been several years ago, or to moneylenders, or to both.

He read each report again, slowly this time, looking for anything at all that might constitute a connection. In his notebook, he listed the addresses that were given as the deceased's place of residence. A pattern emerged: all the lodgings were in half a dozen streets in the Chinatown area, from Mosque Street in the north to Sago Lane in the south. He sketched out a rough street plan from memory and marked the locations. It was too small and specific an area to be a coincidence. He read through the reports a third time, looking for something else that might link the victims or their abodes. A couple of them attended a temple on Ayer Street; three had sought help from a *sinseh* on Chin Chew Street. An opium den on Nankin Street was mentioned. He read back through the reports once more.

Spent all his money at Lew Min's opium shop on Nankin Street...
Opium den...
Last seen alive on Nankin Street...
Opium seller, maybe Hokien Street...

Hokien Street. Or maybe Nankin Street, which was one street south? The detective senses he'd earlier doubted had found the connection he was looking for. He put the files back on their respective shelves and returned to the front desk.

'I need to use your telephone.'

He instructed the operator to connect him with the Marine Police station on Empress Place.

'Djulkifli? Find Quek and put him on to me.'

When a slightly out of breath Quek answered, Betancourt barked out instructions.

'See what you can find out about an opium shop in Nankin Street. It may be licensed to a Lew Min. There's a coffee shop on the corner of Hokien Street; the coffee's almost drinkable. Meet me there at eleven o'clock tomorrow morning. And bring what you have about Lew Min.'

'Got it, boss.'

'What did the engineers say about the gas stove?'

'Nothing, boss.'

'What do you mean, nothing?'

'It was gone, boss. Nothing there.'

'You got the right room, didn't you? Room 6?'

'Yes, boss. The constable on guard showed me. The whole room had been cleared up.'

'Did you ask the constable who had been in the building?'

'Yes, boss.'

Betancourt waited for Quek to apprise him of the results of this enquiry, but it wasn't forthcoming. 'And?'

'And what, boss?'

'What did he say when you asked him?'

'Ah, OK. He said a soldier had been in. A British soldier.'

The bomb squad man, Reeves, had said he was no longer interested as it wasn't, according to his technical definition, a bomb. Could he have changed his mind? He'd get hold of Reeves and find out.

'All right. Leave that with me.' He was about to hang up when he remembered Alex.

'I may regret asking this, but where is my motorcycle?'

'Here, boss. At the station. Just like you asked. I told you I could ride it OK.'

Betancourt breathed a sigh of relief.

'Just a couple of small dents,' the sergeant continued. 'Easy to fix. No problem.'

Quek sounded genuinely pleased with himself. Oh, well. It could have been worse, Betancourt supposed. As his Aunt Theresa used to say to him, be thankful for small mercies.

Chapter Sixteen

Having not seen the inside of the Raffles Museum for over twenty-five years, Betancourt now found himself entering the edifice for the second time in a week.

Mohammed, defender of the lobby, immaculate in his white dress tunic and black velvet *songkok*, stood motionless at his usual post at the foot of the grand staircase. Recognising Betancourt, he stirred and gave a small, courteous nod. 'You came back.' He delivered his words with what seemed like a tone of vague regret, which left Betancourt wondering whether the concierge considered his return a wholly positive event.

'I'm told that a Mr Lenehan is giving a talk, here in the museum.'

Mohammed shook his head.

'No?' said Betancourt.

'No talks in the museum.' Mohammed stretched out an arm and pointed across the expanse of foyer to the other side of the building. 'Talks in the library.'

Had it been anyone else, Betancourt might have put the

pedantic correction down to contrariety, but he was sure that, to Mohammed, it was nothing more sinister than the little things in life mattering.

Another uniformed attendant stood outside a pair of French doors, waving in the guests as they arrived. A board next to him announced the subject of the event:

Straits Asiatic Society
Artefacts and Their Origins
(Mr Thom. Lenehan – Secretary)

Betancourt looked up. The doors reached almost to the corniced ceiling, far above his head. It was as well, he thought, that the doors were painted and not shellacked; his friend with the tin-can stilts would never have reached the tops had he been called upon to varnish them.

Betancourt was unsure if this was supposed to be a members-only affair, but when he approached, the attendant offered no challenge and simply gave him a murmured, 'Good evening, *tuan.*' Nor was there a registration desk inside, or anything else that might have required Betancourt to identify himself and explain his interest in the evening's proceedings, so he took a seat at the rear, where he could keep an eye on the audience.

The chairs were the wooden-slatted, foldable type and were laid out ten to a row, either side of a central aisle. There was still ten minutes to go before the talk was scheduled to begin and he estimated the hall was already near to being full. The origins of artefacts seemed to be a more popular draw than he might have imagined.

Scanning the room, he wondered if Molly Ridpath would be here. There couldn't be that many archaeological talks on the local agenda, and if she was as keen on the subject as her collection of paperwork indicated, he'd expect to see her. He spotted her eventually, a few rows forward on the other side of the room, semi-obscured by a large, fluted pillar. She appeared preoccupied and wasn't paying any attention to the surrounding conversations.

The rest of the audience was much of a muchness – mostly male and mostly European. One attendee stood out. In the front row sat a striking-looking woman. Her face was immaculately but tastefully made up and her coffee-coloured hair swept back and fixed with a long-toothed tortoiseshell comb. She wore an evening gown that would have looked more in place at a reception at the Governor-General's *istana* than at a talk at the museum, and matching green jewels. He noticed that no one occupied the seats on either side of her. A few of the guests stopped briefly when passing to wish her a good evening, but she stared straight ahead, impassive, barely acknowledging their presence. Betancourt had the sense of being in the presence of royalty.

On the dot of seven o'clock, a man who Betancourt presumed was Lenehan mounted the stage and called the meeting to order. He was somewhat seedy looking, the wrong side of forty, and bearing the hallmarks of having already conceded his personal battle with the scales. He wore a three-piece brown striped suit and a full beard, into which streaks of grey had insinuated themselves. He looked to Betancourt as though he'd turned up twenty years too late.

He began with a few points of order: subscriptions were due at the end of the month, and could everyone do their best to pay on time this year? No one, Lenehan was sure, wanted a repeat of last year's debacle. Sales of raffle tickets had been disappointingly low and, yes, he realised there was a war on in Europe and belts were being tightened, but if everyone could sell just a couple of books, that would be jolly good. Finally, a call for proposers and seconders for continuation of the incumbent committee was readily answered.

The main event followed. An assistant set up a projector facing the rear wall, into which a reel of film was fed and set in motion. Lenehan called for the lights to be lowered, and for the next thirty minutes or so, he spoke over the hissing and crackling of the projector, which showed images of points of interest around Singapore's coast, some of which Betancourt recognised. The talk, such as it was, seemed to be a summary of Lenehan's own work in recovering items of Chinese porcelain. As each successive image filled the screen, he explained where he found the piece, what it represented, and why it was important. It was all over Betancourt's head. Not because it was difficult to understand, but because the items of porcelain all seemed to be recent – within the last hundred years – and not, as far as he could tell, of any great scientific interest. As the talk dragged on, the thrust of Lenehan's argument became clearer: he seemed to suggest that because his arte-facts were of relatively recent antiquity, it showed that Singa-pore's significant history was also recent, and other attempts suggesting Singapore had a more ancient past were fanciful at best. This view seemed to meet with the approval of a good number of the crowd, although there were, Betancourt was pleased to hear, a few barely concealed mutterings of *Rubbish!*

The talk came to its end, the assistant stayed the flapping tail of the film, and the lights came up again.

'We come now,' Lenehan intoned, 'to the final item of the evening's proceedings. I refer, of course, to the sad news of the passing of our dear friend, Richard Fulbright.' Murmured echoes of approval rippled around the room. 'Richard, as we all know, was an able scholar, and you'll doubtless have seen one or two of the pieces he contributed to the Society's news-letter.' He expanded on the highlights of Fulbright's life: his date and place of birth (13th February 1908; Newport, Rhode

Island), his academic background (Yale, and then doctoral studies at Cambridge under the late, also lamented Dr Donald Ridpath), and a summary of his career to date (digs at the Valley of the Kings and Alexandria before coming east to Asia: to Angkor, in the French colony of Cambodia; Sumatra, where he was reunited with Dr Ridpath; and thence to Singapore, where his work on demystifying the inscriptions on the Singapore Stone, though considered by some to be controversial − Betancourt took this to mean that he, Lenehan, found them controversial − had met with the recognition of his peers, leading to a nomination for the Farquhar Prize). Lenehan then informed the audience that, given the sudden announcement of Fulbright's death, and despite the shortlist now finding itself one name shorter than previously, the prize committee had informed him it had taken the decision not to reopen the entries.

Lenehan closed by saying he was sure Fulbright would be missed by those close to him (while not mentioning who they might be) and said he was sure he spoke for the assembled company in expressing his sympathies with the bereaved. While the words he used were, strictly speaking, appropriate, there was little about his closing remarks that showed that Lenehan himself would lose much sleep over his fellow scholar's demise.

Betancourt had learned little about Fulbright as a result of listening to the eulogy. Nor, given the nature of the gathering, had he expected to, but something bothered him about the manner of Lenehan's address. Everything he had said about Fulbright seemed, if not quite a deprecation of the dead man's achievements, to damn them with faint praise, just as the obituary had Betancourt thought back to what Molly Ridpath had said about rivalries in the archaeological world and resolved to ask her more about the relationship between Fulbright and Lenehan the next time he spoke to her.

He looked across to see how she was taking all this. Not well, if her appearance was anything to go by. She sat hunched in her chair, her hands balled into tight fists, a scrap of white handkerchief peeping from one, her mouth twisted into an ugly scowl as she tried to stem tears. She rocked slowly back and forth in her seat, and a few of the people seated next to her exchanged whispers and looks of concern.

The smattered applause died away and the hum of low-key chatter resumed. The talk finished, the crowd stood, and he stood with them, intending to speak to Molly Ridpath and offer any help she might require before seeking out Lenehan. What happened next was so unexpected and so bizarre that he was momentarily wrong-footed. The tall, glamorous woman in the front row, still grim-faced and ignoring renewed efforts by various members of the audience to engage with her, collected her things and marched off up the aisle towards the doors, which Mohammed's accomplice was in the process of reopening when a sudden shout rent the air.

'You evil bitch! This is all your fault!'

Pushing chairs and their erstwhile occupants out of her way with equal lack of care, Molly Ridpath careered towards the other woman. There were a few muttered imprecations – *I say!* and *Steady on!* – as she ploughed through the other patrons. Even from his position several rows away, Betancourt could see her eyes were red-rimmed and her face was flushed. Unsure whether to intercede, he watched as she pushed her way to the aisle, not giving any heed to the protests of the people she jostled aside, and faced her quarry.

'It was you. You killed him!'

The taller woman frowned, apparently unsure what was going on. She shook her head, as if dismissing some minor annoyance – the way she might dismiss a merchant seeking to show her his goods, or a street urchin asking for coins – and brushed past without saying anything, but her assailant wasn't to be dismissed so easily. Molly grabbed at the billowing sleeve of the other woman's dress. The sound of tearing silk echoed round the room, putting a stop to any conversation.

The tall woman spun round, an expression of shocked surprise soon giving way to one of anger.

'What the hell do you think you're playing at? Do you know how much this dress cost?'

Betancourt did not know what the motivation was for Molly Ridpath's assault, but he parked those thoughts as it was clear the situation was about to get ugly. Half-hurdling, half-stumbling across the now-scattered chairs, he reached the two women in time to prevent hostilities escalating. Lenehan, he noticed out of the corner of his eye, hovered nearby, close enough to show that he was concerned about this embarrassing incident, but not close enough to actually do anything that could effect its resolution.

'Stay there,' Betancourt ordered Lenehan, and then, thrusting out an interceding arm between the two women, said, 'Let's take this outside, shall we?'

'Who the hell are you?' the tall woman demanded, shaking off the hand Betancourt had laid on her arm.

Betancourt identified himself. 'Whatever it is that's going on here needs to stop.'

'Don't tell me, tell *that*!' The tall woman pointed a long finger at Molly. 'She's stark, staring mad. If you're a policeman—'

She looked him up and down, as though not fully prepared to believe the evidence of Betancourt's warrant card.

Why don't you arrest her?'

'Nobody is arresting anyone. I suggest we all go home. Whatever this is about, things will look different in the morning.'

The tall woman threw back her head contemptuously, and

with an accusatory '*Typical*' she strode to the front entrance where a cream coloured Lagonda stood, door open, ready to receive her. Without the slightest acknowledgment of the liveried syce who held the door, she threw herself into the back seat, and Betancourt watched as the car purred away into the night.

To give Molly Ridpath her due, the anger on her face had dissolved, to be replaced with a look of acute embarrassment. She glanced around apologetically, as though she'd only just noticed the assembled throng, all of whom were staring at her in fascinated horror. So much for the British being a race that believed in minding one's business, he thought.

'That's enough, ladies and gentlemen. The show's over.' He caught a few remarks to the tune of *Who's he to tell us what to do?* but one by one the onlookers melted away, most of them towards a long table that held bottles and glasses and a bucket of ice.

'I'm sorry. I don't know what came over me.' Molly shivered and pulled her light throw closer about her shoulders.

'What was that all about?'

She shook her head, as if trying to banish the memory of her behaviour. 'It was nothing. Really. I shouldn't have done it. It's just that when I saw her sitting there, so smug and self-satisfied, I couldn't stop myself.'

'Who is she?'

'Don't you know?' She seemed surprised, as though everyone should recognise the tall woman on sight. A spasm of anger flashed across her face again, and when she spoke, she almost spat the words out. 'That's Vita bloody Westaway. Whatever happened to Richard, she had something to do with it. I'm sure of it.'

He'd been right. There was another woman in Richard Fulbright's life. Or, leastways, there was *a* woman; whether she was *another* woman remained to be seen.

'Look, I need to speak to Lenehan. I believe Dr Trevose is going to arrange for you to identify the body?'

She gave a small timid nod, the flare of anger banished again. 'Yes. She called me. She asked me to go in tomorrow. At four o'clock.'

'Fine. I'll meet you there. We can speak then.'

Having seen her to the door, and made sure she was all right to get home on her own, he returned in search of Lenehan. He found him at the bar table, a large glass of something brown in his hand. Lenehan made his excuses to the linen-clad couple to whom he'd been talking and ushered Betancourt away from the crowd.

'Bit awkward, that. Not the usual sort of behaviour we expect at one of these affairs. Women, eh? Emotional.'

Betancourt chose not to respond to this psychological analysis of womankind and instead redirected the conversation to the reason for his visit.

'Were you and Dr Fulbright close?'

'Professionally speaking, do you mean?'

'In any way.'

'We knew each other, of course – ours is a small world – but, no, I wouldn't have called us close. What's all this about, anyway? Fellow drowned; that's what I heard. What's it to do with me?'

By this time, Betancourt had taken a thorough dislike to the pompous Lenehan, and he continued to ignore the man's questions.

'I'm led to believe there was a strong rivalry between the two of you.' Molly Ridpath hadn't said that at all, but Lenehan didn't know that.

'Well, you know how it is...'

'No, I don't know how it is. Why don't you tell me?'

'Well, Fulbright and I both worked in the same field: South-East Asia. His field was archaeolinguistics, of course. Mine is ceramics.'

'Archaeo-what?'

'Linguistics. He specialised in ancient languages. Him and old Ridpath, they tried for years to decipher the inscription on the Singapore Stone. Ridpath was convinced that if he could translate the inscriptions, it would prove that there had been a Majapahit empire hundreds of years before Raffles arrived.'

'I take it that Dr Fulbright agreed with Dr Ridpath's theory, and you don't.'

Lenehan gave a pig-like snort. 'Boy's Own adventure stuff. Pure fantasy. This godforsaken lump of rock was uninhabited until the first Siamese settlers came here in the seventeenth century, as I lay out clearly in my book, *Singapore: A Siamese Seaport*.'

It sounded to Betancourt that he was being extended an invitation to request Lenehan to expound further on his theories, but he was more interested in the here and now.

'Do you also work here, for the museum, with Dr Fulbright and Miss Ridpath?'

'No. My work is self-funded.' He paused for a moment before continuing. 'In any case, Fulbright didn't work for the museum. Neither does Miss Ridpath.'

'What do you mean? I spoke to Miss Ridpath in her own office upstairs not two days ago.'

'Yes. They all work, or should I say worked, *from* the museum. The benefits of having Cambridge backing you.' He said this with a touch of what Betancourt took to be jealousy. 'But they don't work *for* the museum. The trust just rents rooms.'

'What trust?'

'The Donald Ridpath Trust. That's who rents the space.

Although, I heard that Fulbright had been a bit, you know, slow with the payments.' Lenehan elongated the word slow.

Betancourt recalled that Molly Ridpath had mentioned going to visit her bank. Was this what it was about?

'On stage, earlier, you mentioned that both you and Dr Fulbright were up for a prize.'

Lenehan's eyes lit up. 'The Farquhar Prize. Every ten years, the Royal Society in London offers a prize for the most important archaeological findings in the preceding decade. Five thousand pounds.' The man almost licked his lips.

'And you're up for it? Who else?'

'Apart from me, there's an Australian named Halliday who did some minor work on the limestone tombs at Kamhantik in the Philippines, and a French crowd who do hill-tribe excavations in Laos. All trifling stuff, compared to *Singapore: A Siamese Seaport*.'

'That's it? Just the three entrants?'

'Well, obviously there was Fulbright for his Majapahit work, but, alas, he's no longer with us and, as I said earlier, the committee has decided it's too late to consider another entrant.'

Betancourt wondered how much influence Lenehan might have had in helping the committee reach their conclusion. He put away his notebook. He'd had enough archaeological intrigue for one night.

'One more thing. Vita Westaway. What was she doing here this evening?'

'Mrs Westaway often attends the talks. She's a much-valued patron of the museum. I even suggested she might wish to consider a donation to my work.' His face took on a sour aspect as he considered this memory.

'No luck?'

'Sadly, no. It seemed that by that time she had become a

confirmed Majapahitian. Fulbright had got his talons into her, of course.'

'Dr Fulbright and Vita Westway were friendly?'

Lenehan gave a dirty laugh. 'I'd say they were more than friendly, but I don't like to gossip.'

I bet you don't, thought Betancourt.

Chapter Seventeen

Betancourt arrived at Bill Allenby's stables early the following morning to find the old Australian discussing the health of one of his charges with Osman, his *mandore*. When he saw Betancourt approaching, he removed his dusty, sweat-stained old bush hat and scratched his head. He stared hard, as though unwilling to trust what his eyes were telling him.

'Well, lookie here. If I'm not mistaken, it's Inspector Betancourt, gracing us with his presence. Looks like him, anyroads. Mind you, been that long since we seen him, I could be wrong. What do you reckon, Osman? Reckon that's him?'

Osman looked confused, but Betancourt knew he'd worked for Allenby long enough to recognise when it was advisable to stay out of such conversations. Betancourt, too, knew to tread carefully around Allenby's caprices.

'I've been busy.'

'Busy be buggered. Bone idle, more like. Take it you haven't lost interest in the 'osses, you being so busy and all?'

'Always interested in the horses. You know that.'

The two men strolled together around the stable yard,

Allenby giving him updates on the horses Betancourt knew and potted histories of the few newcomers that had arrived since he'd last visited the yard. Hearing the inmates nickering as they approached, Betancourt regretted not bringing a few carrots or a handful of sugar lumps. He loved this place, and he didn't know what he'd do without it.

They reached the last horse in the row and retired to the converted stable on the end of the row Allenby used as a combination feed room, tack room, and office.

'Take a pew.'

Allenby gestured to a sack of chaff, turned on its side. A deep indentation suggested he'd been making use of it as his own seat. Betancourt turned a steel feed bin upside down. 'This'll do me.' He took a grunt from the trainer as appreciation.

Allenby plugged in an electric kettle and set about arranging mugs and teaspoons on a bale of hay. When the water had boiled and the tea had been made, he arranged his ample backside on the sack of chaff.

The appearance in the doorway of a small tweed-clad figure, stooped-shouldered and diffident-looking, brought their conversation to a temporary halt.

'Not interrupting anything, I hope. I saw you coming in, Inspector, and thought I would say hello.'

Quietly spoken, endlessly sanguine, and rarely seen without a beatific smile on his face, Major Melrose was a likeable old chap. He'd retired from something or other in the army and used his pension to buy a small tin mine outside Ipoh, which he now ran as a sort of hobby. His other hobby was betting on horses. Betancourt had no idea if Melrose was any good at tin mining, but he was very good indeed at the other. It was Melrose who had purchased Victory Parade when a neighbour was going to have the animal shot, and it was he who had masterminded the coup that had made them all – Melrose himself, Allenby, and Betancourt – if not exactly rich, then comfortable. Following Betancourt's dismissal from the CID, he had ploughed all his energy, and his savings, into searching for Anna. Melrose's coup and his own cut of the proceeds had saved him, and he was grateful.

Allenby had trained horses for Melrose since they were both young men, and Melrose usually had one or two in training. On their tour of the yard, Allenby had introduced Betancourt to the latest member of the collection, a mare named Topsy, which Melrose had imported from New Zealand.

'Bill showed me the new one,' Betancourt said. 'She looks well.'

'I've had three or four from that mare. They all won. Let's hope this one is as successful.'

Bill Allenby usually liked to give his newcomers a race or two to find their feet; to get used to racing in the heat. On the other hand, Melrose rarely made the long trip down from Ipoh unless he fancied the chances of one of his runners. Betancourt looked at Allenby and raised an eyebrow.

'If you're going to the races on Saturday,' Allenby said, 'you might want to think about strapping on your betting boots.'

Major Melrose winked, and his trademark smile grew even wider than usual as he walked away to his car.

'Well, I take it you didn't come up here for tips? Wanted that, you'd have been up here sooner. What can I do you for?'

'A horse. Fast Crowd. You didn't mention it when we were walking round. One of yours, isn't it?'

'Was. Ain't no more. Used to be called Bintang Emas. Remember him?'

Betancourt nodded. 'You always said if you could convince him to settle, he'd win races. Pulled a bit, didn't he?'

'A bit?' Allenby chuckled. 'Pulled like a train with no brakes. Just needed a bit of time. The one thing owners never

understand is time. A pommie owned him. Got fed up waiting, so he sold him. What you wantin' to know about the 'oss
for?'

'I'm more interested in who owns him now.'

'I see. Police business, eh? Not going to tell your old friend
what's going on? That about the size of it?'

Betancourt smiled. 'Tell me about the horse.'

'Well, it were like this,' Allenby said. 'The pommie – the
first one, the one who owns the 'oss when he's still called
Bintang Emas – he gets fed up waiting for the 'oss to come
right, so he sells him to another pom. The second pom
changes the 'oss's name. Well, I say it was him what changed
the name. Reckon it was his missus. She's the one what wears
the trousers. Anyroads, you know the old saying: change a
name, change your luck? Sure enough, the 'oss wins first time
out for them. Couple months back, it was. I put you onto him,
didn't I?'

'You said you reckoned he might have a chance.'

'Wasn't sure if I'd got him right. Only had a few dollars on
him myself. Nothing extravagant. Beer money. That's all.'

'This pom – the one who bought the horse. Does he have
a name?'

'Westaway. *Captain* Westaway, he said I should call him.
Cheeky bugger.'

Bingo.

'He's not married to a Vita Westaway, is he? Tall, looks
like a Hollywood actress?'

'That's the one.'

'You said he calls himself captain. Is he army?'

'Didn't ask, but stands to reason, I suppose.'

Betancourt showed Allenby the owner's badge he'd found
inside the race programme in Fulbright's room.

'Inner Circle Stable. Was that the stable name the horse
raced under?'

Allenby nodded. 'Westaway's missus seemed to think it was a bit of a joke. I reckon it was her that Westaway bought the 'oss for. He didn't seem the type. Her, mind you... Fast Crowd.' He gave an ironic snort. 'She looked like a fast one to me.'

'Liked a bet, did he, this Westaway character?'

Allenby shrugged. 'Can't say as I noticed. She did, though. Threw tickets around like they were confetti. Not even as though she was doing it for the money. Reckon it was all a bit of a game to her.'

'Did you ever see her with a young American?' Betancourt showed him Fulbright's picture.

Allenby unfolded a pair of spectacles and peered at the picture. 'I remember him. Never came here, but I saw him with Her Ladyship at the races. Funny name. What was it, now...'

'Fulbright.'

'That's him. Remember thinking he was batting above his average with that one. Husband wasn't too happy about it either.'

'What do you mean?'

'The usual. It was after the 'oss won that time. I warned them beforehand the 'oss might not be ready, but they wouldn't hear a bar of it. I remember her giving the boy his orders.' It was typical of Allenby to refer to anyone under fifty as 'the boy'. 'Backed it like it was going out of fashion, the pair of them. Don't recall seeing her giving him any money, mind you. Reckon it must have been his own he was spending. Anyroads, I'd gone down to the saddling boxes to see about the 'oss – make sure he was all right. The lot of them came down, glasses in hand. As me Irish mate would have said, "drink had been taken". I told them to shift. Didn't want a glass getting broken and the 'oss standing on it. Mrs W was draped all over the boy. Ask me, she looked like she was doing it on purpose, to get a rise out of her old man. Kept looking over at him, as if to say, "Well, what you going to do?" Eventually, the husband had enough and dragged her away by the arm. Gave her a right good talking to.'

'How did she react?'

'Laughed in his face. Went back to the boy and the pair of them disappeared. Give the young 'un his due, he didn't look too happy about it. Kept looking over his shoulder at the husband. Reckon he was worried Westaway was going to cop him one.'

'Well, he won't need to worry about that any more.'

'That right? Sorry to hear that. Seemed like a decent sort of bloke. Just got in with the wrong crowd. What happened to him?'

'His body was found in the sea off Pasir Panjang.'

'Drowned?'

'Doesn't look like it.'

Allenby raised an eyebrow. 'And you reckon the jealous husband might have had something to do with it?'

Betancourt shrugged. 'It's possible. I'm still trying to paint a picture. Who he was, what he did, who he did it with. That sort of thing. You said the horse is gone. What happened?'

Allenby emitted what could only be described as a growl. 'Bloke sends me an 'oss. Not Westaway, another bloke. A filly. Princess Poppy. Nice little thing, but they'd been running her all wrong. I told him I'd win a race with her, but he needs to be patient. One night, after evening feed, Osman's going round, doing his last checks. Finds the bloke at the 'oss's box. Got a mate with him. Osman sees the mate climbing into the box, so he shouts and asks them what they're up to. Tells 'em nobody goes near the 'osses if I'm not around. Bloke says he's the one paying the bills and he'll see his 'oss whenever he wants.

'Then Osman sees the one who's climbing over the bars

MARK WIGHTMAN

has got a syringe, so he gets straight onto the blower to me. I come up here and check on the 'oss. She's a bit quiet, but she seems all right. Next morning, when I look her over again, I see a lump on her neck. No idea what they gave her, but I had to scratch her. Risk my licence if I didn't. Could've been anything in that syringe.

'Next thing, the owner turns up at the races and hears the 'oss is scratched. Drives round here lookin' for a blue. Said I had no right. I told him to get himself off my property or I'd hand him his arse. And he could take his 'oss with him. All mouth and no trousers, he was. Skulked away, saying I'd pay for it. Forty-five years I've been training 'osses and never once been accused of doping. Him and Westaway must've been muckers because the next thing I know, Westaway's took Fast Crowd away too. Last time I saw the 'oss in training, he was back to his old ways: carting the riding boy all over the place. Bloody owners.'

He spat into the sawdust, making it abundantly clear what he thought about the people who paid the bills.

'This friend of Westaway, was he another army type?'

'Nah. He was a local. Some sort of doctor. Name of Loong.'

'Loong? The *sinseh*?'

'If you say so.'

Fulbright, Vita Westaway, her husband, Loong. Betancourt drew four circles in his notebook and added each of the names to a circle. He joined the circles with thick lines and added a large question mark. Fulbright had been having an affair with Westaway's wife. He'd also consulted Loong for his opium addiction. Loong knew Westaway, and Westaway had a reason for wanting Fulbright out of the way.

He put away the notebook and leafed through the pages of the programme once more, hoping to divine something from within its pages. He found nothing.

160

'All right if I use your phone?'

Allenby gestured to the unit screwed to the stable wall. 'Help yourself. Reckon I'll go see to me 'osses. Blokes killing blokes. Gives me the willies. Don't know how you do it. Give me 'osses any day. 'Oss might pinch a bit of next door's hay, but you won't see 'em killing each other.'

Chapter Eighteen

I t took a few calls before Betancourt tracked down his contact, a bookie's runner named Ah Long. When Betancourt was still in CID, he'd broken up an illegal betting ring run by Ah Long's father, also known as Ah Long, and had spared the junior version on condition he alerted Betancourt to any developments in the field of illegal gambling. Neither man's name was actually Ah Long; Ah Long was Cantonese street vernacular for a loan shark and carried with it menacing overtones of violent retribution for slow payers. Whether the name carried the same threat in the bookmaking industry, he wasn't sure.

When he eventually got hold of him, he told Ah Long he'd meet him at the coffee shop on Hokien Street, the one he was due to meet Quek at later. Ah Long initially declined Betancourt's offer and said he'd rather not be seen in such a public place consorting with a member of His Majesty's police. Betancourt told him it was his choice: he could either meet as suggested, or he could have his every move shadowed by a young police sergeant who was keen to impress his superiors and would relish the opportunity of ruining the bookie's credibility. Ah Long relented.

The coffee was good. Betancourt finished his cup and checked his watch. He'd said ten o'clock. It was now a quarter-past and there was still no sign of Ah Long, Jnr. He was about to give up when a loud hissing sound coming from somewhere behind him caught his attention.

He turned.

A head poked through the doorway that led to the kitchen. It was Ah Long, disguised, or so he no doubt thought, by a pair of sunglasses and a woman's headscarf. He beckoned furiously to Betancourt, who shook his head and beckoned back, signalling he'd no intention of entering the kitchen and that Ah Long should emerge from his hiding place and join him at his table. Ah Long stepped gingerly out into the main part of the coffee shop. When he did so, Betancourt saw he hadn't stopped with the headscarf and sunglasses. In addition, he wore a woman's black dress, several sizes too small and riding up his thighs, black stockings, seams surprisingly straight, and a pair of black high heels on which he teetered precariously.

Betancourt placed his head in his hands. Coffee or no coffee, it was too early in the day for this.

'What on earth are you doing?'

'In disguise, *lah*. Cannot be seen.' Ah Long wriggled onto a stool.

'Where did you get that lot from?'

'My sister. Not bad, huh?

'Look on the bright side. If you ever decide you've had enough of working for the bookies, you could always find work entertaining the sailors down Bugis Street.'

Betancourt was as eager as his informant to be done with this charade. He showed Ah Long Fulbright's photograph.

'Can't see,' said the bookie.

'That's because you've still got your sunglasses on. Take them off.'

Ah Long removed the sunglasses and squinted.

'I need you to ask around,' said Betancourt. 'Find out if this man owed money. Horses, probably, but check if he owed for anything else. And who to.' He tore a page from his notebook and handed it over. 'If you find anything, call the station and leave a message.'

Ah Long scowled at the name on the piece of paper. 'How you say this?'

'*Full-bright.*'

His informant practised it a few times, under his breath, before pronouncing himself satisfied. 'OK.' He told Betancourt that Fulbright's name didn't ring any bells and he was sure the American owed nothing to his family, but he would ask the other runners.

'Maybe the Lucky Seven,' Ah long suggested.

'That might make sense. See what you can find out.'

With that, Ah Long attempted to dismount, but found getting his skirt-clad backside off the stool less easy than it had been getting it on. He made one Herculean effort to launch himself back onto terra firma and succeeded only in splitting his sister's dress up to the waist. With one hand carrying the shoes and the other trying to protect his modesty, Ah Long disappeared back through the swing door into the kitchen.

'I despair,' Betancourt said to no one in particular.

Chapter Nineteen

'It's that one.' Quek pointed to a nondescript shopfront that looked much like any other in the row, except that its shutters were closed and there was nothing to proclaim what purpose the establishment might serve, save for a dented red tinplate sign nailed to the wall just below the eaves, bearing the den's Monopolies Commission licence number. Betancourt made a note of the number.

'What do we know about the owner?'

Quek shrugged. 'Just what you said. His name is Lew Min. He's held the licence for two years and it has another year to run.'

'All right. Here's what we're going to do. When we go in, you detain the owner. Ask to see the licence. When he produces it, make a big show of examining it. Copy all the details down. Pretend you're comparing it to your notes, that sort of thing. Question him about where he got it and who issued it. Give him a thorough going over.' He handed Quek Evelyn's list of names. 'Be specific: ask him about these names. He probably won't know, but that doesn't matter. Check the account book. See if you find the names. Then, when you've finished doing that, check the patrons too. Make sure they have their permits on them. Check the photographs. Wake a few up, if necessary – that should create a bit of stir. Take as much time as you can; I want to have a good look around.'

Betancourt waited until Quek had finished writing his instructions in his notebook before rapping on the door. A slat opened and a rheumy eye appeared. This was a government-licensed establishment, so there was no reason the proprietor shouldn't admit all-comers. The door opened a crack and a small, wizened man with an old-fashioned rat's tail moustache peered out.

'Lew Min?'

The man nodded but said nothing. Betancourt pushed open the door, brushing him out of the way.

'Inspection.'

Lew Min shrugged, as though one inspection more or less made no difference to him, and retreated behind a desk upon which were an abacus, a cash box, and an open ledger. Under the terms of the government licensing scheme, the proprietors of opium dens like this were required to keep an account of all sales. Betancourt didn't doubt there were sales records in the book, but whether the proprietor had recorded *all* the sales was another matter.

He nodded to Quek. 'Right, get started. Make sure no one leaves until we're finished.'

He then addressed Lew Min. 'Where's your storeroom?'

With the merest flick of his head, the man indicated the rear of the building.

'Is it locked?'

No answer.

'I'll take that as a no. Sergeant, make a note. It's compulsory all licensees store opium under lock and key.'

He waited for some sort of excuse, a protest, anything, but

the opium dealer's thoughts were unfathomable. Either he was a master of brinkmanship, or he had nothing to hide after all.

The den comprised one long room stretching through to the rear of the building. Betancourt presumed it had once served another purpose as there remained traces of paint, green and rose pink, on the walls and on the cornices of the ceiling. But mostly it was shorn of decoration – there were no pictures, the light bulbs were naked, and the beds were bare planks of wood, twisted and split by the humidity and the heat, resting on crudely cut legs. The rows of forms stretched all the way along the walls of the room, like rough-hewn pews in a primitive church. On the beds a succession of prone figures lay on their sides, blocks of wood acting as crude pillows. A tray containing smoking impedimenta separated each pair: pipes made from bamboo tubes terminating in a small porcelain bowl; spirit lamps for warming the opium, to release the vapours; a needle to skewer the balls of opium before holding them in the flame. The stone floor was thick with ash and stoor. Those who had been imbibing when Betancourt had barged in watched him with incurious eyes, waiting to be told it was all right to resume. Those who had finished their pipes before the interruption slept, and a few gentle snores were the only sounds in the room. Betancourt gave a small involuntary shake of the head, but it was as much one of pity as of censure.

He found the storeroom easily enough. The hasp was open, a padlock hanging from it, a brass key protruding from the lock. He pulled at the door, and it swung open. A small window, covered in dust and cobwebs, admitted the only light, and it took a few moments for his eyes to adjust to the gloom.

To one side of the room, a galvanised pail and a mop that looked like they'd seen little recent action stood next to the incongruous form of an old bicycle – tyres flat and the frame showing signs of rust. Other than that, the room contained four stacks of wooden boxes, each box about a foot square and six inches high. He picked up a box from the nearest stack. In form, it was like a miniature tea chest, and was surprisingly light. The number 3742 had been burnt into the lid using some sort of branding iron. This, presumably, was a quick way of ensuring that the opium reached the correct licensed premises. He checked it against the licence number he'd written down. They tallied. Below the shop number was a description of the contents: *40 hoon 384 pcs.* He lifted a few more boxes. They all carried the same marks. He grasped the lid of one of the boxes and tried to pry it free. It was nailed down and refused to budge. Scanning the room, his eyes alighted on a thin metal bar with a flattened end. It was smooth and rust-free and must have been in regular use. Betancourt guessed it was what Lew Min used to prise open the chests. Grasping the bar, he levered off the lid. At first glance, the box appeared to be filled with straw, but when he pulled the packing aside, the real contents revealed themselves: rows of sealed aluminium tubes, each marked with a red label. He opened another box. The contents appeared to match the description on the lid.

He did a quick count. Around fifty boxes. One hundred and twenty-eight tubes per box. Three balls of opium per tube. Each tube had a retail value of about seven dollars. So, here had to be getting on for fifty thousand dollars' worth of opium in this small, unlocked room. Tempting fate? Or had the owner reason to know his investment was safe?

He lifted a tube from each of the opened boxes and pocketed them. He'd ask the lab boys to check them, but he didn't expect them to find anything untoward. He replaced the lids on the boxes he'd opened and set up about restacking them. Something caught his eye. When he'd removed the boxes to sample, he'd left a space. At the very bottom of an adjacent stack, one of the boxes bore a mark resembling some sort of stylised creature. He peered at it more closely. It was a dragon. Not the fire-breathing type that St George battled in the English storybooks his teachers had made him read at school, but a writhing, twisting, serpent-like dragon of Chinese folklore. He checked the boxes he'd opened previously. None of them bore a similar mark. He quickly removed the rest of the pile and opened the box with the dragon on it. At first, all appeared normal. The box contained a layer of straw covering metal tubes laid out the same way as the ones he'd examined. He pulled from his pocket one of the tubes he'd taken as evidence and laid it on top of the tubes in the box. The aluminium tubes themselves appeared identical, and the hermetic seals showed no sign of having been tampered with. The red labels looked the same. And yet, something jarred. What was it? He peered closer. It was subtle, but close up he could see that the labels on the new tube bore a row of tiny perforations down one side. He broke the seal on the tube and tipped the contents into his hand. It was *cacak*.

An argument had broken out in the main salon. Quek's stalling techniques must have reached their limit. Betancourt stuffed the *cacak* back in the tube and, taking another one from the crate for good measure, stowed the evidence into the pocket of his jacket. Hurriedly replacing the lids on the boxes he'd opened, he returned them to where he'd found them. He had just made sure he'd re-hidden the box with the dragon emblem on it when the hinges of the door creaked behind him. He turned to find Lew Min staring at him.

'Everything seems in order.' Betancourt held out the two legal tubes he'd taken so the den owner could see the labels. 'I'm taking a couple of samples to check. You've no objection, I assume?' He gave Lew what he hoped was a disarming smile. 'I'll give you a receipt, if you want.'

The den owner didn't reply. His gaze pivoted from the

opium in Betancourt's hand to the stacks of crates and back. His eyes flashed with anger. Finally, he found his tongue.

'You go. Now.'

It would do Betancourt no good to arouse any more suspicion than he'd already done, so he retraced his steps and grabbed Quek.

'Come on. I've a feeling we've outstayed our welcome.'

Chapter Twenty

Betancourt walked swiftly away from the opium den, trailing Quek in his wake. He quickly checked up and down the street to ensure they weren't being followed. Satisfied no one was paying them any undue attention, he hauled the bemused sergeant into the doorway of a nearby steam laundry.

In as unobtrusive a manner as he could manage, he slipped the sergeant two of the tubes – one of the legal ones and one suspect. 'Take these. Go straight to the laboratory at the General Hospital and have them tested. Tell them they're from me and I want the express service. Tell them we've a dead American and the Assistant Commissioner himself is crawling all over you for answers and, unless they want him crawling all over them, too, they need to make it snappy.'

Quek's eyes were like saucers. 'Is the AC crawling all over me?'

'No, but they won't know that, will they?' Quek looked disappointed, as though he would have welcomed some personal attention from the top brass. Give it time and a few haulings over the coals, Betancourt thought, and he'd learn that keeping his head below the level of the parapet paid bigger dividends in the long run. 'Take a taxi; I don't want you walking the streets with that lot in your pocket. And don't forget to ask the driver for a chitty or *I'll* have Bonham crawling all over me, and neither of us want that, do we?' Quek shook his head in earnest agreement. 'Right, get going.'

He had about half an hour before he was due to meet Molly Ridpath at the Crypt to complete the formal identification of the body. Not that it made any difference now – Gemmell's kangaroo inquest was history, but at least Evelyn would be able to square away the paperwork in the proper manner. He decided he'd make use of the time by following up on the information Lenehan had given him the previous evening.

Returning to the *kopi tiam* on Nankin Street, he exchanged ten cents for the use of the telephone. The operator placed his call and the now-familiar voice of Mohammed, the concierge, sounding sadder than ever, if that was possible, greeted him.

'*Mem* Ridpath is not here, I'm afraid. Do you want me to give her a message?'

'No, it's actually Mrs Rosario, your accountant, who I want to speak to.'

'One moment.'

There was a crackle of static, followed by Mohammed's disembodied voice. 'Go ahead.'

'This is Mrs Rosario here. What can I do for you?' The woman spoke English with an affected accent. 'More English than the English' was a term he'd heard used, and it suited.

'Inspector Betancourt. Special Investigations Unit.' He omitted the Marine Police bit; it wouldn't add anything to the current conversation. 'I'm investigating the death of Dr Fulbright. I believe you had dealings with him.'

'That is correct. A regrettable business.'

'What was? His death or your dealings with him?'

There was a brief silence before the accountant said, a little haughtily, 'I was referring to Dr Fulbright's unfortunate demise.'

'What exactly was your business with the doctor?'

'I deal with all matters financial. The museum has an arrangement with the Donald Ridpath Trust. The trust pays us for the use of facilities. Latterly, Dr Fulbright represented the trust.'

'Latterly?'

'After Dr Ridpath returned to England.'

'When you say he represented the trust, what were Dr Fulbright's responsibilities?'

'Minimal, really. He signed the leases for the rooms. His only other responsibility was to ensure he paid the rent on time.'

'And did he? Pay it on time?'

'I really can't discuss private matters such as that.'

'Oh, you really can, you know. You can do it now, over the telephone, or I can send a constable down there to escort you to the police station. What would your staff make of that, I wonder?'

Betancourt had guessed Rosario was the type who set great store by her image, and it seemed his guess was correct.

'No, no. That won't be necessary. Ask your questions.'

'I asked if the rent was paid on time.'

'Initially, yes. Then a few payments were late, and for the last few months, they have been non-existent.'

'How much does the trust owe?'

There was a rustle of paper as she checked her figures. 'One thousand, one hundred and sixty-eight dollars and fifty-seven cents. Interest is accruing at two per cent per month.' Anyone but an accountant would have rounded the sum up or down. Mrs Rosario preferred precision, apparently.

'You said Dr Fulbright signed the leases. What happens now he is dead?'

'Nothing. The contracts stand. Dr Fulbright signed the contracts on behalf of the Donald Ridpath Trust. The trust is responsible for its debts.'

'And who are the trustees now?' He suspected he knew the answer, but wanted to hear it, anyway.

'You would really need to speak to whoever set up the trust, but I believe Dr Ridpath's daughter is now the sole trustee.'

Betancourt thanked the woman, who hung up without acknowledgement, and pondered his next move. Given that the bankbook he found in Fulbright's room was for the Royal Edinburgh & Imperial Bank, it was a fair bet the trust would have used the same bankers, and if the Royal Edinburgh held the account, his friend Sir John Cluny might be prepared to divulge more about the trust's financial position. Even if the trust did its banking business elsewhere, Cluny knew everything that happened in Singapore's financial circles, and if another bank was carrying the trust's debt, he could be relied upon to dish the dirt.

Some years previously, Betancourt had, as a personal favour, rescued Cluny's daughter, Victoria, from an uncertain future as the underage bride of a wastrel of an Irish subaltern. Cluny was duly grateful, as was Victoria, after time had passed and her broken heart had mended, and ever since, Betancourt and Cluny had enjoyed a largely harmonious relationship. If Betancourt heard rumours of financial legerdemain, he passed them on to Cluny. Even if the rumours didn't affect Cluny directly, he was a man to whom knowledge was power, and he was always pleased to receive anything Betancourt cared to pass on. In return, if Betancourt needed to know which way the financial tides were running at any given time, Cluny was his man.

He had the number of the banker's private line, and usually when he had a piece of information to pass on, he would telephone. But when he wanted something from Cluny, he visited the great man in person. It reinforced Cluny's sense of power, having people who needed something from him sit before him. So, half an hour later, a paeon ushered Betancourt into Cluny's eyrie above the waterfront. There Cluny sat wreathed in cheroot smoke, dressed as always in a black serge frock coat, bewhiskered and bespectacled. Betancourt had noticed before that whenever he sat in Cluny's visitor's chair, the banker managed to give the impression of looking down on him, like a king looking down on a subject. Cluny wasn't a particularly tall man, and Betancourt wondered if he'd had a dais built behind his desk, just to reinforce his status. He'd never had the nerve to look.

'What is it today, Inspector? Business, or pleasure?' In Cluny's parlance, business meant Betancourt's business and pleasure meant his own. Money, in other words.

'Business. The Donald Ridpath Trust. I was hoping they might be clients of yours.'

'Everyone important is a client of mine.'

Betancourt raised an eyebrow. 'Is the trust important?'

'Not in financial terms, no. But by association. Sometimes relationships are tactical and sometimes strategic. Ridpath had a lot of wealthy patrons in his heyday.'

'Had?'

'The whole thing's gone to pot since his death. Ridpath was a clever man, but he was no businessman. No judgement. He had some American running things. Bad choice.'

'The American is why I'm here. His name was Fulbright. He was fished out from under a *kelong* a few days ago.'

Cluny grunted. 'Is that right?' He unscrewed the cap of a fountain pen and scribbled a note to himself on his desk jotter.

'Last night I attended a talk on broken porcelain organised by an outfit called the Straits Asiatic Society. The talk was given by a man named Lenehan. An archaeologist, like Ridpath and Fulbright. Lenehan told me the Donald Ridpath Trust has been having a few problems paying its bills.'

'How did this Lenehan character know that?'

'Archaeology's a small world, I'd imagine. At least in Singapore. Tight-knit community, gossip, the usual. I called the accountant at the museum, and she confirmed. The trust owed a thousand dollars. Not the end of the world, but…'

Cluny picked up the telephone. 'The Donald Ridpath Trust. Yes, Ridpath, with an '*i*'. Bring it up, quick as you like.'

A few moments later, there was a timid knock at the door.

'Come!'

An anxious face edged its way into view.

'Let's have it then, man.'

The paeon to whom the face belonged handed over the file and beat a hasty retreat. Cluny consulted the file.

'Seems your man, Lenehan, was right. It's not just the museum they owe money to. Ridpath explained the business to me once. There's more to it than a few boffins with trowels and brushes. Those excavations they do last for months. Materials, wages; it all adds up. They owe money all over town.'

'Including to your bank?'

Cluny nodded. 'I financed them, yes.'

'Whose name is the debt in?'

'Strictly speaking, it's in the trust's name, but when Ridpath was still alive, he signed a mortgage document agreeing to underwrite the trust's debts. I expect he meant it to cover the existing credit line.'

'There's been more?'

'Your American, Fulbright, drew down several thousand dollars. I see he was careful to keep his own name off the papers.'

'What will happen now?'

'I wouldn't be much of a banker if I let people fritter away my money. If the trust can't meet its commitments, then I'll have to call for a repossession, under the terms of the mortgage agreement.'

'What did Ridpath give as a guarantee?'

Cluny checked the account details again and then paused a moment. 'It says here there's a house involved. The Arches, Send Marsh, Surrey. It belongs to the wife, Mary Ridpath.'

'Did she sign the document?'

'Didn't need to. What's hers was his.'

Betancourt wondered if Molly knew about the debt.

'Could you do me a favour? Could you hold off on calling in the debt?'

'I suppose so. The next account review isn't until the end of the month. I'll give you until then.' Cluny eyed him keenly. 'What are you up to?'

Betancourt gazed out of the window at the bumboats skirting the waterfront below. What was he up to? The truth was, he had no idea, but it wouldn't do to let Cluny know that.

Chapter Twenty-One

T he sun had receded from its scorching zenith, but despite the cover provided by the canopy of the rickshaw he'd taken from Battery Road, by the time he reached Clarke Quay his shirt was damp and sticky and the cool of Evelyn's subterranean cavern was welcome.

She was working on a cadaver when he entered, and he waited until she had finished what she was doing.

'Your rickshaw puller from the Excelsior.' She stood back to let Betancourt have a closer look.

Given the extent of the damage to the man's face, she'd done a remarkable job. The eyes were closed and the lacerations to the face sewn shut. She had, presumably, rearranged the bones beneath, as there was little sign of the crushed skull. There wasn't much that she could have done about the nose, but she'd cleaned it up and the whole effect was a lot less gruesome than it might have been. He was sure she'd even gone so far as to restore some of the man's complexion with a touch of make-up. Martha had once told him it was something Evelyn liked to do. 'The doctor likes to leave them with a little dignity,' she'd said. The old man looked at peace, and Betancourt was grateful to her for that.

'Thank you,' he said.

Evelyn put a hand to her hair, as if to check it was still there, and no one had made off with it while she was concentrating. He'd caught her off-guard, and for a brief moment she was flustered. She gave a quick, shy nod of acknowledgement, and then the moment was gone.

There was a knock at the door and an orderly showed in Molly Ridpath, looking none the worse for the previous evening's altercation with Vita Westaway. Martha trundled out Richard Fulbright's body and Betancourt retreated, to allow the formalities to be completed. Molly gave a short, anguished cry and then a quick nod of recognition before turning away, tears running down her face. Evelyn thanked her for coming in and asked her where she would like the body sent.

'I've no idea. We were only colleagues. Surely it shouldn't be up to me.'

She sniffed as she spoke, and Betancourt wondered once again if her assertion that her interest in Fulbright was solely professional was the whole truth.

'Do you know if there's a next of kin?' Evelyn asked.

'He never spoke about family, but he must have had them. I'm sorry, I wouldn't know who to ask.'

Betancourt stepped out of the shadows. 'The American Consulate are aware. They like to know when one of their own is involved. I presume they'll want to repatriate the body.'

'Fine. In the meantime,' Evelyn said, 'there's an undertaker we use, in cases like this, when there's no direct family. I'll contact them. They're very good.'

Molly Ridpath gave Evelyn her contact details and made for the door. Betancourt caught up with her.

'Do you mind if I accompany you? I have a few more questions.'

'No, not all. In fact, I could rather do with the company right now.'

'The sun is glorious. It cleanses the soul, don't you agree?' Molly had stopped beside a park bench shaded by a flame tree and turned her face to the sky.

Betancourt didn't agree. In fact, he'd never understood the European fixation with the heat. To locals like him, the sun and the warmth it generated were just facts of everyday living that had to be tolerated rather than being subjects for continual examination. He was sure his soul could be perfectly well cleansed if it was inside, preferably inside somewhere that had air conditioning.

She looked around, as though taking in her surroundings for the first time. 'I'm famished. Do you mind if we have tea? I'm afraid I don't know anywhere. Do you have any recommendations?'

He pointed in the direction of the museum. 'There's a place up that way. My wife used to talk about meeting friends there.' He realised with a regretful start that it had been a while since he had used Anna's name when referencing anything. There had been a time, not that long ago, when her imagined presence had been the nexus of his thinking. Was he really letting go of her memory? It was an unwelcome thought and he forced himself to dismiss it from his mind.

Molly retrieved a pair of oversized sunglasses from her bag and put them on, and they walked in silence until they reached a coffee shop on the corner of Ord Street and River Valley Road. The exterior of the shop was ornately decorated with intertwined painted roses and cherubs dancing around a triangular shaped edifice, which Betancourt was pretty sure was intended to be a reproduction of the Eiffel Tower. He'd seen a photograph of the real thing and, while the scale was all wrong, there were enough similarities to make the connection. Pretentious or not, the cafe's European styling made it popular, and there appeared to be few free tables. The proprietor, a plump Chinese woman, greeted Molly while ignoring her *Serani* companion.

'A table, madame?'

'Yes. We'll take that one.' Molly pointed to a table in a quiet corner that was being cleared.

'I'm afraid that table is reserved, madame.'

'Excellent. We won't be disturbed then, will we?'

Betancourt was impressed. If he'd tried that move, he'd probably have been shown the door. Unless he'd introduced his warrant card into the discussion, of course, but that always felt like cheating.

The proprietor, knowing when she was beaten, led them to the newly laid table. She handed them menus, which declared the establishment to be named *Le Pâtisserie*.

'*La.*'

Betancourt frowned. 'What?'

'It should be *La Pâtisserie*, not *Le*. It's French.'

Betancourt felt it was the sort of thing he should have known, not least because his wife was the daughter of French colonials.

'Yes, I'd gathered that. I'm not totally ignorant, you know.'

She put a finger to her cheek and looked away, as if considering his claim, and then laughed. Maybe there was something in her assertion about the restorative properties of the sun's rays.

A young woman dressed in a black smock with a white lace collar and pinafore took their order. After that, they sat in silence for a minute, neither eager to be the one to start the conversation.

He spoke first.

'Thank you for coming today. I realise it must have been

difficult. It's important we have the body formally identified or the case just sits in limbo. Now it's all official, Dr Trevose can endorse the inquest result.'

'They've done the inquest already? I didn't realise... I mean, I didn't expect it to happen so quickly. I would have attended, had I known. Someone should have been there.'

'There was a lot of interest in high places.' He told her about his meeting with Garfield, the American consular assistant. 'My superior is keen to stay on the right side of the Americans. Doubtless, he'll have played a part in having the inquest prioritised.'

'I see. And what did they say? At the inquest, I mean. What was the verdict? Is that what they call it? A verdict?'

'Officially, Dr Fulbright went swimming, became entangled with a stray fishing net, and, sadly, lost his life. Misadventure.'

'But what about the opium?'

'Officially, there was no opium.'

'You've used that word twice now: *officially*. What about unofficially?'

He thought for a moment about how well he really knew this woman. And whether he could trust her. His instinct told him he could.

'Unofficially, I think someone killed him.'

'But who? And why?'

'I don't know yet.'

'Is that why you wanted to speak to me again?'

Betancourt nodded.

'But if the inquest has given a verdict of death by misadventure, surely that's it. Why are you still investigating?'

'The inquest is enough for Fulbright's body to be released to his family, but the case isn't complete yet. Although I'm sure the Assistant Commissioner will be after me to draw a veil over things as soon as possible.'

'And will you? Draw a veil over things?'

'Not yet, no. I'll just have to stay out of his way until I'm happy I have investigated everything that needs to be investigated.'

'You're quite the Machiavelli, aren't you, Inspector?'

'I haven't read Machiavelli. Do you recommend him?'

'If political machinating is your game, and I suspect from what I've just heard it is, then, yes, I'd recommend him very much.'

The young woman in the pinafore returned with a tray bearing sandwiches, cream cakes, and a pot of tea. When they'd helped themselves, Betancourt decided it was time to shift gear.

'What was he like to work with?'

'Richard?' She pursed her lips, as though considering the question for the first time. 'Intense. He didn't say a lot. Not to me, anyway. I got the impression he wasn't too keen on working for a woman.'

'You were his boss?'

'Don't sound so surprised. It happens, you know.'

He shook his head. 'I didn't mean that. It's just you spoke highly of Dr Fulbright's abilities, but you've said nothing about your own.'

Dr Fulbright. Had he been putting his foot in it?

'I'm sorry. Should I have been referring to you as *Dr* Ridpath?'

She gave a small, bitter laugh. 'No. You're all right. I'm not a doctor. I studied at Cambridge, you see?'

He didn't see, and it must have shown.

'*Ladies*,' she said, her voice oozing with irony, 'don't graduate from Cambridge. We're welcome to study there and, of course, to pay fees, but that's all. No degree for me, let alone a doctorate.'

Betancourt tried to imagine Lucia pouring her heart and

soul into her studies, only to be told at the end of it her efforts wouldn't be recognised. He couldn't.

'That doesn't seem fair.'

'Of course it isn't fair. It's bloody outrageous. But that's Cambridge for you.'

'Then why didn't you go somewhere else? Like Liverpool?'

She wrung her hands together. 'My father…'

It sounded like the famous Dr Ridpath had a lot to answer for.

She looked at him inquisitively. 'Why Liverpool?'

'What?'

'You asked why I didn't go somewhere else, like Liverpool. What made you say Liverpool?'

It was the first place that had entered his head. He knew roughly where London was, but as for Cambridge or Oxford or any of those other places that English expatriates seemed to hold so dear, he couldn't have pinpointed any of them on a map if his life depended on it. But when Evelyn had told him she gained her degree at Liverpool, he looked up where it was in the station atlas.

'I know someone who studied there. Dr Trevose, actually. And they let her call herself *Doctor*, too.'

'Ah.' She gave one of those enigmatic, knowing, infuriating smiles women seemed to specialise in. At least, the women in his life did. It was time for a change of tack.

'What was last night all about?'

She let out a long, resigned sigh. 'I shouldn't have done it, but she's evil, that one. I've seen women like her before. They're like Black Widow spiders. They lure their prey into their webs, and once they're finished, they spit out the husk and move on to the next one.'

There was genuine dislike in her voice. Whether there had ever been anything romantic between Fulbright and Molly, or whether their relationship was platonic, as she'd intimated previously, the Westaway woman had clearly come between them.

'Do I take it, then, that she and Dr Fulbright were... involved?'

Molly looked away again, a wistful, faraway gaze in her eyes as she considered his question. When she next spoke, she sounded calmer and more circumspect.

'Richard used to be different. His work always came first, but he could be easy-going and approachable, even friendly, in his own way. Then he met Vita. They met at the races. He took me a few times when I first arrived. He seemed to enjoy hanging around the owners' stand, having a bet, drinking champagne. I think it must have been so different from academic life that he became swept up in the illusion. It made him feel like – oh, I don't know – like he was one of the smart set.' She sipped her tea. 'He took me again, about a month ago. I don't know why he invited me – he knew I had no time for that crowd, and, in any case, he hardly spoke to me all afternoon. He'd met Vita by this time. He was besotted with her. Couldn't keep his hands off her. I stayed for a few races, but I decided I'd rather go back and work than have the beautiful people looking at me piteously. "Poor little Molly, poor little wallflower." So, I caught a taxi and went back to the museum. Besides, I could see things were about to turn ugly.'

'What do you mean?'

'Richard was making all the running, but Vita wasn't exactly telling him to stop. She was as bad as he was, and Peter had a look like thunder on him.'

'Peter?

'Her husband.'

'Her husband was there, watching all this?'

'They had a runner that day. I don't think Peter was terribly interested in the horses, to be honest with you. It was Vita's thing. Peter would do anything to indulge her. She has that effect on men. Anyway, the horse won, and they all made a packet.'

'The horse; Fast Crowd, was it?'

'It might have been. Sorry, I'm not interested in horses. Dangerous brutes, if you ask me.' She paused and thought about it for a moment. 'Fast Crowd. It's how Vita refers to her and her little gang: the Fast Crowd, so it would make sense. How did you know that?'

'I searched Dr Fulbright's room. I found a race programme. He'd marked the entry for Fast Crowd and had made a note of what looked like a bet. Did he make a lot of money that day?'

She laughed. 'I very much doubt it. Richard was a terrible gambler. He might have won a few dollars when the Westaways' horse won, but he'd have lost twice as much on the rest of the card. He used to put bets on whatever she told him. She might have had an eye for picking men, but she was hopeless when it came to horses.' Her face grew more sombre. 'Richard was in debt. He owed a lot of money.'

'Did he tell you that?'

She nodded. 'He came to me a couple of weeks ago. He sounded desperate.' She pushed her plate away, apparently having lost her appetite. 'He asked me for a loan.'

'Did you give him money?'

She shook her head, and Betancourt could see tears forming in her eyes. 'I feel so mean. If he hadn't got into debt because of her, I'd have gladly helped him, but... And now I can't help him any more. Perhaps, if I had, none of this would have happened.'

She looked ashamed, even though there was nothing he could see for her to be ashamed of.

'We don't even know if his death had anything to do with money. And whether it did or not, none of this is your fault.'

She sniffed and tried her best to summon up a smile. 'Thank you.'

'Before I forget.' Betancourt reached inside his pocket and withdrew an envelope. He removed Molly's photograph and handed it to her. She placed the picture on the table, beside the condiment jars.

'There,' she said. 'An improvement, don't you think?'

Looking at the photograph again in this new and incongruous setting, Betancourt realised he'd previously only focused on the picture's subjects. Behind the three figures, the blurred and grainy background showed a few cars parked next to a low concrete wall topped by a tubular steel guard rail. Beyond the wall, white-capped waves lapped against the shoreline.

'Where was this taken?'

'At Pasir Panjang, by the Sea Moon Hotel. We went there for chilli crab. It was just before my father...'

Betancourt picked up the photograph and stared at it. He was taken again by the directness of Fulbright's expression. The jut of the jaw. The steely gaze. It was as if his eyes contained a challenge. A challenge to whom? Then it clicked. There must have been four people in the party, not three: Molly, her father, Fulbright, and whoever took the picture.

'What are you doing?' she asked.

'What? Oh, nothing important. It's just something I do. I try and reimagine scenes. Try and get inside them. It's silly.'

'It's not silly at all. I do exactly the same thing when I find an artefact. I try to imagine myself there. Using it. Amongst the people who left it.'

'Tell me, who took this photograph?'

'Thomas Lenehan.'

'If they were such fierce rivals, what were he and Lenehan doing dining together.'

'It was my father's idea. Anyway, the rivalry wasn't that

fierce in those days. That picture was taken before the shortlist for the Farquhar Prize was announced.'

'Lenehan wrote Fulbright's obituary. In the *Straits Tribune*.'

'Did he? I didn't read it. Did he have anything nice to say?'

'Not really, but then it was an obituary notice, not a eulogy.'

'That's Thomas for you. Never has anything good to say about anyone. Not even when they're dead, it seems. My father put up with him out of professional courtesy. He believed all archaeologists were members of one big supportive community. I wish that was true, but he couldn't see that some men are driven by greed and ambition, rather than some noble calling.'

'And where do you sit?'

'Me?' She looked away for a moment. 'I'm no longer sure. I used to think what we did was important, but now with my father gone, and Richard, I'm not sure I have the stomach for it any more. I think I might leave it to the vultures.'

'Like Lenehan?

She gave a small smile. 'I couldn't possibly say. Did you find anything else?'

'I found this.' Betancourt unfolded the map he'd found in the drawer of Fulbright's desk. 'Mean anything?'

'We use maps like this all the time to mark our finds. There are dozens like this back at the museum. But they're my father's maps. Fort Canning mostly. As for this one...' She turned the map around and studied it. 'This is Bukit Chandu. It overlooks the bay at Pasir Panjang. There's an opium packing plant there.'

'Was Fulbright digging out there?'

'If he was, I wasn't aware of it.' She thought for a moment. 'Richard had a theory. When he was in Sumatra with my father, they discovered that the Majapahit built a series of forts on neighbouring peaks. He may have thought that if artefacts had been found at Fort Canning, then there might be more, further along the coast.'

So, could he have been on some sort of treasure hunt?'

She tutted. 'Hardly, Inspector. Richard was a serious archaeologist. But, yes, it is possible he'd been doing excavations on Bukit Chandu. This map would certainly suggest so.'

'These excavations, would he have been looking for evidence of dragons, by any chance?'

'Dragons? What an extraordinary question. No. Why?'

'Nothing. Just something that someone mentioned.'

He refolded the map.

'Are you planning to hold on to that, Inspector?'

'It might prove helpful in tracking Dr Fulbright's movements. Is there a problem?'

'I don't suppose so. Automatic reaction. We archaeologists like to keep hold of things. It's almost a prerequisite for the job.'

'Miss Ridpath—'

'Molly. Maiden aunt. Remember?'

'Very well. Molly, when we spoke at the museum, I asked if Dr Fulbright's mood had changed recently.'

'Yes, I remember.'

'And you said you were both busy and no longer saw each other outside work. Can I ask what your relationship with Dr Fulbright was?'

'My relationship, as you term it, was strictly one of professional colleagues, though if it had been anything else I'd tell you not to be so impertinent.' An amused twinkle in her eye betrayed the sternness of her words.

'In that case, what did you mean by "*we no longer saw each other*"?'

She looked out of the window, at some indeterminate

point in the distance, as if the answer to his question might be found there.

She began hesitantly. 'He was older than me. When I was younger, when we were both at Cambridge, I suppose I thought there might be something… And then when we met again, here in Singapore, he took me out to dinner a few times, and to parties, that sort of thing. I'm sure he was only being civil, introducing me to people, but I wondered.'

'But nothing came of it?'

She shook her head, a little sadly, Betancourt thought. 'He was jollier in those days, of course. Before he met Vita.' She looked at her wristwatch. 'If there's nothing else, Inspector, I'd better be getting back.'

'Yes, of course.' He called to the waitress and asked her to bring the bill. 'There's one thing I don't understand. Why Singapore?'

'What do you mean?'

'All this digging and cataloguing and studying that you do. I could understand if it was ancient Egypt or somewhere like Greece, but I don't understand the fascination for this place.'

'Come on,' she said, standing up. 'Pay the woman and follow me.'

'Where are we going?'

'Back to the museum. There's something you need to see.'

Chapter Twenty-Two

Outside, the sun was falling, casting long shadows on the five-foot way outside the café. They crossed River Valley Road and headed north up Clemenceau Avenue. As they passed Fort Canning, Molly pointed out various places where her father had completed digs and described what he'd found there. Her descriptions of the artefacts – mostly ceramics, cooking pots, and the like – did little to satisfy his curiosity about what the scientific community found so interesting about Singapore.

When they arrived back at the museum, she led him through to the public galleries. She said nothing further until they arrived at a display room filled with glass cabinets.

'How much do you know about archaeology?' she asked.

'Just what I've seen in newsreels at the cinema. Burial tombs and bones. Howard Carter and the curse of King Tutankhamun. That sort of thing.'

She smiled, appearing not to have taken any offence at his ignorance.

'What we do is practical history, really. Going back to the start of civilisation, people have been interested in who came before them. Sometimes there are written accounts telling what life was like, but not always. That's where we come in: when there are no written records and all we have are artefacts. Bones and burial chambers, as you say. That's what makes the news – the great kings and queens – but we're interested in far more than that. By studying the remnants of the lives of previous generations, we can piece together what those lives were like and, ultimately, how our lives came to be the way they are. Like these.' She approached one of the cabinets. It contained necklaces, amulets, and what might have been an armband. They looked similar to Malay trinkets he'd seen worn at weddings or on special occasions, but he suspected these might have been a bit more valuable. They looked like they were made of gold, and on many of the items, crudely cut gemstones glinted as they reflected the cabinet lights. He glanced at a card inside the glass frame. *Majapahit jewellery. Sumatra. 12th century.*

She continued walking around the room, him in tow, and she described the artefacts in each case with a zeal and a passion Betancourt found both impressive and a little intimidating.

She finally came to a halt at a lone cabinet, larger than the others, that took pride of place in the middle of the room. Inside the cabinet, nestled on a bed of red velvet, was a block of weathered sandstone, covered with marks, etched into the rock, that appeared to represent some sort of hieroglyphics.

'This is it: the Singapore Stone.'

She announced it as if she was a proud parent presenting her offspring. So this is what Lenehan was talking about the previous evening. Judging by the look on her face, he got the impression she expected him to be aware of the artefact, at the very least. She was wrong. Before Lenehan's talk, he hadn't even heard of it and he had no idea what it was, but he wasn't prepared to show his ignorance.

'Ah, so this is it. I thought it might be.'

She smiled. It was clear she'd seen through him.

'This stone brought my father here in the first place. He made it his life's work to disprove the popular view of Singapore's history.'

'Which is?'

'That before Raffles set foot on the island, there was nothing here but jungle and mosquitoes and a few Bugis fishermen who parked their boats in the Singapore River to shelter from storms.'

'And that isn't the case, I take it?'

'Far from it. The history of this current society may be a short one: an Englishman claimed the island for King and Empire in 1819, and history from that point onwards is well documented. What my father was interested in – what I'm interested in – is what happened before then. You heard what Lenehan said last night. He thinks Singapore was uninhabited until a few Siamese traders stumbled across it. The truth is that this island was occupied and re-occupied over the centuries, and it's had as many names as it's had occupiers. A map produced by Ptolemy in the second century AD identified an island he called *Sabara*, off the southern end of the Malay peninsula. Ninth-century Arab sailors referred to it as *Ma'it*. Mongol annals show that an expedition came here looking for elephants to take back to China. They called it *Long Ma Yen* – Dragon's Gate Teeth. For centuries there have been references in texts to the so-called Silk Road of the Sea: a wealthy island kingdom that acted as the hub of a trade route connecting China with India, and beyond.

'And I take it that island was Singapore?'

'It's what my father believed, although it wouldn't have been called that then. Which brings us to this.' She gestured to the stone. 'From what we know, it was part of a set of two much larger stones that once guarded the entrance to the Singapore River.'

'The Mongol's dragon's teeth?'

She shrugged. 'It's a theory. Sadly, this is all we have left. An English officer named Stevenson decided the stones were in the way of some building work he wanted done, so he dynamited them. Another officer rescued a fragment of the stone, but even then, the fragment was too large to lift, so he had one of his coolies break it up into three pieces. The pieces were sent to Calcutta, supposedly for safekeeping. In 1918, the museum requested the stones be returned, and they deigned to return one of the pieces. This one. They said the other two were lost.'

'And what was Fulbright's role in all this?'

'Archaeolinguistics.' She repeated the word, almost wistfully, as though reminding herself of another time. 'It's difficult to explain.' He'd seen that look before. The confused, frustrated look of someone who understood a subject perfectly, but struggled to explain it to someone who didn't. She picked at a loose thread on her skirt, as though she might be able to pull a satisfactory explanation from the fabric. She decided to have a stab at it.

'I don't mean it's difficult to explain what he did – that's easy. He deciphered ancient languages – extinct languages – and translated them. But there was far more to it than just decoding the written words. He had a gift for understanding how the words would have been used by the ancients. What they really meant.' She looked at Betancourt, to see if he understood what she was trying to explain to him, and decided he didn't. She was right. 'You see, it's like this. When we discover physical artefacts, they act as clues. If we find a cooking pot, we can assume the civilisation that made the pot cooked their food. If we find the pot is blackened, we can assume they cooked with fire. But, in a way, all that is quite superficial. What Richard was able to do was probe the souls of those societies; he gave us insight into what was really important to them.' Her face had lit up as she spoke. 'He was quite brilliant, you know.'

She glanced at him to gauge his reaction. 'Trust me, it's exciting if you're an archaeologist. See here?' She pointed to a series of scratches or indentations in the stone, about three-quarters of an inch wide. They looked identical to the drawings he'd seen in Fulbright's room. 'No one has ever been able to decipher these marks. It became my father's obsession. He believed these marks are a form of Sanskrit, symbolising a language used by the Majapahit – a wealthy and powerful kingdom that ruled much of what is now the Dutch East Indies in the tenth and eleventh centuries. The army were doing some digging up on Fort Canning Hill, drains or some such thing, when a sapper hit something with his spade. That headband, over there.' She pointed to one of the trinkets. On closer inspection, Betancourt could see where a fold in the metal had been straightened out and polished. 'They took a bit more care after that. They found another dozen artefacts. That was when my father was sent over from Sumatra, where he was working, to inspect them. He wrote to me about the finding – I was still at school in England, I must have been about sixteen at the time – and I could tell how excited he was. The Majapahit were like the Incas of South-East Asia. The artefacts he'd found in Java and Sumatra suggest they might have been fabulously wealthy. If he could prove they'd conquered Singapore, well, the possibilities are endless. That's what Richard was doing: trying to decipher the inscriptions.'

'So, your father believed these inscriptions might be the key that would unlock some sort of treasure chest?'

'Not exactly. He didn't consider the stone to be some sort of holy grail, but those original stones were put there for a reason, and he believed if Richard could decipher the writings, well… who knows where they might lead? That's what makes archaeology so compelling: it's about what you *might* find as much as what you do find.'

'And was Fulbright successful?'

'He was definitely onto something, but we hadn't discussed his progress for a while. Maybe he found something at Bukit Chandu, which allowed him to make a breakthrough. He was hopeless at documenting things. I was always on at him about it. Now, I wonder if we'll ever know.' The regret in her voice was almost tangible. Archaeology, it seemed, had its disappointments.

'If Fulbright had discovered something significant, would it have been enough to tip the scales in his favour for the Farquhar Prize?'

'Definitely.'

As they walked together back to the foyer he asked, 'If your father loved Singapore and its history so much, why did he leave?'

'He would have settled here if he could, but for all he loved Singapore, Singapore didn't love him. The climate didn't agree with him and eventually he developed pneumonia. His doctors insisted he return to England to recover. He was never right again, though. In public, he was quite stoic about not being able to spend his life out here, but in private he resented it. Like one resents having been rejected by a suitor.' There was a pain in her voice as she spoke. It was obvious she'd been devoted to her father. Betancourt wondered if her affection had been reciprocated.

He headed back out into the dusk bemused. He'd come to the museum hoping to find out a bit more about a dead American and he'd ended up with an ancient history lesson. But the status of the Farquhar Prize had taken on a new significance.

Thursday's special at Mr Tan's *kopi tiam* was seafood *bee hoon* — fried rice vermicelli with prawns, clams, scallops, and fish balls. Food, that's what he needed. And then a little quiet contemplation while he considered everything he'd learned that day and tried to weave the parts into some coherent whole.

The twenty-five-minute walk back to Duxton Hill didn't appeal, and he went in search of a rickshaw. He cut down a narrow lane connecting Armenian Street with Hill Street, where he'd have a better chance of finding an available carriage.

The lane was little more than an access way, providing ingress for delivery to the rear of the shops and restaurants and other miscellaneous businesses that fronted the main thoroughfares. Most of the day's business being done, the lane was empty, save for a small group of British soldiers who stood huddled in a doorway about halfway down, smoking and laughing at some comment one of them had made. Betancourt wondered briefly what they were doing there, but they didn't look lost, so he ignored them. As he passed the group, one of the soldiers peeled off, and the point of his shoulder cannoned into Betancourt's chest, winding him. He'd no sooner let fly with an expletive at the man for his carelessness when a pair of hands grabbed him from behind, clamping his arms to his side. A rapid series of punches to his solar plexus, his heart, his testicles, quickly put an end to any resistance, and he slumped to the ground. Lying on the stinking surface of the lane, he was vaguely aware of someone rummaging through his pockets. The search ceased as suddenly as it had begun, and he heard a clipped 'C'mon, lads. We're done.' One last boot to his ribs and they were gone.

Chapter Twenty-Three

After being turned down a few times by rickshaw pullers convinced he was drunk and incapable and likely to turn *amok* on the journey, he finally found one he could convince to take him home. A couple of crumpled dollar bills had gone a long way to settling the man's concerns.

He closed the door to the flat behind him and locked it, something he rarely did even when he was absent.

In the bathroom, he stripped off his clothes and sluiced himself with cold water until the throbbing diminished a little. He looked in the mirror and examined the angry damson welts that stippled his body. He winced as he touched one of the angrier-looking ones. He ran his tongue around the inside of his mouth. No teeth missing. He tentatively stretched his arms above his head and then from side to side. He took a few deep breaths, as much as his lungs would hold. No broken ribs. He'd live. It could have been worse. While the bruises looked bad, and they hurt like hell, his assailants didn't appear to have done any serious damage. He squinted in the mirror again. There wasn't a mark on his face. If he hadn't been undressed, it would have been difficult to know the assault had taken place. Maximum hurt with minimum evidence. The attack had been no casual coming together; the soldiers had been waiting for him, and whoever had done him over was an expert.

He thought about calling Evelyn and asking her to put some strapping on his ribs, but while he could reasonably explain away one attack as being bad luck, he was sure she'd consider two in three days careless, and he postponed her admonishments until another time.

When he'd had the flat done up, Lucia had insisted he install a medicine chest, replete with plasters, dressings, bandages, finger stalls, iodine, monkey blood, antiseptic cream, aspirins, a thermometer, a syringe (for what purpose, he'd no idea – she'd seen it in the chemist's shop and added it to the list), a pair of scissors, hygienically wrapped, and a first aid manual published by the Queen Alexandra's Royal Army Nursing Corps, as yet unopened. He unwrapped a crepe bandage, tied one end to the handle of the bathroom door and, pirouetting like a dancer, albeit a slow and awkward one, wound the bandage tight around his chest. After confirming he could still breathe without too much difficulty, he found the bottle of pills Evelyn had given him when she was patching him up at her flat, shook out three of them, and swallowed them with half a glass of whisky. He refilled the glass and eased himself onto the sofa.

He ran through the attack again, like a cinema reel in slow motion, frame by frame. Had it just been an unfortunate incident? Had the men simply not liked locals and taken exception to his presence in the lane? Maybe they'd been drinking and fancied some sport. But the assault had been swift, brutal, and efficient. Something hovered on the fringe of his memory, knocking, waiting to be allowed in. Then it came to him. While he was on the ground, fighting not to lose consciousness, one of the men had gone through his pockets.

'C'mon, lads. We're done.'

He retrieved his jacket from the floor of the bathroom and returned to the sofa. He checked the pockets. His wallet was still there, so they hadn't been after his money. So too was his warrant card. He carried little else. He thrust his hand inside the outer pocket. Apart from the label he'd cut from Fulbright's trousers in the Crypt, it was empty. The opium he'd taken from Lew Min's storeroom was gone.

The Tiger beer sign that hung above the entrance to the bar across the road cast a coruscating band of colour across the wall of the living room as it winked on and off. Picking up Jack London, he stared at the pages with unseeing eyes for a few minutes before giving up. With the day's events swirling in his head, he couldn't concentrate and, while he'd rather forget about dead American archaeologists, hostile British squaddies, and opium for a while, he knew he wouldn't be able to settle until he'd marshalled his thoughts. He found a stub of pencil and collected his mail from the stand in the hall. He had no interest in the contents of the letters, but the envelopes made useful notepaper.

He licked the end of the pencil and began to write.

According to Ramsay, the harbourmaster, the body of the dead American could have drifted on the tide from somewhere around the area of the docks and had most likely been dumped in the water somewhere around the harbour before drifting with the tide to the *kelong* at Pasir Panjang. The port was busy at all hours, even at night, so if someone dumped the body there, why had no one seen anything? It was, of course, entirely possible someone did see something, and decided it was none of their business. But the other possibility was that he hadn't been dropped off in the harbour area. Ramsay had also suggested the possibility that Fulbright's body could have entered the water near to where it was found, at Pasir Panjang. Given Fulbright had been digging at Bukit Chandu, he made that interpretation favourite.

He thought again about what Molly Ridpath had told him. A couple of things nagged at him. Fulbright was a respected archaeologist. His excavation work would have been carefully planned and executed. What, then, was he doing digging up Bukit Chandu, where there was no evidence of any artefacts having been found? And why in secret? Why hadn't he shared it with his colleague?

Fulbright was involved with Vita Westaway, and her husband was aware of it. Was that enough of a motive? Perhaps, but an Englishman would be more likely to defend his honour with a pistol. Two balls of opium forced down the throat seemed out of character. Then again, if this affair had been simmering for a while, Westaway would have had a while to plan it.

Because of his affair with Vita, Fulbright had got himself into debt. According to Molly, Fulbright spent his money betting on Vita's, usually unsuccessful, racing tips. It was conceivable that if the Fulbright well had run dry, then his straitened circumstances might have been enough for Vita to become bored with him, but no one kills just because their lover has run out of cash. At least, no one he'd ever come across. So that left whoever Fulbright owed money to. Bookies weren't afraid of going to extreme lengths to extract the money they were owed, but he hadn't heard of one actually killing someone over a debt. It was counter-productive, apart from anything else.

Whatever else, he needed to know more about both halves of the Westaway union.

The upper stratum of Singapore's expatriate society was a close-knit one and it viewed outsiders with suspicion, if not outright distrust. Betancourt was granted temporary access by virtue of his marriage, but he had never been welcomed in his own right, and when Anna disappeared, so, too, did his membership credentials. While he didn't miss the social circus, it was useful to have occasional access to its inner circles, and no one in the colony had better access than Marjorie.

A servant answered and asked him to hold while he went to fetch her. There was a lengthy hiatus before she picked up.

'Is this business or social?'

'Business, I'm afraid.'

'Why am I not in the least bit surprised? Don't tell me, you need some information about someone, and no one knows more about what's going on in society than I do, so here you are. I suppose I should be flattered. But, before you ask for whatever it is you're going to ask for, I should warn you I'm not as au fait with goings on since…'

…Since her divorce. She'd put on a brave face, but he knew the toll French's actions had taken. She'd withdrawn from the society which, for so many years, she'd been an integral part. Kid gloves, Betancourt.

'A name came up today. Vita Westaway. Know much about her?'

'I may be out of touch, but not so out of touch I don't hear what the likes of Vita Westaway are up to. Is this something to do with your dead American?'

'Fulbright's colleague at the museum gave me her name. She said they were having an affair.'

'Were they indeed? Well, you've got me there. I hadn't heard that, but it doesn't surprise me. Perhaps I have been out of circulation too long. It's about time I started reconnecting. Want me to make a few calls and see what I can find out?'

'If you could, I'd appreciate it. I've no idea if the affair had anything to do with his death. It seems a long shot, but I've precious little else to go on at the moment. What else do you know about her?'

'Where do you want me to start? Vita and your American

sound like par for the course. She was always one for the men. And the women – she's not fussy, if the stories are to be believed. Vita's the original wild child. She comes from a long line of distinguished army men; her father was a brigadier. Ormond, I think his name was. Stationed in Hong Kong. Peter Westaway, her husband, was the old man's ADC. That's how they met, but for the life of me, I can't see the attraction. He's a bit of a stick-in-the-mud, nothing like her. Married life doesn't seem to have tamed her appetites. She's quite the party girl. Loves to throw big shindigs. Catered by Raffles, Cristal all round, that sort of thing. In fact, she's hosting a fundraiser this week. To raise money for the museum, funnily enough. Everyone who's anyone will be there.'

'Sounds expensive.'

'I should say.'

'Where does she get the money? Allenby said he calls himself captain. How much does a captain in the British army earn?'

'He isn't in the army any more. He cashed in his chips after he married Vita. Works for the government now. But you raise a good question. It's one a few people have asked, but no one seems to know the answer.'

'This fundraiser. You're invited, I take it?' It was a safe bet. Despite her hiatus, she remained a fixed star in the Singapore social firmament and received dozens of invitations. Her self-imposed withdrawal from society would be deemed temporary, no matter how long it lasted.

'Of course, but they'll have to do without me on this occasion.'

'Are you sure? It would do you good to get out again. You said yourself it was about time you were back in circulation.'

'Oh, Max, I don't know...'

'I'd be happy to accompany you, if it would help you decide.'

'You? I remember Anna having to drag you out of the house to get you to attend anything.'

'People change, you know.'

'Hmm... Especially when they want something. You plan to do some sleuthing, don't you? And I'm your key to the door.'

'Well, perhaps a little sleuthing. But it really would be my pleasure to escort you.'

'You know what? You're right. It is about time I pulled myself out of this funk. I'll go. Come here at seven o'clock. We'll go in my car. Don't be late. And it's black tie.'

'Tomorrow. Seven. Black tie. Looking forward to it.' He thought about the state of his one remaining half-decent suit. 'One question – when you say black tie...'

'Dinner suit. You do possess a dinner suit, don't you?'

'Of course.' He tried to sound offended at her implication but failed. 'It may require a few alterations, but I know a very good tailor.'

He rang off and let out a long sigh. Dinner suit? Black tie? This was exactly the sort of thing Anna would have dealt with. He felt in his pocket for the label he'd removed from Fulbright's trousers in the Crypt. Well, Sam Fong, Tailor to the Stars, let's see if you can perform miracles.

Chapter Twenty-Four

The following morning, he was preparing to leave for Sam's when the sound of the telephone arrested his departure. It was Quek.

'I'm at the hospital, boss. I came to get the results of the samples.'

'And? What did they find?'

'The man in the laboratory said they'd already been collected.'

'*What?*' Who by?'

'Somebody wearing an army uniform. They said you had sent them to pick everything up — the sample, the container, and the results. You didn't ask anyone, did you?'

'Of course not. So, we have nothing?'

'Not exactly.'

'The man I spoke to said he was the same man who did the test on the contents of Fulbright's stomach. The sample that Dr Trevose sent in. He remembered doing the first test and said the opium in the tube was the same as the opium that was in Fulbright's stomach.'

Betancourt grunted. That was something at least.

'All right. Get the man to give you a statement,' he said, before hanging up.

Twenty minutes later he pulled up outside Sam's shop.

'I'm attending an event this evening. Fancy affair. Black tie. They'll all be wearing those penguin suits. You said the other day my suit needed a bit of attention.' Betancourt held open his jacket, as if modelling it. 'Could you do something with it by this evening?'

Sam Fong, self-styled tailor to the stars, looked offended. 'Inspector, everyone knows I'm the finest tailor this side of Geylang. I'm a genius, but I'm not a magician. The best thing you could do with that suit is give it to the *karung guni*. They might take it off your hands. If you gave them some coffee money.'

'Well, could you make me something?'

'Jacket, trousers, cummerbund, all that silk edging… Even if I put my fastest seamstress on it, I couldn't do a dinner suit by tonight. It's impossible.'

Deflated, Betancourt considered his options and decided he had none. He couldn't let Marjorie down. He briefly considered trying to borrow a suit, but everyone he might be on borrowing terms with, and who might own a dinner suit, was a different shape and size to him.

'Any ideas?' he asked.

Sam regarded him, apparently deep in thought.

'You still friends with Bill Allenby?'

Sam was an enthusiastic, if hapless, gambler. He had a system, which he'd expounded to Betancourt during a previous fitting a few years previously. It involved the first letter of the name of the horse – some letters being more auspicious than others, the number on the horse's saddlecloth,

Sam's lucky numbers as decided by his numerologist, and the month according to the lunar calendar. After he explained the detail of how this formula worked, Betancourt offered his considered opinion, which was that Sam would enhance his chances greatly if he just stuck one of his tailoring pins into the newspaper at random.

He could see the direction in which this conversation was heading.

'What if I said yes?'

'You give me a good tip; I give you a dinner jacket.'

'I thought you just said you couldn't make one that quickly.'

'Not make, but alterations I can do. Wait here.'

When Sam returned, he carried a suit on a hanger, covered in a brown paper sleeve with his *Tailor to the Stars* logo embossed in red ink. He removed a silk jacket and a pair of matching trousers from their cocoon and hung them up.

'Dinner suit. Ready for final fitting.'

'Won't the owner mind if you give it to me?'

'No problem. Not coming back.'

'How can you be so sure?

'Dead. No need for a dinner suit any more. Good fit for you. Same size.'

'What happened?'

'Drowned. Now you try it on.'

Drowned? 'Wait a minute. Who was this suit made for?'

'Fulbright. He ordered suit. Now he don't need it.'

'I can't wear a dead man's suit.'

'Why not? Already paid for. Come, you try it on.'

Betancourt racked his brains, but off the top of his head he couldn't come up with any legal impediment to repurposing a murder victim's clothing. He'd long since given up trying to resist the irresistible force of fate. He removed his own jacket, gingerly. His ribs were screaming out for a day off, but they'd just have to manage with his self-applied strapping for a while longer.

Sam busied himself with his tape measure, barking out measurements to his uncle, who, mouth still full of pins, wrote them down in the big order book.

'Five o'clock,' Sam said, when he was finished. 'Now, you give me tip.'

Betancourt gave a silent prayer to a God he didn't believe in, asking for Allenby's forgiveness in advance. 'Tomorrow. Race number six. Topsy.'

Sam nodded gleefully and set to work, tearing out the tacking stitches that held Betancourt's newly gained dinner wear together.

His next stop was the Customs Service HQ on Maxwell Road.

As much as he could, Betancourt stayed out of the seemingly interminable power plays between the upper ranks of the profusion of factions of the colonial government, and, for the most part, he had a good working relationship with Callan, Bonham's counterpart in Customs.

Callan had worked his way up through the ranks, starting as a raw probationer in Rangoon, patrolling the outer reaches of the Irrawaddy, and had now reached the relative comfort of a desk in Customs House and a Superintendentship. He was a short, stout man, plagued by dyspepsia, and gave the appearance of having gone to seed somewhat. Any ambition he might once have held had dissipated, and he seemed happy to see out the few years that remained before he retired.

A few months previously, Betancourt had picked up a bit of wharf-side scuttlebutt about a new ring of toddy farms operating in the north of the island, in the jungle around Mandai village. He passed on the tip, and a squad of Callan's men from the Woodlands station rounded up the farmer's crew and impounded the stills.

Callan had invited Betancourt along to observe the confiscation and he explained, as they bumped their way along the tracks that led through the rubber trees to the illicit stills, that he'd no particular issue with yet another farmer producing palm liquor and selling it to the locals who worked in the rubber plantations of the area. Not in principle, anyway. His job was to ensure His Majesty's government was paid its full complement of toddy duty. Betancourt watched with grudging admiration as the Customs man offered the farmer two options. Option one: the man could reclaim his equipment, start logging his production, and pay his duty on the dot each month. Alternatively – option two – he could spend a couple of years in gaol considering the error of his ways, no time off for good behaviour. In fact, there was every possibility of an extension, if the gaolers decided he was acting as a bad influence on his fellow prisoners, which Callan was almost certain they would do, given he intended to bring the idea to their attention.

After considering the matter for a second or two, the farmer chose option one. It was a good outcome for all concerned. The distiller regained control of his livelihood, Callan received a mention in dispatches from the Chief Superintendent for swelling HMG's coffers, and Betancourt was due a favour, which he now intended to collect on.

He eased himself into Callan's visitor's chair, wincing as one of the arms brushed against his rib.

Callan regarded him with renewed interest. 'Everything all right?'

Betancourt adjusted his position until he found one that was tolerable. 'Fine. Just been overdoing it a bit recently.'

'I see,' Callan said, obviously not believing a word.

Betancourt declined Callan's offer of tea and came

straight to the point. He unfolded the chemist's analysis report and handed it to the Customs man.

Callan scowled and unwrapped a bismuth lozenge, which he popped into his mouth before speaking. 'What's this?'

'An analysis of an opium sample.'

'I can see that. Where did it come from?'

'I'm less interested in the opium itself than I am in the man that it killed.'

Callan grunted and sat back in his chair, apparently placated for the moment.

'Tell me more.'

'The body of a dead American, name of Fulbright, was found in the sea off Pasir Panjang. When the police doctor carried out the post-mortem, she found a large quantity of rough opium in his gut.' He pointed at the sheet of foolscap that still lay on Callan's desk. 'That. She also said she'd had a dozen similar deaths in the last few months, but the others were all local. Needless to say, one dead American will make twice as much noise as twelve dead Chinese. Dr Trevose supplied me with a list of the names of the other victims. I looked into them, to see if I could find anything in common.'

'What did you find?'

'I went through the witness statements from the inquests. It wasn't easy to spot at first, but a theme emerged. All the dead addicts lived or worked within half a mile of a certain opium shop on Hokien Street.'

'Lew Min's den.'

Betancourt nodded. Callan, like many of his fellows, was territorial and, favour or no favour, he wouldn't appreciate it if he thought Betancourt was treading on his turf. He knew he would have to play this next bit carefully.

'My sergeant and I did a bit of snooping.'

Callan's face suffused with colour, and he fixed Betancourt with a stare.

'And what, exactly, did this *snooping* involve?'

'I paid Lew Min a visit. Quek kept him busy while I searched the storeroom.'

Callan shot out of his seat. 'You did what? You had no bloody jurisdiction! My men have been watching that place for months. If there is – or should I say *was* – anything irregular going on there, Lew Min and his confederates will be on their guard. Three months' worth of surveillance down the drain, thanks to you.'

'It's a murder inquiry. I was perfectly within my rights.'

'If you'd come to me first instead of charging in like a bull in a china shop...' Callan slumped back in his chair and reached for another bismuth lozenge. 'At least tell me you found something useful and the whole thing wasn't just a great big time-wasting cock-up.'

'I checked the crates of opium. Everything looked normal. Then I found a crate buried under the others at the back, which looked different.'

'Different how?'

'It had a symbol of a dragon burned into the wood.'

'Did you open it?'

'Yes. It was filled with tubes, just like the other crates. I took a couple of samples, intending to have them analysed before Lew Min interrupted me.'

'Have you got the samples with you?'

'Not exactly.'

Callan rubbed his face wearily. 'What, *exactly*, does not exactly mean?'

'I gave one to Quek to take to the lab, and I kept one myself.'

'Why do I get the impression there's a but coming?'

'I was beaten up by a bunch of squaddies on the way home. They took the tube of opium.'

'Squaddies? You mean squaddies as in British soldiers?

Jesus. I'm beginning to wish I hadn't come in this morning. But there's still the other tube. The one your man took to the lab.'

'That's gone, too, I'm afraid. Someone got to the lab before my sergeant and told them I'd given instructions to pick up the sample and the results.'

Callan gave him a withering look. He picked up the analysis sheet again and scowled. 'If this is what the doctor found in your man's stomach, then he was eating *cacak*.'

For now, Betancourt was happy to play the naïve inquisitor and instead of letting Callan know he'd already discussed the report with Evelyn, he let Callan do the talking.

'It's like this,' Callan said, warming to his task. 'The *chandu* we make here comes from Bengal. That's where they grow the best stuff. But it's also more expensive. Let's say your average opium fiend doesn't want to pay the going rate for government opium, so what does he do? He goes to his local backstreet den and buys *cacak*. There's been a plague of the stuff recently. I've got my men checking the port, the railway station, the Johor causeway… Nothing. I can't figure out how it's getting in. Now, although you've gone about it all cack-handed, stuffing up my investigation in the process, you may have given us something we can use.' The Customs man appeared somewhat mollified.

'How much of this *cacak* is sold in the more respectable outlets?'

It was a common misconception, particularly amongst the expatriate community, that opium was only consumed in backstreet hovels, away from polite eyes, where it could be ignored. There was plenty of that, of course, but the wealthy were as fond of smoking the drug as the poor were, and there were clubs where rich Chinese and, occasionally, their European guests could go to smoke a few pipes, be entertained by *pipa tsai*, and talk business.

Callan pursed his lips. 'Not much. Asking to be caught, that would be. In any case, like I said, government *chandu* is the highest quality. Bloke frequenting the kind of place you're talking about: he's wanting to impress his friends. And the ladies. He's not going to do that by offering them cheap dope.'

'How easy is it to tell the difference?'

'Very easy.' Callan reached behind him and picked something up. 'Here, see for yourself.'

Although he'd confiscated plenty of raw opium in his time, Betancourt realised he'd never seen the finished retail product. He took the object and examined it. It was a small packet, about an inch on each side, and covered in white paper. He turned it over. On the obverse side was a red label, bearing the words 'Monopolies Commission' and a mixture of numbers and letters.

'How much is in here?'

'Three *hoons.*'

Enough for about six pipes. In the opium dens around the docks, that would cost an opium smoker about fifty cents. The average rickshaw puller or dockyard coolie earned about a dollar a day. If his hankering wasn't too bad, six pipes might last him a couple of days, but if the craving was strong, he'd easily get through the lot in a day, and have no money for anything else. And so, the spiral into destitution began.

'Are they all like this?'

'They come in different sizes, but they're all packaged like that.'

'Can I open it?'

'Help yourself.'

Betancourt carefully removed the white paper to reveal another parcel, this one formed from some sort of woven leaf. Poppy would have been his guess. He opened the packet and uncovered three pea-sized balls of waxy brown opium.

'What happens to it before it gets to this stage?' Betancourt had a good idea of how the government opium got as far as the docks – he'd watched it coming in often enough – but he was sketchier on how it got from the Bengali boats to the opium shops of the city. Callan liked to talk, and he was happy to listen.

'Well, considering how much revenue it brings in, there's not actually that much to it. After the poppy flowers die, the farmers tap the seed capsule with a knife and collect the latex. Once the latex has dried in the sun, it's pretty much raw, unrefined opium. It's packed into chests for market, and our agents in India buy up boatloads of the stuff and ship it over here. After it's landed at the docks, my men check the paperwork is all in order and then it's taken to a factory at Telok Blangah, where they cook it to remove the impurities. Once it's cooked and cooled, it's pure *chandu*, ready for packing. That happens at the plant out at Pasir Panjang. You got boys?'

'A girl.'

'My condolences,' said Callan, looking wistful. 'I've got three girls myself. Took 'em up to see the plant, and they weren't in the slightest bit interested. Amazing place, if you're interested in engineering. Boys would be fascinated.'

Betancourt sincerely hoped Lucia would have no interest in any aspect of the production of a pernicious drug, no matter what a feat of engineering it was. He, on the other hand, was keen to see the process for himself.

'Any chance I could watch it being made?'

'Which bit? The production or the packing?'

'Both.'

'I could get you in to watch the manufacturing at Telok Blangah – I'm in and out all the time – but Pasir Panjang is a different kettle of fish. They run a tight ship up there and they don't appreciate visitors.'

Betancourt managed to contain his annoyance. It was precisely this sort of divide-and-rule attitude that led to the pissing competition between Onraet and the top brass at Customs in the first place.

'I thought—' He started to put his objection, but before he could finish, Callan stayed his utterance with a raised palm.

'I know. You thought we did the whole thing, soup to nuts, as our American friends would say. It would be a damn sight simpler if we did, but we don't. We have to make sure the money finds its way into the coffers, but the actual production is done by the boys and girls at the Monopolies Commission.'

Betancourt had long suspected the British must be the world's experts at creating committees and sub-departments. Divide and rule, he supposed. It said little to him about the trust in which they held their public servants.

He had a growing certainty that not only was the opium Evelyn had found the cause of Fulbright's death, it was also central to *why* he died. Tight ship or no tight ship, he wanted to see inside both plants.

'I'm investigating the murder of an American citizen. I couldn't care less what the Monopolies Commission appreciates or doesn't appreciate.' That one might come back to haunt him, he thought. Especially if it reached Bonham's ears.

Callan shrugged his shoulders. 'It's your funeral.'

'When can we go?'

'To Telok Blangah?' Callan took a handful of bismuth lozenges from the jar on his desk and stuffed them into his pocket. 'No time like the present. They're due a visit from me.'

Chapter Twenty-Five

'I 've called ahead,' Callan said, as he climbed into his car. 'They're expecting us. I told them you were assisting me with a case. Try to look suitably assistant-like, would you? There's a good fellow.'

Betancourt had declined the offer of a lift and went instead to liberate Alex from the watchful eye of the boy he'd paid to guard her.

He wended his way down Anson Road, past the Seamen's Mission and the old Parsi burial ground, along what would have been the shoreline in the pre-Rafflesian days. When he'd negotiated his way through the snarl of trucks that were a perpetual feature of the dockyard gates, the traffic lightened, and he completed the rest of the journey in short order. He drew to a halt outside a low building that looked much like any of the other dockyard buildings, with the exception that a chain-link fence and a sepoy standing guard at the main gate barred entry to this one.

Callan arrived a few minutes behind him and gave his driver his instructions. 'Half an hour, and then I'll be returning to Maxwell Road.'

The sepoy guard recognised Callan and smiled and nodded. Callan's terse '*He's with me*' seemed to provide sufficient authority for Betancourt to enter the building unhindered.

'Let me give you the tour,' Callan said. 'We'll start outside.'

They left the building through a doorway at the sea end. Outside, a single rail track ran from the plant to a wooden jetty at which a *tongkang* was moored. Being sited this close to the sea, anything made from iron could be expected to tarnish quickly, but there was no sign of orange rust and the surface of the tracks glinted silver-bright in the morning sun. Evidently, the track was well used.

At that moment, cries broke out from the jetty and a gang of coolies fanned out and picked up the slack on a harness made from thick sisal hawsers that were fastened to a wooden wagon. Betancourt watched transfixed as the men leant forward, sinews straining, as they struggled to pull the wagon up the slope to the factory entrance where he and Callan stood.

Eventually, the wagon trundled to a stop in front of them and the pullers unhitched themselves from their yokes. A couple of them sank to the ground, exhausted. Human oxen, thought Betancourt. He glanced at Callan, but the Customs man appeared uninterested. He'd have observed the scene many times before, and if he'd ever harboured any concern for the workers' welfare, he'd long since mastered the emotion.

A fresh gang of coolies unloaded tea chests from the wagon, laying them in a row on the scrubby grass.

'The government has agents in Bengal who ship the raw opium over here,' Callan said. 'The freighters lie offshore, in the deeper water, and these chaps bring the stuff ashore.'

He gave the foreman an order to open one of the tea chests, and the foreman in turn barked at one of the coolies.

The coolie, having no one inferior to him to pass the instruction on to, picked up an iron bar and prised open the lid of the chest.

Betancourt peered inside. Wrapped in straw were balls of what appeared at first sight to be brown wax. Raw opium. Darker in colour and of more uniform consistency than the stuff he'd confiscated from rogue fishermen in the past. He counted half a dozen balls. He presumed there were more beneath the ones he could see.

'How much in a chest?'

'Twenty-four balls – about a hundred pounds of raw opium in total.'

More coolies were busy emptying similar chests, transferring the balls to rattan baskets, which they hoisted onto their shoulders and carried indoors. Another foreman peered into each basket as it passed him and made an annotation on a piece of paper.

'Follow me,' said Callan. 'Next stage is the cooking.'

Back inside the factory, the first thing Betancourt noticed was the heat. Rows of copper vats ran the length of the building. Beneath the vats, charcoal fires glowed bright orange.

The second thing he noticed was the smell. When he'd entered Lew Min's den, the place had been redolent with the sweet perfume of burning opium. This was different: a sharp, astringent aroma filled his nostrils. Callan must have noticed him turning up his nose.

'That's the additives. The smell of the opium itself is not unpleasant.' He pointed to a vat nearest the door. 'First, they boil the raw material to remove the impurities.' Betancourt supposed referring to the contents of the vats as *material* allowed Callan to distance himself from what was actually happening here. As though it was soap or hair products that were being produced, and not a drug that ruined lives, and for which people were prepared to kill or be killed.

Callan stopped. They'd reached the next stage in the process. A worker held a wooden frame across which was stretched a sheet of muslin while another man ladled the dark, soupy liquid through into a fresh tank. 'After they've filtered it, they boil it again. They'll leave it over a low heat until it's thick. Over here.'

He crossed the room to where another team of coolies was filling moulds with a thick glossy paste, which, if Betancourt didn't know better, he could have taken for molasses.

'Final stage is to dry it. This way.' Callan led him through another pair of doors and out into the sunlight again, where the moulds he'd seen inside were being loaded onto bamboo racks.

'That's it?'

'Pretty much. Once it's dry, it gets carted off to the packing plant at Bukit Chandu and packed into tubes. Like the ones you found.'

Callan removed a small silver penknife from his pocket, the sort of thing a pipe smoker might use to clean his implement. Opening the blade, he sliced off a sliver of opium from one of the sun-baked blocks, a flake so thin the sunlight shone straight through it. The Customs man broke the fragment in half and offered Betancourt a piece. 'Here. Try it. All part of the tour.'

Betancourt's instinctive reaction was to decline the offer, but such was his curiosity he took the opium and, following Callan's lead, placed it on his tongue. He chewed. The taste, as he was now expecting, was sharp and bitter, but then, he reasoned, it wasn't intended to be eaten. At first, the opium had no effect at all, and he wondered why people bothered. Then, suddenly, what he could only describe as a euphoric wave pulsed through his body.

Callan watched him, grinning. 'Take it this your first time?

I'm used to it. Quality control. One of the perks of the job. Want me to have someone bring you a seat?'

Betancourt shook his head, which, as well as providing Callan with an answer to his request, had the effect of defogging his brain. The initial rush had passed, but he was left with a sense of mild elation, a delightful lightness. In those few short moments, he understood why the addicts would do whatever they had to do to get their hands on the drug and made a mental promise to himself to remain well clear of its seductive wiles in the future.

Callan checked a few facts and figures with various foremen, before pronouncing the tour complete.

'You'll be fine shortly. The effect doesn't last long. That's why the dope fiends keep coming back for more. Chasing the dragon, they call it. Trouble is, they no sooner catch the dragon than it slips through their fingers, and they have to chase him all over again. Good for business, of course.' He gestured towards the building behind them. 'Our business, I mean.'

A plain black delivery van was being loaded with opium from the racks and Callan and Betancourt stood and watched until the driver of the van slammed shut the rear doors and took his seat up front.

'Thanks for the tour.'

'Glad you found it interesting. What will you do now?'

It was really none of Callan's business what he did next. Nor under normal circumstances was there any reason the Customs man should care, but Betancourt knew it was his earlier interest in the packing plant at Bukit Chandu that had prompted the question.

'I was thinking of taking a drive along the coast road. Not been out there for a while. There's a place out Pasir Panjang way does a good chilli crab.'

Callan eyed him keenly. 'The Sea Moon? I know it well. Drive carefully. I've heard it can be treacherous out that way if you don't know what you're doing. Don't say you weren't warned.'

Chapter Twenty-Six

Betancourt gave the van a few hundred yards' head start before following, taking care not to get too close. Normally, he enjoyed driving the southern coast road. On the land side, the route was studded with rubber plantations, gambier farms, and every so often, a kampong where there was always a child or two prepared to give him a wave. Out to sea, tramp steamers chugged past on their way to the harbour, black smoke billowing from their funnels. But today he was oblivious to the sights. Callan's words rang in his ears, and he felt an unaccustomed sense of wariness about visiting the factory on Bukit Chandu.

After they crossed the small canal that marked the official city limits, the traffic thinned and Betancourt eased back on the throttle, settling into a gap of about a quarter of a mile or so. It meant the van occasionally disappeared from view as it rounded twists in the road ahead, but as he knew where it was going, he was happy to hang back.

A red-lettered tin sign nailed to a telegraph pole informed passers-by that the Sea Moon Hotel was a mile ahead. From there it was a short distance to Bukit Chandu and the van's final destination. As he rounded the next bend, a straight section of road stretched ahead to where he could see the restaurant in the distance. What he couldn't see was any sign of the van. It had disappeared.

He swung the motorcycle hard left onto a patch of scrub, scattering stones in all directions, and nearly losing control. His strategy of holding back and giving his quarry plenty of distance had backfired. He'd been careful; the van driver would have had no reason to suspect he was being followed, and the van couldn't suddenly have picked up so much speed that he'd lost sight of it. The only logical conclusion was that the driver had turned off somewhere between where Betancourt had last seen him and where he stood now.

Below him was a small beach strewn with flotsam deposited by the tides. He clambered down the slope to the sand and looked back along the coast. There was no sign of the van. No sign of anything come to that except for mangrove trees. At that moment, a cloud cleared, revealing the full force of the sun, and he caught a glint of something through the trees about a hundred yards back in the direction he'd just come.

Climbing quickly back up to the main road, he set off in search of the missing van. Just when he thought he must have gone too far, a gap in the jungle revealed a narrow, rutted laterite track. Had he not been looking for it, he wouldn't have given it a second glance.

He followed the track through the tangle of trees until he came to a clearing. He took cover, making sure he wouldn't be seen. Up ahead, the van had come to a stop outside what appeared to be an army Nissen hut. What on earth would the British want with a storage facility out here, in the middle of a patch of jungle? He'd seen no signposts and none of the usual *Keep Out – Government Property* signs on his way down the track, and he wondered if it might not be exactly legal.

The doors to the van were open and, at first, it looked as if the driver had abandoned it. Just as he considered edging closer for a better look, the man emerged from the hut, followed by a couple of Chinese coolies carrying wooden chests, which they placed in the van's rear. The men went back and forth between the inside of the Nissen hut and the van a few more times before being dismissed by the driver. They melted away into the jungle in the direction of the waterfront and, shortly afterwards, he heard a motor starting, followed by the distinctive sound of a two-stroke engine disappearing into the distance.

The driver secured the hut doors with a large padlock and climbed back into the van. Executing a perfect three-point turn – he'd obviously done this a few times before – he sped off back up the track to continue his journey.

Betancourt retreated further into the tangle of trees as the van passed him. He needed to think quickly. If he sprinted back to where he'd left Alex, he'd just about be able to catch up with the van and follow it to the packing plant at Bukit Chandu. But the detour by the man driving the van was clearly a practised move: if one van had stopped here, others would, too. He needed to find out what the men had transferred into the van. He let the van go and stole back to the Nissen hut, taking care to stick to the shadow of the trees in case the gang had left one of their number behind, on guard.

When he was satisfied that he was alone, he stepped out into the dappled sunlight and circled the hut. It was exactly as it had looked from his vantage point in the jungle: a semicircular arc of corrugated iron formed both walls and roof. He ran a finger along the surface. Apart from the usual dust, the surface was clean. No oxidation. The sun and the salt air hadn't yet dulled the steel, so the hut must have been a recent addition. There were two sets of locked doors, one at each end of the building, and no windows. Apart from the doors, the only way anything could get into or out of the building was through a narrow, galvanised stovepipe piercing the outer skin at the far end.

He stood back and examined the doors the driver had entered previously. They too were made of steel and were about eight feet tall. The heavy-duty padlock securing them was military issue, about six inches across, and specifically designed to stop unwanted visitors like him from broaching the building's defences. He gave the lock a shake, but he knew it was useless; there was no way he was going to get it open. Nor was he sure he wanted to. If whatever was behind these doors was tied to Fulbright's death, he didn't want to scare off whoever owned it. He examined the doors more closely. There was a small gap, about half an inch, where the two halves overlapped. He slipped his fingers into the space and pulled. The outermost of the two doors gave slightly. It was enough to let in a sliver of light. If he could find something to use as a lever, he might be able to prise the doors apart just enough to catch a glimpse of what was inside.

He scouted around him for something to use as a jemmy, but with no luck. The trees above were all palms and had no branches, and the discarded fronds littering the surrounding ground were bone dry and snapped as soon as he picked them up.

A track led from the rear of the building down towards the shoreline and he remembered the earlier sound of a two-stroke engine. The path led to a small wooden jetty. The track leading up to it was well trodden and clear of any vegetation. He stepped out onto the jetty. It swayed as he put his weight on it and he quickly stepped back again. As he did, something caught the leg of his trousers, and he heard the material tear. Another visit to Sam Fong beckoned, he thought. He freed himself from the impediment: a coil of rusted barbed wire. There must have been a fence here at some point, because when he pulled at the barbed wire, he discovered it was attached to a length of equally rusted angle iron.

Perfect.

He separated the wire from the steel post and returned to the rear entrance to the Nissen hut. Inserting his makeshift crowbar between the doors, he leant back, prying the doors apart with just enough force to allow him to see inside without leaving any signs of forced entry. He placed his cheek next to the surface of the door and squinted along the length of metal. It was dark inside the hut, but not completely black; the stovepipe, which emerged over the remains of a charcoal hearth, allowed just enough light in for him to see the contents But he was none the wiser. All he could see were bales of straw, the sort that Allenby would use to bed down his horses. Disappointed, he removed the lever.

He was checking he'd left no trace of his attempt to see inside when he heard the two sounds he least wanted to hear at that moment. The first was that of a vehicle crashing through the undergrowth further up the track, its engine over-revving as the driver negotiated the potholes. He froze. He hadn't expected another delivery so soon after the last one. He looked around. He was about thirty feet from the cover of the jungle. If he made a run for it, the driver would spot him immediately. He looked back towards the sea. If he could make the jetty without being seen, he might be able to wade along the waterfront to safety. That was when he heard the second noise – the *put-putting* of a two-stroke motor, and it was getting closer. It was obviously a coordinated pickup and delivery.

He flattened himself against the rear of the hut. The doors at the other end of the building swung open. There were no voices. Whoever was picking up was doing it alone He heard boxes being dragged and a clang as they were dropped into the rear of the van. Behind him, the outboard motor gave a consumptive cough as it shut down. The boatmen would be tying up shortly. Then, it was only a thirty-second hike from the jetty to where they'd find him. Evasion was now out of the question. Picking up the length of steel, he crept around the side of the building until he could just see the van. At first, he couldn't see the driver. Then he heard the doors of the Nissen hut slam shut and a key turn in the lock. A khaki-clad figure came into view and set about closing up the van. Betancourt stole forward, thankful the space surrounding the hut had been cleared of debris. The chatter of the boatmen's voices floated up through the jungle. Instinctively, the squaddie turned towards the sound. It was now or never. Betancourt winced as he contemplated what he was about to do. Then he swung. He caught the side of the man's head with the edge of the steel rod. The man gave the smallest of sighs as he exhaled, and his body crumpled to the ground. As it did so, it twisted, revealing the man's face. His mouth slackened, and the man looked for all the world as if he was in a drunken stupor, a rictus grin revealing a gap where his front teeth used to be. Memories of the beating Betancourt had taken in the lane came flooding back. The driver of the van was one of the thugs who had waylaid him and taken the opium samples he'd recovered from Lew Min's den. Suddenly, he didn't feel so bad for braining the man.

He jogged back to where he'd left Alex and rode to the Sea Moon Hotel. He reckoned it was no more than fifteen minutes since he'd first heard the van careening down the track. He'd no idea when the next one was due. Leaving Alex in the car park, he took his bearings.

About a hundred yards offshore a platform fixed to a network of bamboo stilts swayed in the tide. It was the *kelong* upon which Fulbright had become caught. He could see the fisherman scampering around the platform, attending to his nets, and he called out and waved, but his words were carried away by the wind and the fisherman carried on with his tasks, oblivious.

The plant itself was about a hundred yards up the Pepys Road, on the right-hand side. It consisted of a series of long, narrow concrete buildings perforated by small windows, which ran along the upper edge of the walls, under the eaves. Without a long ladder, it would be impossible to see inside. An eight-foot chain-link fence topped with coils of razor-sharp barbed wire encircled the compound. If he was going to get in and have a look, it would have to be through the main entrance.

As he crossed the road, he felt a spasm in his gut. It was irrational. He was approaching a legitimate enterprise, in the middle of the day. Dozens of law-abiding civilians were hard at work inside. There was nothing to fear. But the person who killed Richard Fulbright was connected to this plant, and whoever that person was, they had a lot to hide and a lot to lose.

A swing-arm barrier guarded the main entrance and a soldier in a sentry box guarded the barrier. As Betancourt neared the entrance, the soldier stepped out from his box, a bayonetted rifle extended in front of him.

'What do you want?'

The soldier was young, and his voice lacked authority. He seemed nervous, and Betancourt wondered if this was the first time away from the drill square that he'd challenged anyone. He pulled out his warrant card.

'My name is Betancourt. I'm with Special Investigations. I'm investigating a death. I believe...' What did he believe? He had no plausible reason for requesting admittance to the compound. 'Superintendent Callan sent me.' He'd apologise to Callan later. Hearing the Customs man's name was enough to cast a shadow of doubt over the young soldier's face.

'Stay there.'

He marched off towards the main building, presumably to seek further instruction. He stopped outside a window and explained his predicament to an unseen listener. After a further exchange, he stood back and hovered, resting the butt of his rifle on the toecap of his boot. Betancourt guessed that someone higher up the food chain had been summoned. He was right. A few moments later, the door opened and another man, also in uniform, emerged from the building. The younger man said something and pointed back to the gate, where Betancourt still stood. But not for long. The new man was none other than Lieutenant Reeves, the man who'd claimed to be from the bomb squad after the explosion at the Excelsior.

Something that had been puzzling him now made sense. After the explosion, when Chee was lying in the ambulance, broken-limbed and barely conscious, Betancourt had asked him if anyone had enquired about Fulbright's room. Chee had whispered *Amoy*. Except he hadn't said that at all; he'd said *army*.

Thirty minutes had elapsed since he'd left Pasir Panjang. He'd made himself scarce as soon as he'd recognised Reeves. But Reeves had seen him, and even across the expanse of tarmac separating them, he could tell from the man's expression that he'd recognised him. It wouldn't take Reeves and his men long to discover the driver he'd put out of action, and at that point Reeves would put two and two together. There was another consideration he kept trying, unsuccessfully, to push to the back of his mind. Bonham was under the impression his interest in the Fulbright case had ended with the inquest. He was soon going to have to explain why he was still involving himself and why that involvement required his spying on

Monopolies Commission delivery vehicles and beating British soldiers about the head with metal implements. Once Bonham found out, it was nigh on certain he'd panic and call an immediate halt to any further investigation. Betancourt wasn't prepared to let that happen. His best chance of finding Fulbright's killers, not to mention clinging on to his job, would be to have as many of the answers as possible. He needed to find out who Reeves was, and what he was doing at the packing plant, and that meant bearding the lion's den that was the Barracks.

The Malays called it Bukit Larangan – Forbidden Hill. They believed the hill to be the final resting place of Parameswara, the last Malay king of the island, and venerated it accordingly. The British, not considering themselves forbidden from doing anything they chose, renamed it Fort Canning, after Viscount John Canning, the first Viceroy of India, and built a military stronghold there. Later, it was there that Molly Ridpath's father and his team had identified the horde of Majapahit gold artefacts now lying in the museum a few minutes' walk away. Wherein also, Betancourt assumed, was Molly, busy with who knew what.

When, five minutes earlier, he'd parked his motorcycle under the cavernous banyan tree and tipped the boy who guarded it, he'd briefly considered going in to see her. And do what, exactly, he'd debated with himself? Tell her who he believed had killed her colleague, her friend, the erstwhile object of her affections? And how had that happened? He didn't know. Why had it happened? He didn't know that either. Not really. Admitting to himself how little he actually knew had been sobering and had reminded him of the urgency of his need to find out more about Reeves. That was why he now found himself at the main gate of the sprawling complex of colonial buildings that rejoiced in the title Headquarters Malaya Command Operations Bunker. To its friends, it was known simply as *the Barracks*.

He approached the front desk.

'Yes?'

His questioner was a long, lanky, sour-faced individual who regarded Betancourt as though he was something he'd just stepped in and was having trouble removing from his shoe. The Barracks, as well as being a working barracks, was the administrative centre for the British army in the Straits Settlements, and the guards were used to visitors. But that didn't mean their natural inclination wasn't to treat a *Serani* policeman with suspicion.

'My name is Betancourt. Inspector. Marine Police. I'm investigating the death of an American citizen.'

'And?'

'And... during my investigation, I met a bomb squad officer by the name of Reeves. I need to check some evidence with him. I need to know where he's based so I can speak to him again.'

'Serving British officers are not required to cooperate with local civilians. Good day.'

Betancourt reckoned the man could have been no more than half his own age, which only made his attitude even more galling. He bit his tongue.

'I understand. I can see I'll need to ask the Inspector-General to clear it. I was hoping not to have to, as I know he's meeting with the Governor today, but needs must.'

He turned, intending to suggest to the inimical soldier he was leaving to make the call. To give the man his due, he allowed Betancourt to reach the front entrance to the building before backing down.

'Wait.'

Betancourt waited, not turning.

'What did you say the name was?'

Now he turned and retraced his steps.

'Reeves.'

'Rank?'

'He said he was a lieutenant.'

The man gave him an acerbic look.

'Then he'll be a lieutenant, won't he? Stay here.'

He was away for a full ten minutes before his head emerged from behind a glass door, further down the corridor.

'This way.'

Betancourt followed him to an office. After rapping on the door, the man swept it open and stood back. Betancourt entered the room and heard the door being firmly closed behind him.

'He seems happy in his job,' Betancourt said to the room's incumbent.

'He's young. I'll have a word with him.' The man stood and extended a hand. 'My name is Phelps. Captain.'

'Betancourt.'

'Yes, I know. I took the liberty of looking you up. I hope you don't mind.'

Betancourt doubted very much that it would have made a blind bit of difference whether he minded or not. He studied Phelps. Forties, he guessed. Clean-shaven, except for the oblig-atory British army officer's moustache. Full head of wavy brown hair, oiled. Typical officer's khaki uniform: arms rolled up in deference to the heat. Nothing out of the ordinary, he'd have thought, had he not noticed a folded red beret lying on the desk, left where it was meant to be noticed. Phelps was Military Police.

'I believe you are looking for...' He opened a folder and glanced at the contents, as if to remind himself why Betan-court was here. It was an affectation: Betancourt was sure he remembered the name. 'Ah yes, Lieutenant Reeves. Do you mind if I ask why?'

'There was a gas explosion at a hotel on Shaikh Madersah Lane. I was inside the building when it happened.'

'Sorry to hear that. Communists, probably. No lasting damage, I hope?'

'I'll live. A man describing himself as Reeves from the bomb squad investigated the site and said the explosion had been caused by a booby-trapped gas burner.'

'And do you have some reason to doubt his opinion?'

'I catch smugglers and fish the occasional body out of the ocean. Bombs aren't my area of expertise, but I know they're a bit of a specialist subject. If one of your men worked for the bomb squad, I wouldn't expect to see him manning the office at an opium packing plant in Pasir Panjang a few days later.'

'I see. Help me here, Inspector. What does all of this have to do with the death of an American archaeologist?'

In the time he'd kept Betancourt waiting outside in the corridor, Phelps had done his homework.

'Who said anything about American archaeologists?'

'As I said, Inspector, I made a few enquiries.'

'Honestly, Captain, I don't know. I just know there is a connection, and Reeves is involved. Now, I don't have much time. Are you going to help me or not?'

Phelps leant back in his chair and looked out the window, as if weighing up a decision.

'The corporal told me you're trying to find out where this Reeves is based.'

'That's right.'

'Well, I'm afraid I can't help you.'

'Can't? Or won't?' said Betancourt.

Phelps's gaze bored into his. 'When I say something, Inspector, I mean it. I find it keeps thing simpler that way. I'm unable to help you for the simple reason that there is no record of anyone named Reeves stationed in Singapore.' He started to tidy papers. It seemed the conversation was over.

As Betancourt stood to leave, he glanced at the desk. His gaze stopped on the folder. Reeves's name was typed on the label. If the army had no record of a Lieutenant Reeves, bomb disposal or otherwise, why then did the Military Police have a file on him?

Chapter Twenty-Seven

After collecting the now perfectly fitting dinner suit from Sam, he returned to the station on Empress Place. There he found an exasperated-looking Djulkifli leaning on the reception counter, holding a pink slip.

'*Mem* French, for you. She said I was to give it to you personally, and I wasn't to leave until you had it in your hand. Now, I'm going home. Goodnight.'

Betancourt gave the sergeant an absent-minded wave and read the note.

Call me as soon as you get this or suffer the consequences.

He was seeing Marjorie that evening. If there was a problem and she had to cancel, her tone would have been apologetic, not demanding. There was only one thing that could have got her back up enough to use such strident language: Bonham was on her case.

She answered on the first ring. 'I was just about to leave when your boss, and he is still your boss, may I remind you, stopped me and told me I was to convey an urgent message to you. He recognises, he said, and I'm quoting here, "there is absolutely no point in me leaving a message myself as he'll just ignore it". Because – quoting again – you are "the most inconsiderate, ill-disciplined officer I have had the misfortune to command in my thirty years on the force". End quote.'

Betancourt ran a hand over his face. The last thing he needed was Bonham on the warpath and he was about to snap back a pithy reply. But this wasn't Bonham, at least, not directly. It was Marjorie, so he tempered his tone. 'I didn't think I was *that* inconsiderate. Do you find me inconsiderate? Perhaps he's just a difficult person to consider. Has he considered that?'

Marjorie continued as though he hadn't spoken. 'He then said, as it was me who suggested your name to the Inspector-General in the first place, and could, therefore, be reasonably held to bear at least a portion of the responsibility for you being here it behoved me – yes, *behoved*; by this point he was in a behoving sort of mood – it behoved me to ensure you received this message before I could leave the office.' Betancourt tried to interject, but Marjorie was in full flow, and she wasn't for stopping. 'Say nothing, just listen. You persuaded me to go out this evening. Perhaps you recall? It's now gone six o'clock, and instead of being at home soaking in a warm bath, I'm here, sitting at my desk, babysitting you.'

He sensed an apology was in order, but he wasn't sure exactly what he'd done wrong, so he opted to keep it non-specific.

'I'm sorry. Give me the message and consider your duty done.'

'What?'

'The message. From Bonham. You said he wanted you to give me a message.'

'Oh, that. Major Melrose called. He wishes to speak with you as a matter of some urgency.'

Melrose? When they'd spoken at Allenby's yard, they'd done little more than pass the time, discussing Topsy's prospects for the weekend.

'Why on earth is Melrose using Bonham as a messenger? If he wanted to get hold of me, why didn't he leave a message with Allenby?'

'How should I know? Mine is to do, not to question why.'

That wasn't true, but given Marjorie's mood, Betancourt decided it wasn't the time to remind her he knew who really wore the trousers in that relationship.

'When was this?'

'When was what?'

'The phone call from Melrose?'

'Half-past five. Why am I so sure, you ask? Because I looked at my watch as I was leaving the office. Half an hour ago.' Her tone was becoming decidedly frosty.

'All right.' The sooner he wound up this conversation, the better. 'Where am I supposed to find him?'

'Who? Bonham? Unlike me, he's gone home.'

'No, not Bonham. Melrose.'

'Again, how should I know? You're the detective, aren't you? Do some bloody detecting. And get a move on.'

'Melrose said that?'

'No, I'm saying that. You're picking me up at seven and you'd better not be late. And for God's sake, Max, call Bonham. Better still, come in and see him. You'll push him too far one of these days.'

Betancourt assured her he'd bear her advice in mind and rang off.

What could Melrose possibly want? They rarely had more than a few words for each other. The major spent most of his time on his estate, overseeing activities and tending to his orchids, and only came down to Singapore when he had a runner at the races. And if he wanted to speak, why had he gone through Bonham to make contact?

He called the operator and gave her Allenby's number. He hoped he was still at evening stables. Instead of waiting until her two parties were connected, the operator hung up. Perhaps she didn't approve of horse racing and didn't want to sully herself by facilitating connections between the gambling fraternity. The distant extension continued to ring. Betancourt imagined the horse in the next stall to Allenby's feed room where the phone was situated, wondering what the noise was, and whether it would result in a carrot, or a piece of sugar.

Osman, Allenby's *mandore* answered. Betancourt didn't need to give his name – the two men had spoken often enough. Yes, *tuan* Allenby was around somewhere. Osman would go and find him. When Allenby eventually picked up, he was still in the middle of a previous conversation and Betancourt had to wait as the trainer delivered a torrent of barked instructions to do with feeding routines to some hapless employee.

'What?' Something had put Allenby in a black mood. The old Australian didn't appreciate small talk at the best of times, and Betancourt knew to dispense with the niceties and get to the point.

'Major Melrose.'

'What about him?'

'Apparently, he wants to see me.'

'News to me. Never mentioned nothing when I saw him at evening stables. Talked about the 'oss, Topsy. Said he's having a bet. That was it. What would he be wanting to talk to you about?'

'No idea.' If Melrose had mentioned nothing to Allenby, then it was odds on that whatever he wanted to talk about wasn't anything to do with racing. 'Any idea where he stays when he's in town?'

'Some sort of gents' club on Cuscaden Road. The Hermitage, I think it's called. Took me for a beer there once. Not my kind of place. Full of poms. Just stayed for the one.'

Betancourt thanked Allenby and rang off. Recalling the operator, he asked to be put through to the Hermitage. He asked if Major Melrose was available. When he was told that he wasn't, he left a message.

'Tell the major I'll meet him in the foyer at nine o'clock tomorrow morning.'

———

He pulled at the collar of his dress shirt and craned his neck.

'Will you stop that? Anyone would think you'd never worn a dinner suit before.'

He thought it best not to tell Marjorie that he hadn't, in fact, worn a dinner suit made for a dead man before, and no amount of chastisement from her would induce him to feel comfortable.

He'd been late arriving at her house on Nassim Hill, and she was still annoyed. This party represented her re-entry into a social world that had once considered her its epicentre, and people were bound to be curious. Naturally, she was nervous, and the least he could have done was turn up on time. He'd underestimated how long it would take to get home from the station, bathe, and dress. Worse still, Sam the tailor had neglected to mention that the black-tie component of the ensemble was a single length of satin ribbon that Betancourt was required to assemble into a bow by his own efforts. In previous times, Anna would have ensured he left the house properly dressed. Now he faced wrangling the beast into shape on his own. He did battle with the tie for a quarter of an hour before giving up and tying it the way he would a shoelace.

'Come here.' Marjorie pulled apart the gnarled knot and reassembled the fabric into the shape for which it was designed. She straightened the shoulders of his jacket and pulled at the lapels, so that they were level. 'Better,' she pronounced.

When Betancourt tried to climb into the front seat of Marjorie's car beside the driver – an old habit – she forbade him and told him to sit in the back with her.

'You're supposed to be my escort for the evening, not my bodyguard.

Betancourt swapped seats, and asked, 'Where is the Westaway mansion, anyway?'

'Hardly a mansion. It's a standard government issue bungalow on Pepys Road.'

'Pasir Panjang? But that's where the opium packing plant is.'

'Why should that be a surprise? Peter Westaway is manager of the plant after all. The bungalow comes with the job, I should imagine.'

He turned in his seat and stared at her. 'What, Westaway manages the packing plant? You left out that rather crucial piece of information. You told me he worked for the government.'

'He does. He works for the Monopolies Commission. And if you keep up that attitude, I'll have the driver turn around and take us back home again. Don't forget, I'm your entrance ticket to this particular piece of sleuthing.'

So, Vita Westaway had been involved with the dead Fulbright, who had discovered something when digging near the opium packing plant run by her husband, who employed the mysterious Lieutenant Reeves. Individually, each of these facts could be explained away as coincidences; but considered together, they pointed to murder.

By the time Marjorie's driver deposited them at the

entrance to the Westaway's bungalow, the party was in full swing.

In the entrance hall, a thin bespectacled Chinese man, also dressed in a black suit and tie, stood holding a clip-board. Marjorie gave her name and the man immediately said, 'Good evening, Mrs French,' and made a small mark on his piece of paper. Betancourt couldn't decide if it surprised him that Marjorie had kept her married name, at least for public consumption. The name linked her inextri-cably with the disgrace brought down by Ray French's behaviour. On the other hand, to revert to her maiden name was to draw attention by omission to her connection with French, and to the expatriate community that would carry its own stigma. An indictment, he thought, of what the people who stood inside the room beyond considered the greater disgrace.

When Betancourt gave his own name, the man pushed his glasses further up the bridge of his nose and held the clip-board away from him, scanning the page. He found the name at the bottom of the page and applied a tick of approval.

'Betting-cot.'

Betancourt didn't bother correcting him.

'Inside, please.' The man waved an arm in the direction of the party inside.

Beyond the entrance, the room was filled with groups of three and four, some talking animatedly, as white-jacketed waiters circumnavigated the room bearing silver trays stacked with glasses of variously hued liquids.

The noise level dropped a level or two as they entered, but quickly returned to its former volume as the company exchanged comments. Fragments of conversations floated across the crowded floor.

Marjorie French? Who'd have thought it…

I'm surprised she has the nerve…

Don't tell me she didn't know what was going on, she was his wife, for God's sake...

Who's that she's with? Is that her driver?

He felt as much as heard Marjorie take a deep breath. She drew back her shoulders and put on a wide smile. 'Show time,' she muttered out of the side of her mouth.

Betancourt followed her round the room as she reintroduced herself to the great and the good. At first, she seemed stiff – almost a little awkward – but, slowly, years of practice kicked in, and her social graces returned. Before long, she was enjoying herself as much as ever. Betancourt, on the other hand, was reminded why he would normally do anything to avoid situations such as this.

Marjorie excused herself and he was left momentarily on his own. He felt a presence at his elbow. He turned to see Vita Westaway. She was dressed in a plunging carmine silk dress and wore a suite of white-stoned jewellery that he had no trouble at all believing were diamonds. She held out a thin cheroot in a long ebony holder.

'Do you have a light?'

He flicked the wheel of his lighter.

'I remember you,' she said. You were at the talk at the library. You played Sir Galahad to that mousy little thing who works at the museum. Has she calmed down yet?'

He told her he hadn't seen Miss Ridpath again. Not true, but then it was none of her concern.

'They tell me you're a policeman,' she said. She eyed him up and down. 'Most of the bobbies I've met were flabby numbers with flat feet. You, on the other hand, scrub up quite well.'

He could have taken the compliment and just waited for Marjorie to return, but he was no use at social niceties, and he'd decided that he didn't much like Mrs Westaway.

'What they told you was correct. I am a policeman – a

detective inspector, actually, and I'm investigating the death of Dr Richard Fulbright.'

He watched her carefully to gauge her response to his bluntness. She looked away, across the room. He couldn't decide if she was avoiding his gaze or was just practising a carefully curated response.

'Poor Richard. I was so sad to hear the news. A tragic accident.'

'You knew each other, I believe.'

'Yes. I sponsored his work. It was fascinating. He was so passionate about everything he did.'

'And what about outside his work?'

'I can't think what you mean.'

'I'm asking if you saw each other socially. Were you, perhaps, involved?'

Vita drew silently on her cheroot for a minute, and when she spoke, she was perfectly calm.

'A piece of advice, Inspector. You want to be very careful about slinging around scurrilous accusations like that. See that man over there, by the verandah? That's my husband, Peter.'

He followed the direction of her long finger. She was pointing to an insubstantial figure wearing a black cravat instead of a bow tie. It was the man Betancourt had seen at the coroner's inquest with Reeves. He was close to understanding it all – who had killed Richard Fulbright and why. 'My husband is well connected, Inspector; *very* well connected. And through him, *I* am well connected. A word in the right ear and you could find yourself on traffic duty. If you wish to point fingers, I suggest you point them in the direction of Miss Ridpath. Then, at least, you might find yourself closer to finding out the truth. Enjoy the party.'

She walked away, elegant to the end, as though Betancourt's questions were nothing more than a minor inconvenience. He watched her as she crossed the room. She stopped a boy carrying a tray and gave him an instruction. A few moments later, the bomb squad-cum-plant security man, Reeves, appeared. She spoke to him animatedly and pointed back across the room towards Betancourt. He could almost feel Reeves's stare boring into him.

By this time Marjorie had returned. 'That's enough for my comeback appearance,' she said. 'I'm out of practice and I need to pace myself. Shall we go?'

'Of course, if you like. I enjoyed myself. I never realised what interesting conversations you could have at these parties.'

Chapter Twenty-Eight

He'd read somewhere that the original hermitages were retreats that provided a haven for men who, weary of the sins and temptations of the mortal world, wished to live out their days in ascetic isolation. He'd also read that those early retreats had been caves or small buildings in deserts, mountains, and forests, or on islands. This Hermitage was a grey, charmless building set back from Cuscaden Road. A stark grey granite wall protected the inner sanctum from the prying eyes of passers-by.

A sepoy *jaga*, dressed entirely in white, from pith helmet to puttees, guarded the entrance to the enclosure in which the major's club sat. Betancourt gave his name and waited while the man checked to see he was expected. It seemed he was, and the *jaga* waved him in.

The entrance foyer was clad in mahogany, and the preponderance of wood sucked in the light and left the atmosphere gloomy and oppressive. A doorway led to what looked like a dining room where several Europeans were taking breakfast and reading newspapers. The place reminded him of the government rest houses found in small towns up country: spartan and functional rather than opulent and comfortable, and he wondered why someone like Major Melrose, who couldn't be short of funds, lodged here when he was in town.

Another layer of security sidled up to him. A Chinese man wearing a dark suit and the haughty air sported by major-domos everywhere.

'Yes?'

Apparently, *Serani* in scruffy suits didn't merit a 'sir'. Betancourt wafted his warrant card in front of the man's eyes, for no good reason other than to intimidate him a little.

'I'm here to see Major Melrose. At his invitation.'

The man inclined his head to one side. A look of vague disappointment clouded his narrow face, as if he was regretting these changed days in which he now found himself, when even a *Serani* policeman could be invited onto the premises. 'The major is in the reading room. Follow me.'

Betancourt found Melrose ensconced in a rattan armchair in a small nook off the main room, his face all but obscured by a copy of the *Daily Telegraph*. WE NEVER SURRENDER, the headline proclaimed.

Betancourt's shadow coughed into his hand. 'You have a visitor, Major. A *policeman*.' He managed to make this latter part of the announcement sound pregnant with warning, as if to say, '*If he gives you any trouble, just call for me. I'll see to him.*'

Melrose clambered to his feet, hand extended in welcome, his face wreathed in its habitual smile.

'Good of you to come. Tea all right? Ask them to bring tea for two, would you, Goh?'

Goh disappeared and Melrose made small talk, relating what he'd read about the progress of the war in Europe in the newspaper. It was telling, Betancourt thought, and typical, that despite having long since settled in Malaya, the major's primary interest appeared to lie in events on that distant continent, rather than on the increasingly parlous situation in the north of this one.

When Goh had delivered a tray with a teapot and cups and had departed again, closing the doors behind him, Melrose leant forward, his face suddenly serious.

'Perhaps you would be so good as to tell me what is going on, Inspector.'

His demeanour had changed so quickly it took Betancourt aback.

'I don't understand. What do you mean, "What is going on"?'

'You'll remember a man named Montgomery?'

Betancourt did indeed remember him. He was a spook. Something to do with Military Intelligence. Montgomery had appeared from nowhere one day during the Sleeping Tigers case, riding roughshod over protocol and taking control of the case. What did a normally avuncular retired tin miner and racehorse owner have to do with a man like Montgomery?

'I remember him. Why do you ask?'

'Last night, Montgomery received a call from a man named Phelps in the intelligence unit at Fort Canning. Phelps told him a Eurasian police inspector had been in, asking questions about security at the opium packing plant at Bukit Chandu. That would be you, I take it.'

Betancourt was baffled by the way the conversation had turned. He was also struggling to control his annoyance at the way Melrose was speaking to him.

'Just be thankful Montgomery is—' Melrose paused before continuing. 'Attending to affairs elsewhere. Instead, you have me to deal with, and believe me, that is the lesser of two evils.

Betancourt stared. Gone was the mellow, agreeable, slightly absent-minded, all is well with the world and all who sail in her Melrose, and in its place was a very different version, one he hadn't seen before. His normally placid grey eyes were hard and cold, the smile replaced by a thin, hard look. The overall impression was of a man of action – one who knew exactly what he wanted, and how to get it.

'Major, I'm confused. What does any of this have to do with you? And how do you know about any of it?'

Melrose hesitated, but the steely gaze continued unabated. 'Before we go any further, Inspector, I expressly forbid you from repeating anything you hear in this room this morning to anyone. Do I make myself clear?'

Betancourt gave as good as he was getting with the flinty looks. 'I'll decide what I say and to whom I say it.' He kept his voice low. He wasn't going to let the old man bully him. 'Either *you* tell *me* what is going on or I'm going straight to the Assistant Commissioner to inform him of this conversation.' Of course, he had no intention of speaking to Bonham about anything at that or any other moment if he could avoid it, but he figured his superior's name should carry some weight. To reinforce his threat, he stood as if he was about to leave.

Annoyingly, Melrose smiled. 'For God's sake, sit down,' he said. 'You appear to have forgotten why you're here.'

'I'm here because I received a message stating you wished to speak to me. The message didn't say why or what about.'

'And who gave you the message?'

Betancourt suddenly felt very foolish. In his blustering attempt to gain control, he'd completely ignored the fact that it was Marjorie who had passed on the message. It was at Bonham's behest he was meeting with Melrose.

'Sit down, Inspector.'

Betancourt sat.

'That's better.' Melrose's own anger had subsided, and he was more like the major Betancourt knew and preferred. 'Shall we begin again?'

'All right.'

'Good. But before I say any more, I really must ask you to

keep what you're about to hear to yourself. It's imperative no one else knows. Not Bonham, not Marjorie French, not Bill Allenby, no one.' The grey eyes took aim. 'Not even Dr Trevose. It's a question of national security. Agreed?'

A sense of unease and a thrall of excitement gripped Betancourt simultaneously. What the hell was going on? It looked like the only way he was going to find out was to accede to Melrose's demand. He nodded slowly. 'Agreed.'

'Very well. In that case, I'd better establish my credentials. Phelps called Montgomery after your visit because Montgomery is regional control for the coordination of intelligence in Malaya. In other words, although the official reporting lines show different, Montgomery is Phelps's boss.'

'But how on earth did you come to know about all this?'

'Because I am Montgomery's boss.'

Betancourt wasn't sure how long he sat with his mouth open, but it probably wasn't as long as it seemed.

'Hold on. Until now, you were a retired tin miner from Ipoh who owned a few racehorses and liked a bet now and again. Now you're telling me you run military intelligence for the whole of Malaya?'

'You make it sound much more dramatic than it really is. I don't run military intelligence. Not exactly. That's Montgomery's job. My job is to run Montgomery. And a few others,' he added, under his breath.

'I see,' said Betancourt, although he was having trouble taking all this in. 'And what, exactly, do you want from me?'

'Let's start with your interest in the opium packing plant.'

'I'm investigating a death.'

'The death of the American, Fulbright?'

'That's right.' There was no point in asking how Melrose

knew. If he was military intelligence, there would be little he didn't know or couldn't find out if he wanted to.

'I'm given to understand the inquiry into Dr Fulbright's death decided the cause of death was suicide. Why, then, are you still investigating?'

'Dr Trevose found lacerations in Fulbright's throat. She believes the opium she found in his stomach was forced down. That's a crucial piece of evidence the coroner ignored.'

'And you trust Dr Trevose's judgement?'

'Completely.'

'I see.' Melrose didn't expand on what it was he saw. 'Carry on.'

'Someone murdered Fulbright. The question was, why? Why would someone want to kill an archaeologist? I decided to follow the opium, to see where it led me. I had it analysed. The lab confirmed it wasn't government issue, it was an illegal form of the drug known as *cacak*: poor quality – rough, unrefined, but, in this case, also highly potent. Dr Trevose mentioned she'd seen an alarming number of deaths recently due to ingestion of a similar product. I followed up on those deaths and I narrowed them down to a den on Hokien Street.'

'An illegal den?'

'No, that's the strange thing: it's a licensed shop. I had a look around and I found some of the illegal product. I confiscated a sample, meaning to have it tested, but I was attacked on the way home and relieved of the evidence.' Betancourt smiled at the memory.

'Do you find being beaten up amusing?'

'Anything but. But it's ironic, given we're having this conversation. The men who attacked me were British army.'

Melrose narrowed his eyes. 'Are you sure?'

'Unless they were on their way to a masquerade ball dressed as squaddies then, yes, I'm sure.'

'And where does Reeves come into it?'

'There was an explosion at the hotel where Fulbright was staying. I was there. Shortly after, a man calling himself Reeves emerged from the building. He said he was with the bomb squad. Seemed reasonable enough at the time. But now I wonder if he might have had some other reason for being there. Then I thought I saw him at the coroner's inquiry.'

'You *thought* you saw him?'

'He wore a mask at the hotel, a sort of kerchief thing. For the dust, I thought, but it may have been to hide his face. Anyway, after I was beaten up, I knew for certain the opium was central to whatever had happened to Fulbright. I took the sample results to Callan at Customs, and he confirmed his men were finding more and more of this illegal stuff. He said they'd redoubled their surveillance activities, but they still didn't know how it was getting into the dens. I asked him to show me the factories. He took me around the boiling factory at Telok Blangah, but he said he couldn't get me into the packing plant at Bukit Chandu. So, I had a look for myself.

'What were you looking for?'

Betancourt shrugged. 'I don't really know. Anything that might lead me closer to understanding how Fulbright died. If I understood how he died, I'd be closer to understanding why he died. And if I understood why, I'd be closer to knowing who killed him. Standard detective work. One thing leads to another. It's my job to follow the trail.

'I followed one of the vans from Telok Blangah. It made a detour at a Nissen hut. After it had gone, I had a look in the hut. Then I tried to get into the plant, but a boy on sentry duty stopped me. He told me to wait, and who should come out from the plant?'

'Reeves.'

Betancourt nodded.

The room was quiet, save for the distant clatter of breakfast dishes being loaded onto trays. Betancourt broke the silence.

'What happens next?'

'As I said, I must ask you to keep this conversation strictly between us. If opium smuggling is being facilitated by anyone in the British army, then naturally it would have to be taken care of, quickly and quietly.'

'Phelps said that Reeves didn't exist. Are you now saying he is army?'

'Are you sure Phelps said that?'

'All right, then. He said that there was no one named Reeves enlisted in Singapore.'

'You can leave Reeves to me. I'll speak to Phelps again.'

'I just want my murderer, Major. You're welcome to the rest of it.'

Melrose said he'd let Betancourt know what he had found out that afternoon at the races.

'You're going to be there, I take it?'

'Wouldn't miss it, Major. I've had a tip. Straight from the horse's mouth, you might say.'

Melrose stood and put out his hand to be shaken. 'I'm glad we had this chat, Inspector. We can trust one another, can't we? We're on the same side, after all.'

Betancourt laughed aloud. He couldn't help himself.

Melrose's eyes narrowed. 'I seem to have amused you.'

'I'm sorry. You'll have to excuse me. It's just that sometimes I'm unsure what the sides are, let alone who is on which one.'

Chapter Twenty-Nine

U pon entering the comparative luxury of the air-conditioned grandstand, Betancourt headed straight for Melrose's usual spot: an isolated corner of the trainer's stand where, strictly speaking, he had no right to be, but he'd stood there for so long that successive generations of racecourse officials had come to treat him as part of the furniture. There was no sign of the spymaster.

He checked his watch. The runners for the first race would enter the pre-parade ring soon, and Allenby had a runner. He found the old Australian making his way towards the saddling boxes, a well-worn saddle over one arm and a pair of binoculars slung over the other. Betancourt fell into stride alongside.

'I'm supposed to meet the major. You haven't seen him, have you?'

Allenby gave him a sideways glance. 'This about your secret rendezvous? You blokes and your secrets. It'd give me the colic. I told you, give me 'osses any day. You know where you stand with 'osses. Well, most of the time, anyroads. If the major ain't sitting where he usually sits, then your guess is good as mine.'

'If you see him, tell him I was looking for him.'

Allenby ambled off to saddle up his runner, and Betancourt leant on the fence encircling the pre-parade ring, studying the runners as they ambled past. It was something Stanley had drummed into him when he was young.

'*Get your nose out of the tip sheets, boy. Learn to read the horses for yourself.*'

And he had. He'd learned to tell which horses had the conformation to stand up to the rigours of galloping on the hard-baked tropical turf and which ones would hold themselves back, trying to protect themselves. He'd learned how to differentiate between the compact, powerful-looking ones that were destined to be sprinters and the leaner, rangier types that would require a longer distance to show their best. Above all, he learned early on how to recognise when a horse was yet to reach its peak and when it was fit to run for its life.

He checked his race card. Allenby's runner was called Garden Party. He watched with a critical eye as the horse wandered past him and made a mental note. (Nice looking horse. A bit dull in the coat. Will come on for the run.)

Next up was a tall bay mare. She had a loose, effortless walk, and unlike Garden Party, her coat glinted in the early afternoon sun. When she reached the point where Betancourt stood, he saw she had a calm, intelligent eye. The saddlecloth bore the number seven. He checked his card again. Prima Donna. Another of Stanley's axioms was to never give a good horse a bad name. Betancourt took the view that it was unlikely Prima Donna knew what connotations her name held and was unlikely to run badly as a result. She would carry his hopes and his cash.

There was still no sign of Melrose, so he went to place a bet. Allenby always fixed him up with a badge for the members' stand, but if he had to choose between the rarefied atmosphere of the air-conditioned enclosure above him and the swirling mass of humanity that was the public area, he'd choose the latter every time.

A gate linked the two compounds, monitored by a tall, heavily set Sikh. He raised an eyebrow as Betancourt approached. His job was to keep the badgeless riff-raff from crossing the line and not to stop the badged elite from going the other way, so, presumably deciding his was not to question why, and it was Betancourt's business if he wanted to cross the divide to join the great unwashed, he swung open the gate, gave one of those huge expansive smiles that no race could do like the Sikhs could, and let Betancourt pass.

A Malay man, immaculately turned out in a bright red *baju melayu* and *songkok*, perched on top of a crate by the fence that lined the track. He called himself *The Prophet*, and he was a regular on race days. The scarlet silk of his outfit was no mere fashion statement: his mostly Chinese patrons considered red the colour of good luck, and anything that attracted more custom was a good investment. He called out:

'*Gentlemen! Come closer. I have a horse!*'

One hopeful approached him proffering a bank note, which the soothsayer happily accepted. In return, he passed his new client a folded slip of paper upon which he had written today's advice. Each piece of paper he sold bore the name of a different horse, so there was always someone who won and who was ready to sing the tipster's praises. Nearby, working men in cotton singlets and shorts stood clouded in cigarette smoke, slapping folded newspapers against the palms of their hands as they argued about the likely outcomes of the seer's predictions.

With another fifteen minutes until post time, the queues in the betting hall were light.

'Number seven. Win.' Betancourt didn't back horses each

way. *If it's good enough to run a place, it's good enough to win.* Another Stanleyism. Betancourt agreed with this one, but his rationale was mathematical: the odds just didn't justify betting on horses to place. He handed over a ten-dollar note and the woman behind the grille passed him a ticket in exchange.

He realised he was hungry. He could return to the owners' stand, and eat cake and drink tea, or he could eat some real food. The best recommendation for any food outlet, he'd always thought, be it the grandest restaurant or the humblest *kopi tiam*, was the length of the queue waiting to taste its offerings. Tucked away in a shady spot beneath the main stand, a hawker, enveloped in clouds of steam, dispensed pale, soft white dumplings filled with sweet bean paste to a lengthy queue of hungry punters. He joined the queue. When he reached the front, he ordered two and found a quiet spot on the fence near the furlong marker to eat his lunch in peace.

Dumplings dispatched, he turned his attention to the ritual of the race.

'*The starter's calling them in... Still one or two stragglers... That's it... He's got them in a line... And they're off! Prima Donna broke well on the inside...*'

Prima Donna proved not to be a prima donna at all and willingly gave her jockey everything she had. She won easily, and Betancourt collected his winnings. A nice stake for Topsy later in the afternoon.

He returned to the owners' stand in search of Melrose, but before he had a chance to look, he found Evelyn instead, standing near to the entrance to the paddock. She was with Alistair Grey and a couple he didn't recognise.

'Ah, Inspector,' she said. 'There you are. Do you know the Nicolls? John and Susan. They own Garden Party. And you know Alistair, of course.' Alistair Grey nodded but said nothing.

Betancourt shook hands with the Nicolls. 'I had a look at Garden Party before the race. She's a fine-looking horse.'

John Nicoll looked concerned. 'I hope you didn't lose too much on her.'

'No, not much at all.'

'I'm afraid you'll have to excuse us. I need a word with the inspector.' Evelyn's words were light and casual, but her eyes, when she glanced at him, conveyed urgency. 'A work matter.' Evelyn smiled to the Nicolls, and then, to Alistair Grey, said, 'I'll see you later.'

Grey appeared less than happy about the idea of losing his inamorata, even temporarily, to Betancourt.

'Must you do this now? How long will you be?'

'I don't know. It's important. I'll make my own way home.' And then, as though regretting her tone, she gave Grey an almost fraternal pat on the arm.

'What was all that about?' said Betancourt once they were back inside the grandstand. 'Were you bored?'

'Of course not. I was having a perfectly pleasant afternoon.' There was a brief silence. 'All right. Maybe a little bored.' She laughed. That tinkling, musical laugh he'd found so intoxicating the first time he heard it. 'But I really do need to speak to you. I have something for you. Something big.'

He raised an eyebrow. 'I'm all ears. We'd better find somewhere quiet.'

They found an empty table at the rear of the stand. A waiter came and hovered beside them until Evelyn waved him away impatiently. Betancourt glanced around, checking no one was paying undue attention to their conversation.

He stopped. 'Look, over there.'

'Where?'

'The table by the window.' He indicated with a nod of his

head in the direction of a large table at the front of the grand-stand where a party of racegoers enjoyed an uninterrupted view of the next lot of runners making their way to the start.

'See the woman? The one dressed up to the nines? All over the young man with the blond hair?'

Evelyn nodded. 'Should I know her?'

'That's Vita Westaway. She was having an affair with Fulbright. According to Molly Ridpath, she just about bank-rupted him. Got him to place her bets for her, using his own money.'

Just then, Vita pointed to her race card, touched the young man's arm, and laughed coquettishly. The current object of her affections rose from his seat and headed towards the betting windows, checking his wallet and frowning as he did so.

'If he's running short of funds already, I don't fancy his chances for the rest of the afternoon.'

'The other man,' Evelyn said. 'The one with the face like thunder on him. I've seen him somewhere before.'

'That's Peter Westaway, her husband. You saw him at the inquest.'

'I remember. He was sitting down at the front. Next to a soldier.'

'Westaway is involved in Fulbright's death. I went to a party last night, at their bungalow.

'You did what? You don't go to parties.'

'I went to this one. With Marjorie. She smuggled me in as her escort for the evening. I recognised Westaway from the inquest, but it was Marjorie who told me who he was. And get this, he manages the opium packing plant at Bukit Chandu.'

He told her about everything that had happened since they'd last spoken: Molly and Fulbright and the trust owing money; his encounter with the squaddies in the lane; his visit with Callan to the opium factory; following the van and discovering the illegal drop-off; his interview with Phelps; the party and his encounter with Vita; and his meeting with Melrose that morning.

'I'm supposed to meet him here. He's going to find out what Reeves is up to.'

'You certainly have been busy,' she said when he'd finished.

'The illegal opium is coming in directly to the packing plant at Bukit Chandu, and Fulbright must have caught wind of it, through his affair with Vita, and was killed as a result. Westaway is devoted to Vita, but he can't afford her lifestyle. So, he must have hit on this scheme. Reeves provides the muscle for the operation. Whether it was Westaway's idea in the first place, or he has a silent partner, I've yet to find out.'

'I may be able to help you there,' she said. 'That's what I've been wanting to talk to you about. Remember the other night? At my place?' She blushed faintly.

'What about it?'

'Remember you told me about the *sinseh*? The one who claimed to be a trained doctor?'

'Loong?'

'Him. Well, he isn't a doctor.'

'So, the story about studying at Cambridge was all nonsense?'

'Not exactly nonsense, but let's say he took a few liberties. I looked him up; he did study at Cambridge, that bit was true, but he didn't study medicine.'

Betancourt shrugged. 'Does it matter? He doesn't need western qualifications to practise Chinese medicine.'

'True, but there's more.' Her eyes were afire. She was enjoying this. 'When you told me about him, there was something about his story that didn't ring true, but for the life of me, I couldn't think what was bothering me.'

'I remember.' He wished she would get to the point, but he forbore from saying so.

'You said he claimed to have worked at the Anti-Opium Clinic. I remembered that was where I'd met him. Chen Su-Lan who ran the clinic is now a director at Tan Tock Seng hospital, where I just happen to have a patient.'

'Don't tell me: your patient became in sudden need of an urgent consultation.'

She grinned. 'When I was there, I paid Chen a courtesy visit. We got chatting, and I said I'd met a doctor named Loong. A white lie. Everyone's allowed the odd one of those. Chen looked blank at first and said he didn't know any doctors named Loong, but when I gave him the description you gave me, he said I must be mistaken because the Loong I had described wasn't a doctor. I did my silly-female-forget-my-own-head-one-of-these-days act and said he was quite right. I then asked him if the rumours I'd heard about Loong being sacked were true. He said they were. And get this: they caught him selling drugs to the very patients he was supposed to be helping recover from addiction.'

'Pretty low behaviour for a doctor.'

'That's what I said. And then Chen asked what had made me think he was a doctor. I told him Loong had said he was, and Chen said no, he was a chemist. His job was to make up preparations to help the patients.'

'And instead of helping them, he was slipping them drugs.'

'Exactly. Chen seemed bitter about the whole business. When I pushed him, he said that until then the clinic had been successful; recovery rates had been good, and they were receiving increasing numbers of donations from local Chinese businessmen. Chen said he tried to keep Loong's actions out of it, but eventually the news got out. The clinic was already struggling because the Chinese business community was diverting funds to the war against the Japanese in China. Chen had no choice but to close.'

'Why didn't he get the police involved?'

'I don't suppose he saw any point. The government wasn't in favour of the clinic. The idea that opium addiction was an illness that could be treated didn't fit with their view of it being an intrinsic weakness in the oriental character, not to mention it being bad for opium sales. Apparently, they were delighted when it was closed down.'

'This is all very interesting, but what does it have to do with Fulbright?'

'I'm coming to that.' Evelyn leant forward, her eyes alight again. 'I assumed that if these patients were opium addicts, then it must have been opium that Loong was selling to them, but Chen said no, it was worse than that. Loong was selling them pure refined thebaine.'

'Which is what, exactly?'

'It's a constituent of opium.'

He must have looked blank, so she explained.

'What we call opium is actually a cocktail of different drugs – all related, but with different potencies and effects. Codeine and morphine are two of the better-known ones. Let's say you're an opium addict. You smoke the drug, or you swallow it. Or, in Fulbright's case, someone forces it down your gullet. The drugs enter your bloodstream and are carried to your brain where they have their effects.'

'And?'

'And, when Chen mentioned thebaine, it jogged my memory. It isn't something that comes up in conversation every day, and yet I remembered reading something about it recently. It was in the sample report from the laboratory – the one on the opium found in Fulbright's stomach. So, I went and dug it out. Sure enough, the report mentioned thebaine. My pharmacology is a bit rusty, but we had a lecture on this at university, and I remembered thebaine is also a component of opium. I asked the laboratory to recheck the sample results. They agreed with me: the levels of thebaine appeared to be unusually high.'

'Why the hell didn't they say something at the time?'

'Because they didn't have the context; I just asked them to analyse the sample. Your idea, remember?'

He shuffled in his seat. 'Did they say why it was so high?'

'No, but I think I've figured it out. The Bengali opium that the government imports comes from *Papaver somniferum* – the opium poppy, but that contains relatively small amounts of thebaine. So, the opium found in Fulbright's body can't have been made from government opium.'

'Then what?'

'There's only one type of plant that has that high a concentration of thebaine: *Papaver bracteatum* – the great scarlet poppy. It would take a trained chemist to isolate thebaine. A chemist like Loong.'

Betancourt sat quietly for a moment, taking in everything Evelyn had told him.

'It all makes sense,' he said, eventually. 'Loong said he'd treated Fulbright and the now-dead rickshaw puller. What if he wasn't treating them at all? What if he was supplying them? If he was caught selling drugs to the patients at the addiction clinic, it isn't unreasonable to assume that the drugs were of his own making. He's a trained chemist, after all. I'll tell Callan to raid the shop on Kitchener Road. See what's going on in the back room. I've a pretty good idea what he'll find. But there's one thing I still don't understand. Callan has had a double watch on all the shipping traffic from India. Why aren't they finding this opium when it comes in?'

'Simple. Because it isn't coming from India. The great scarlet poppy is also known as the Persian poppy. That's where it's originally from. I'd suggest that if Callan wants to find the opium, he starts checking boats from the Persian Gulf. Oh, and there's something else. Most Indian opium is made from the sap of the plant. Thebaine is made by crushing the whole of the plant. Tell Callan to look for poppy straw, not resin.'

The bales of straw in the Nissen hut. Not bedding for animals, but the makings of a dangerous drug.

'He was waving it in my face the whole time.'

'Who was waving what?'

'Loong. He said he'd taken up painting when he was at Cambridge. He had one of his pictures in pride of place in his office. It was a watercolour of a great scarlet poppy.'

'What will you do now?'

'I need to find Melrose and see what he's found out about Reeves. Then I'm going to find out what Fulbright discovered that was worth him making a map for. I could do with some exercise; an early evening hike up Bukit Chandu might just hit the spot.'

He left Evelyn reunited with Grey and the Nicolls and went in search of Melrose, stopping at the tote window on his way to place a bet on Topsy. By this time, the major was back in his accustomed position in the top corner of the stand.

'I was wondering where you'd got to.'

'Chasing after your man Reeves, that's where I'd got to. Thought I was going to miss the race. Anyway, I'm here now.' Melrose regarded Betancourt sternly. 'Do you have any idea what sort of hornet's nest you've stirred up?'

'Me? All I want to do is find who killed Richard Fulbright.'

'I got Phelps to do some digging on Reeves.'

'He told me there was no record of Reeves being in the British army. Is that right?'

'Phelps's intelligence was sound as far as it went. His name is Michael Reeves, and he didn't serve in the army here, but he did in Hong Kong. He started off in the NAAFI, running the stores. There were all sorts of accusations, from watering down the whisky and pocketing the profits, to selling counterfeit cigarettes and taking bribes from suppliers – you name it, Reeves had a hand in it. There were also stories, hushed up, from some of the army wives that he'd been a bit…'

Melrose paused. Betancourt cocked an eye.

'A bit rough with them. You know, in the bedroom. He was lucky not to be cashiered then, but one of his girlfriends came to his rescue. Found him a posting with her father, a Colonel Ormond, who was in command of the Supply Corps. Daddy put Reeves in charge of contracts. His job was to award tenders for the building contracts. He was soon back to his old tricks, taking kickbacks from the contractors, and, in return, he turned a blind eye to shoddy workmanship. The contractors made back the money they'd given to Reeves by using substandard material. There was a fire. People were killed. It was a miracle it hadn't happened sooner and more often. The scam was exposed, and Reeves was court-martialled and drummed out of the army. Then he disappeared, before turning up in Singapore a year ago. Westaway took him on as head of security at the packing plant. Strange choice – he must have been aware of Reeves's record – but there you go, he's the boss.'

Ormond. Why did he know that name?

'Marjorie,' Betancourt said, the memory flooding back.

'Mrs French? What's she got to do with this?'

'Nothing. At least, not directly. Marjorie knows everything about everyone in expat society. I asked her about Vita Westaway. She said Vita's father's name was Ormond.'

'And she was Reeves's girlfriend.'

'And now she's married to Peter Westaway, who employs Reeves as the resident heavy at Bukit Chandu. That will be how Westaway and Reeves met. It may even have been Reeves's plan from the start. Get the daughter; get the father. And they all have a link to Fulbright.'

'What do you intend to do now?

I need to go up there myself and find out exactly what it was Fulbright saw that got him killed.'

'Do you know where you're going?'

'I have Fulbright's map.'

'Well, you'd better be sharp about it. There's an almighty storm brewing between Phelps, Bonham, and Callan about who gets to move in for the kill. I'm staying out of the way and letting them get on with it. Right, enough of that. Starter has them lined up.'

Chapter Thirty

Topsy romped home and after he'd collected his winnings, Betancourt waited for darkness to fall before setting out for Pasir Panjang. Hiding Alex behind a clump of mangrove on the seafront about fifty yards from the plant, he stole across the road.

He stuck close to the fence, circling the plant until he could see the sentry box. A taller, lankier version of the youth he'd dealt with the previous day was on duty. Perhaps the night shift was quieter and there were fewer visitors to deal with. Whatever the reason, the new man appeared bored and wandered around outside his hut, smoking a cigarette and batting away the mosquitoes that were attracted by the arc-lights illuminating the plant.

He ducked down into a hollow and kept watching the sentry, waiting for an opportunity to cross the road without being spotted. He didn't have to wait long. When the sentry had stubbed out his cigarette, he took a good look around him in all directions and, believing he was alone, parked his rifle in the hut and slinked off into the shadows to relieve himself.

Staying low, Betancourt sprinted past the now-empty

sentry box and into the scrubby jungle where he wouldn't be seen. He'd brought a torch with him, and with his back to the plant, he cupped his hand around the light and examined Fulbright's map. His target was at the top of the hill, which meant he'd have to pass the Westaways' bungalow without being spotted. The track that led to the bungalow looked steeper and more twisting than it had from Marjorie's car last night, and he would need to stay a good fifty feet away from the track if he was to avoid being seen. The night was inky black and the jungle dense, but with the aid of the map, and judicious use of the torch, he reckoned he should be able to reach the summit of the hill without attracting attention.

The trek proved more arduous than he'd expected, constantly upward with no flat spots where he could recover his breath, and the thick jungle prodded and scratched at him until blood flowed freely from his arms, legs, and face. Stopping to wipe himself clean, he glimpsed a weak light up ahead. The Westaways' bungalow. He struck out to his right, deeper into the jungle, before resuming his climb. He slowed as he drew level with the bungalow. As he did, a sound like a rifle crack echoed through the still night air. He spun round and peered into the gloom. He could see nothing and wondered if he should risk the torch again. He waited, his whole body tense. After a minute had passed and there was no further sound, he relaxed, satisfied it must have been a heavy-footed pangolin, or an inquisitive mousedeer, stepping on a dry twig.

He inched forward until the trees thinned and he could see the bungalow clearly. If he could see the building clearly, then in theory, anyone inside could see him too, but firstly, they weren't expecting him, and secondly, he was looking into the light, whereas they, even if they bothered to look out, would be looking into the pitch black of the jungle.

Through an open window in the side of the house he

could see Vita and Westaway. They appeared to be having a blazing argument. Westaway's face was flushed red, and he was shouting, shaking his fist, and pointing out of the window. At one point he raised his arm above his head, and Betancourt became concerned for Vita's safety, but she looked to be giving as good as she was given. Suddenly, all the emotion seemed to escape from the altercation, like the air leaving a punctured balloon, and they were both quiet. Westaway threw on his jacket, said something to Vita, his mood more subdued now, and left the room. Betancourt waited a while longer until Westaway emerged from the bungalow and headed off down the road towards the packing plant. He gave a few more minutes just to be on the safe side and then ploughed on up the hill.

When he was out of sight of the bungalow and safe in the darkness again, he took out the torch. The spot Fulbright had marked on the map was about twenty feet off the track, in line with something he'd shown as a square box. Up ahead, Betancourt spotted the box. It was a green-painted junction box, for electricity, or possibly for telephone lines. He reached the box, turned through ninety degrees, and counted off the steps. He hadn't needed to worry about accuracy; before he reached the twentieth pace, his foot caught a flagstone, and he was sent sprawling. The pain in his ribs as he hit the ground was excruciating, and it was all he could do not to cry out.

The fall had dislodged the torch from his hand, and he scoured the undergrowth looking for it. He found it eventually, half-buried in the humus that had accumulated beneath a tangled bush. He switched it on. It still worked. More than that, the torch had landed at the spot Fulbright had marked on the map. It wasn't an archaeological dig at all; it was some sort of low cellar, cut into the hillside and crudely covered with bracken and fern frond. Brushing aside the vegetation, he squatted down and peered into the void. A foot or two inside was a hatch, the wood damp and rotted. On the surface of the hatch, someone had stencilled a series of letters, now faint and algae covered. Even with the torch, it was difficult to make out what the letters spelt out. The cellar must have served some sort of military purpose at one time, perhaps an ammunition store or similar. He turned the torchlight onto the ground. Where he'd cleared away the bracken and ferns, the ground was bare. Nothing had grown there for a while. Someone had opened the door regularly. There was a rusted iron ring attached to one side of the hatch. He grabbed it and pulled. The hinges creaked in protest, but the door opened easily enough.

He'd had half an idea what to expect, and he wasn't disappointed. Inside the cellar were boxes identical to the ones he'd seen in Lew Min's storeroom. He pulled one out where he could see it more clearly. It had no lid, and inside were rows of metal tubes. He picked a couple up and gave them a shake. Empty. He checked the labels. They were all but identical to those used for the official government opium but carried the small mark of a dragon he'd seen on the boxes in Lew Min's den. Whether they had been specially manufactured or syphoned off from the official stock in the factory, he'd no idea. Nor did it matter.

Callan had been looking for an illegal packing plant large enough to package the illegal opium, but all the time it was being packed here, at the official plant, and included amongst the legal shipments.

He felt the presence before he heard it. He tried to spin round, but he was crouching and his movement was limited. He was too slow. The last thing he remembered was the sight of a figure holding a rifle by the barrel. He saw, too late, the butt end of the weapon as it carved an arc through the air. And then everything went black.

Chapter Thirty-One

S lowly, he came to. At first, it seemed pitch dark, but as he emerged from his stupor, he realised that a stream of weak moonlight was filtering through a small window in the top of the wall, casting a shadowy pallidity across the room. Sensations began to return, the first being that his cheek was next to something cold and hard. Stone, perhaps, or, more likely, concrete. As his eyes became accustomed to the moonlit gloom, he took stock of his prison. He was sprawled across a floor, his head near a door and his feet under what seemed to be some sort of table. The rest of his feelings kicked in and he realised his head hurt like hell. He lifted a hand to explore it. His fingers, when he withdrew them, were wet, wet with something grey. No, that couldn't be right. It must be blood. He sat up, and in doing so, he realised his leg was attached to the table. He reached forward. A handcuff joined his ankle to the leg of the table. He grabbed the leg. It was made of steel, like the ones Evelyn used for storing her instruments when performing post-mortem examinations. He shook it, but it didn't budge. Further examination revealed that the table leg was bolted to the floor. He shuffled around, and bracing his feet against the wall, he pushed, but the table barely moved.

He yelled. All the usual sorts of thing a person yells when they find themself incarcerated in a small, dark, concrete prison with no idea of where they are, why they are there, or how they got there. Things like '*Help!*', and '*Let me out!*', and '*Oi!*'. No one answered his cries. There was nothing to do but wait. But wait for what, he'd no idea.

He had drifted back into a half-coma when, sometime later – it could have been five minutes or five hours for all he knew – distant voices entered his conscience, echoing down what he presumed to be a corridor outside the room. Bracing his back against the wall, he beat a loud tattoo with his heels on the floor and redoubled his entreaties to be released.

Whether his efforts had had any effect, or whether his captors had intended to pay him a visit in any case was never resolved. A key turned in the lock and the door swung back. Light streamed in, and Betancourt shielded his eyes with his arm. The soldier, Reeves, entered the room. He had a fishing net slung over his arm. The *sinseh*, Loong, followed a step behind. He carried a kidney dish containing two large balls of what looked very much like opium, a pair of forceps, a syringe, and a phial of clear liquid. Suddenly, the room felt very crowded indeed.

'Don't worry, Inspector. You won't feel a thing.' Loong proceeded to fill the syringe with whatever was in the phial. He looked down at Betancourt, as though reading his thoughts. 'Thebaine,' he said. 'In low doses it's an effective pain suppressant, but not much use for anything more. But if you know how to refine it, it becomes a potent narcotic.'

'And you know how to refine it,' Betancourt said.

Loong just laughed. He finished filling the syringe. Once he injected the thebaine, Betancourt knew he'd be unconscious in a few minutes. He had to buy himself some time. After that, God knew what…

'I know everything about your operation, you know. About how you brought in the *Papaver bracteatum* and refined it. The clue was in Fulbright's blood tests. Too much thebaine. You'd been doctoring the *cacak* – making it more potent. Callan told me he was convinced the *cacak* wasn't coming in by sea or by road; I knew you had to be making it here, in Singapore. When he showed me the vans shipping the legal chandu from the plant at Telok Blangah, I knew there had to be an intermediate point where the drivers would pick up the doctored *cacak*. It was a simple matter to follow the vans until one of them took a detour. That's how I found the store along the road, down by the water. The one with the bales of opium straw in it. That's when I knew for sure how you were doing it.'

For the first time since he'd entered the room, Loong's face lost all trace of amusement. He threw Reeves an angry look. 'I told you it was too obvious. What if he's told someone?'

'Relax,' replied Reeves. 'He hasn't told anyone anything. Otherwise, there'd be a dozen police and customs vans outside right now. He's trying to scare you.'

'You're wrong,' Betancourt said. 'When I figured it all out, I wrote it up and gave my sergeant two copies, one to give to Assistant Commissioner Bonham and the other one for Superintendent Callan. They'll be here soon.'

'You're lying.' Reeves aimed a carefully placed boot at Betancourt's ribs. It connected, and Betancourt doubled over in agony. Given that Loong was just about to put him to sleep forever, that last act by Reeves was nothing other than pure cruelty.

Betancourt forced himself to straighten up. He had to keep talking or it would all be over. He'd hit one raw nerve. Maybe he could find another. It was time to play his trump card: Westaway. If he told them he knew Westaway was behind the operation, and he could convince them that Bonham and Callan know, too, it might be enough to divert their minds from killing him, even if only briefly. He was guessing, but if he made it sound convincing, he might hit a target. He took aim at Reeves first.

'You were having an affair with Ormond's daughter. She introduced you to Westaway. Westaway resigned his commission and moved to Singapore and took on a post here at the opium packing plant. But Westaway found his wife's spending habits far outstripped his civil service income and he couldn't keep up. He needed money. I'm guessing that's where Loong came in. He'd been sacked by the opium clinic for selling the patients refined thebaine. He figured that if he could get his fortified *cacak* into the Monopolies Commission supply, he'd make a fortune. He needed muscle and he remembered you.'

He stopped for breath and looked at each of the men in turn. He was surprised to find them not returning his gaze, but looking instead at each other, and not with the trapped expressions he hoped for. They looked more perplexed than afraid of being in danger of any imminent exposure.

He tried to press his point home. 'Well? Am I close?'

A laugh from outside the doorway broke the gravid silence.

'As they say in the films, Inspector, close, but no cigar.'

Vita entered the room and stood next to Reeves.

Betancourt realised with a sinking dread that he'd got it all wrong. It wasn't Westaway's scheme; he was just a stooge. The kingpin of the operation was his wife.

'They told me you were smart,' she said. 'Perhaps I should have paid them more attention. No matter, it's all over now. At least for you.'

A voice somewhere inside his head urged him to keep talking. He'd no idea how he'd be able to talk his way out of this, but neither did he have any other ideas.

'If you're going to kill me, the least you can do is tell me where I got it wrong.'

Vita studied him for a moment, like a Roman empress deciding whether to grant a condemned gladiator a last wish before signalling for the final death blow.

'All right, then,' she said eventually. 'Actually, you got a surprising amount right; it was the details that let you down. It all started in Hong Kong. You were right about that. Daddy was in charge of the whole show. He was busy playing soldiers while Mummy drank gin and entertained a string of Daddy's young courtiers. And when I say entertained, I'm not talking about bridge mornings, if you get my meaning. Michael here was in Daddy's brigade, but army life didn't suit him any better than it did me. If you think I'm bad, Michael was a real rotten apple, weren't you, darling.' She dragged a finger down Reeves's face, her nail leaving a scarlet trace. An act of sadistic affection. He didn't so much as flinch.

Michael Reeves. MR. The appointment in Fulbright's diary. He hadn't been with Molly Ridpath at all. He'd been with Reeves.

'Anyway, there I was, 'Vita continued, 'confined to base with a bunch of tedious army wives. I was bored rigid. Michael had made some interesting friends, and he introduced me to them. You wouldn't believe some of the parties we had. That's how I met Loong here. He supplied the party favours. Life became a lot more tolerable with the aid of his little creations. I was introduced to Peter by my father. He was besotted. He couldn't keep his hands off me, dirty lecher that he was. He told me he was moving to Singapore to take up the job at the opium packaging plant. The possibilities were obvious. I let Michael and Loong in on the plan, and we were in business.'

'And what about Fulbright? What did he do to deserve to die?'

She took an ebony case from her purse and lit a cigarette. She took a long draw before answering.

'Richard was a silly fool. He was digging his holes up on the hill. If I'd known, I'd have put him off somehow, but when I found out, it was too late. Then he ruined everything by telling me he loved me, and that we should run away together. He said he knew how to get his hands on some money. I made him tell me what his plan was, and when he told me, well... he had to go. Such a shame. I really liked him, you know.'

His only chance was to keep her here. He had to keep her talking.

'So what was Fulbright's plan? For the money?'

She gave a sigh of irritation. Her interest in him was clearly ebbing.

'He was surveying up at the top of the hill. He came across a cache of Loong's opium in one of the bunkers. I'll say one thing for him: he was clever. He staked out the bunker and watched the deliveries come and go. And he figured out what was going on. He planned to blackmail my husband.' She laughed, a sharp cruel laugh. 'Maybe he wasn't so clever after all.'

'Did your husband know what was going on?'

'Not at first. When he found out, there was nothing he could do without betraying me. And he was hardly likely to do that.'

She dropped her cigarette to the floor and ground it out with her toe.

'Get on with it, then.' And with that command, she swept imperiously from the room without looking back.

Reeves grabbed Betancourt and hauled him to his feet. Loong picked up the syringe and walked towards him, a cruel smile spreading across his face. Betancourt twisted left and then right, but Reeves had his arms locked in a vice-like grip. He felt a needle in his arm, and he went limp, overcome by an incongruous sense of euphoria. His final image would be that of Loong, carrying a ball of opium in the forceps, and saying 'Open wide, Inspector.'

Chapter Thirty-Two

The sound of a distant car horn pricked at his consciousness. At first, there seemed to be nothing odd about this. It was a familiar sound and, as it wasn't close, it couldn't have been honking at him, so there was no need for him to move. Kernels of thoughts, not yet fully formed enough to be memories, swam into focus before dissolving again. *A forest... A room... Darkness... A needle...*

A needle?

His eyes felt gummed together, but he forced them to open. His first complete thought was that he should be wet. He didn't know why, just that he should. But he wasn't. With a rush, other thoughts coalesced, and the events of the previous night returned in a horrifying rush. He sat up bolt upright and he was pretty sure he screamed.

A hand touched his shoulder and a soothing voice, coming from somewhere close to him, said, 'It's all right. It's all right.'

'Evelyn?'

'I'm here.'

'I'm not dead, then?'

'It would appear not. You probably deserve to be, though, going up there on your own.'

'Where am I? Why is it so dark?'

'You're in my bedroom.' Evelyn threw open the blinds, and sunlight streamed in. 'You're going to feel groggy for quite a while yet, so try to stay still. I'll bring you some coffee.'

Betancourt felt around his body. Everything that had been there before still seemed to be there. He explored the now-large lump behind his ear.

'It ought to hurt, but oddly enough, it doesn't.'

'I'm not surprised. Loong gave you enough thebaine to put you out for a very long time. You won't be feeling any pain for quite a while. You were lucky. Molly Ridpath followed you up the hill. She saw you being carried into the packaging plant. Knowing you were in trouble, she ran down to the hotel and called me.'

'Molly? I don't understand. Why did Molly call you?'

Evelyn shrugged. 'She said I was the only person she knew who she could trust to help. It was lucky for you that she did. I thought if anyone would know what to do, it was Marjorie, so I called her. She must have called Bonham, because by the time I arrived at the Sea Moon, there were half a dozen police cars. They surrounded the factory. Vita and the gang tried to make a run for it, but they didn't get far. Quek arrested them. He looked like he was enjoying himself. It was him who found you, you know. You owe him. Again. I managed to treat you before the drugs did too much damage. Another thirty minutes and who knows? You'll be feeling no pain for a while.'

'How did Quek know to send for medical help?'

'He didn't. I drove myself there and arrived at the same time.'

'Why?'

She didn't answer at first, and the room was still and quiet.

'Because… because you were in danger, and I couldn't stand the thought of anything happening to you.'

He had no answer to that, so he changed the subject.

'When can I get up?'

'You'll feel woozy for a while. You'll feel better when you've had something to eat. I'll send out for food. After you've eaten, you should be able to get up.'

He leant back onto the pillow.

'Something is bothering me. Why didn't Molly just call the police?'

'I think you'd better ask Molly that. She's expecting you.'

'It wasn't Westaway. I got that bit wrong. He found out about it of course, but it wasn't his idea.'

'So I understand. Vita. Everyone's favourite party girl. No more parties for her for quite a while, I shouldn't think. I spoke to Marjorie earlier, when you were still sleeping. It seems that man Callan from Customs got wind of what happened and there's now an almighty row going on between him and Bonham over who gets to take the credit. According to Marjorie, Bonham is winning by a short head.

The door with the postcard bearing the legend *History* in mauve ink was closed, but this time Betancourt didn't knock.

The office was in disarray. Papers were strewn everywhere. Molly Ridpath was on her hands and knees on the floor, throwing papers into boxes.

'You're here then,' she said, not looking up.

'Dr Trevose said you were expecting me.'

'Yes.' Her voice was distant, almost ethereal.

'I'm told I have you to thank for saving my life.'

She gave a small, bitter, forlorn laugh. 'Isn't life ironic, Inspector? You're here thanking me, and yet, if it hadn't been

for me, your life wouldn't have been in peril in the first place.'
She looked up at him for the first time. 'You've worked it all
out, haven't you?'

He nodded. 'I know about the opium, and I've a pretty
good idea about the rest of it, but I'd prefer to hear it from
you. Why don't we start with what you were doing following
me up the hill?'

He helped her to her feet, and she sat on the chair at her
desk, hands folded in her lap, like a penitent about to ask
forgiveness from a priest.

'It was that day in the cafe, when you showed me the map
of Bukit Chandu – the one that Richard had marked. He
really was the world's worst for recording finds. I was forever
nagging him about it. I knew that if he'd marked up the map
and kept it, he must have discovered something significant. I
had to know what he'd found. If Richard had proved his
theory about the Majapahit, then, with the work my father
had done, it would have been enough to tip the Farquhar
Prize in his favour.'

'And you couldn't have that, could you?'

She shook her head.

'What happened?'

'You wouldn't let me have the map, so I bided my time.
When you called me and said you intended to climb the hill, I
followed you.'

'But it was pitch dark.'

A small smile touched the corners of her mouth. 'It wasn't
difficult. You'd make a terrible spy. Anyway, I've always been
good at it. When I was young, I would follow my mother
around the house. It was a game. If I could follow her for five
minutes without being detected, I won. I usually won. She
said I was like a cat. I never made a sound. Her little kitten-
cat, she called me. I saw you stop and look into the bungalow.
I guessed you must have noticed something. What was it?'

'Vita and Westaway were having an argument. He looked livid. I actually thought he was going to hit her at one point. I was too far away to hear what it was about, but given what happened later, I can imagine.'

'Peter had found out about the opium?'

Betancourt nodded.

'He was such a sap. He'd do anything to keep hold of her. It was pathetic, the way he let her treat him. I saw him leave the bungalow, and by the time I reached the point where you'd stopped, she was making a phone call. She looked agitated, waving her arms about. That sort of thing. Then she left the bungalow, too, and set off down the hill towards the factory. You had already walked further up the hill, so you wouldn't have seen her. I set off after you. You were using a torch to follow the map. You really are easy to follow.' She smiled apologetically. 'At one point, I strayed off your path slightly and stood on a twig and it cracked. It was so quiet up there, it sounded like a gun going off. You turned around. I was sure you'd see me. Then you stopped and put the map away. I knew you must have reached the spot Richard had marked. Then you just disappeared. It was like the hill had swallowed you up. I was about to move closer when I saw the soldier. I wondered if I should warn you, but I knew that if I cried out, he'd know I was there, too, and I didn't have an excuse ready. Besides, I thought he was probably just on patrol. I thought he might question you, ask you what you were doing there. But, of course, he didn't.' Betancourt put a hand to the lump behind his ear. 'After he hit you, he went away and came back with another two soldiers. They stood around for a moment, like they weren't sure what to do. Then Vita turned up with that man Loong, the chemist.'

So, she knew who Loong was. Another piece of the puzzle fell into place.

'Vita told them to pick you up and take you inside. Then

she turned to Loong and said, "do the same thing as you did with Fulbright". I knew then that you were in danger, so I ran back down to the restaurant at the foot of the hill and called for help.'

'You called Dr Trevose.'

'She was the only person I knew who knew you.'

'But why not just phone the police?'

'I couldn't. You see, I killed Richard.'

Chapter Thirty-Three

'That isn't true, though, is it?'

'It might as well have been.' She looked at him, her eyes fixed, staring, as if she was trying to see inside his very soul, looking for some sort of sign that he might understand what it was she was about to say. 'My father was a good man, Inspector, he really was, but he was useless with money. God knows, he had little enough of his own – the occasional grant or a gift from a benefactor – and what he had he burned through. If it wasn't for my mother...' She trailed off, as if having decided he wouldn't understand after all, and there was little point in continuing.

'He used your mother's money to finance his expeditions?' It was more of a statement than a question. She nodded – a quick birdlike movement – as though she was nodding to herself, confirming her story before continuing. She went on as though he hadn't spoken.

'It was her inheritance. She paid for the digs. And every-thing else for that matter. She always has. Her brother is a solicitor. When she and my father married, her brother suggested she put her money into a trust. She was horrified.

283

She told him it would look as though she didn't trust my father. And she did. Completely. As far as she was concerned, they were one and what was hers was his. My uncle was not only prescient, he was also persuasive. That's how the Donald Ridpath Trust came about.'

'Did your mother know that your father had frittered away her money?'

She shook her head impatiently. 'He hadn't. Well, not all of it. When my father died, my uncle sorted out the will for probate. It was then that we discovered that my father had granted Richard power of attorney over the trust's activities. Most of the money was gone. Much of it couldn't be accounted for. It appeared Richard had just siphoned it off.' She gave a small, bitter smile and looked at Betancourt. 'I stood up for him. I said there must have been some mistake – a misunderstanding. You must think me a very great fool.'

'I don't think anything; I just need to understand what happened.'

'My uncle suggested I come out to Singapore to see if I could shed any light on what was going on. I knew things weren't great, but I still hoped I might sort it all out. Somehow recover my mother's money. When I arrived, I went through the papers. I was wrong. Richard had just about run the trust into the ground. Gambling, parties, Vita Westaway.'

'And then the prize came along.'

Her eyes lit up, as if remembering the hope that the promise of the Farquhar Prize had brought.

'There had never been a prize like it. *Five thousand pounds*. It would have saved us, my mother and me. The submission was all my father's work, but as Richard had assisted him, he'd felt it was only right and proper that Richard's name appeared alongside on the research. I wasn't even that bothered when I heard. Richard might have a small claim on some of the prize money, but the bulk of it would revert to my mother as the beneficiary of the estate.'

'What changed?'

'About a month ago, I received a telegram from my uncle. He'd received a letter from the Society. They told him Richard had withdrawn the original entry and re-entered it in his own name. It was all perfectly legal, according to the rules of the society. The paper now named Richard as the sole remaining participant in the research.'

'Why didn't you or your uncle just go to the committee and explain what had happened?'

'Because they would have just withdrawn the submission altogether and awarded the prize to Lenehan. This way, I thought I could buy myself some time to come up with a plan. I went to Richard's hotel. We had a blazing row. I tried to get him to agree that he'd hand over the money, but he just laughed in my face. I pleaded with him. I even begged him to come to some sort of arrangement.' She looked down, shame-facedly. 'I even offered myself. But what would he want with me when he had Vita Westaway? He told me to get out, so I left, but I returned later in the day. I was still furious. When I got there, the hotelier said Richard had gone out. I convinced him to let me into Richard's room. I told him we were colleagues and Richard had a document I needed urgently.'

'What were you looking for?'

'God knows. I was distraught; I wasn't thinking straight. Anything I could use that might help me recover some of the money he'd spent, I suppose. I found a journal. The stupid fool had just left it lying there on his desk. It described every-thing: names, dates, places. You name it, it was there. How he'd been surveying Bukit Chandu and stumbled across the opium operation. He must have spent days up there, watching. Then the entries stopped for a while. Whether he'd stopped watching or he'd just stopped taking notes, I've no idea. He started writing again about two weeks ago. He'd formed a plan. He'd found where they were storing the illegal opium. That's what he'd marked on the map you found. It wasn't artefacts at all. He was going to steal the opium and elope with Vita. He hadn't told her. Not then, anyway. A few days later, he'd written his final entry. He'd shared the plan with Vita, and she'd laughed at him. She'd called him a silly boy. He'd underlined it so hard he'd torn the paper. He was going to show her. He intended to bring down the operation. He'd listed the names of everyone involved: Vita, Reeves, Loong, all of them.'

'That was when he signed his death warrant. You gave the journal to Vita?'

She shook her head. 'No. I found a business card inside the journal. It belonged to the pharmacist, Loong. There was a rickshaw puller outside the hotel. I got him to take me to the address on the card. I told Loong about the journal. I told him I would hand it over if he could scare Richard off and get him to withdraw from the prize. Loong said he would take care of it.' By now, tears ran down her face. 'I only wanted him to frighten Richard. To make him see sense. He'd taken so much from us. I'd no idea what would happen. I killed him.'

She broke down completely and could say no more.

He waited until she'd composed herself again before carrying on.

'You didn't kill him. Loong and Reeves and Vita killed him. You hadn't intended any harm to come to Fulbright.'

She glanced at the boxes. 'What happens now?'

He didn't answer, and she gave a small nod and then sighed, apparently understanding that his hands were tied.

'Do you think you might give me some time to tidy things up before you arrest me?'

He studied her and then swept his eyes around the room. 'I imagine you must have quite a bit to take care of. How would it be if I gave you twenty-four hours? I'll come back here tomorrow. Would that be enough time?

She nodded dumbly and then gave a small smile. 'Thank you, Inspector Betancourt.'

When he returned to the museum on the dot of noon the following day, Mohammed was back, standing to attention by his desk. As Betancourt approached the stairway to make the now-familiar climb to the History room, the doorman called after him.

'*Mem* Ridpath. She's gone.'

'What time did she leave?'

'Early, *tuan*. About nine o'clock.'

'Did she say anything?'

'She thanked me. That was all.'

Betancourt nodded in understanding and climbed the stairs, anyway.

The room was tidier than he'd seen it before. She'd put the papers and journals in boxes, which she'd labelled and stacked on the shelves in order – research date, subject matter, author. Presumably so that anyone who came after her could make sense of the work. A scientist to the end.

Propped up against the telephone on her desk was a single sheet of quarto paper, folded in half. He unfolded it and read.

I'm sorry. I hope you won't get into any trouble on my account. I had to do it. You can see that, can't you?

He could.

He pocketed the note and left everything else as he'd found it.

Back downstairs, he enlisted Mohammed's help for what

he hoped would be one last time. 'Do you have a copy of today's *Straits Tribune?*'

'In the library, *tuan.*'

In the room where Lenehan had made his empty tribute to Fulbright and where Molly had attacked Vita Westaway, he found a copy of the newspaper and opened it at the *Comings & Goings* section. The *SS Calypso* had been due to leave for Southampton that morning.

'I need to use your phone.'

The librarian handed him the unit, and Betancourt gave the operator the number of a shipping agent named Owen, his contact at the docks. Owen confirmed the *Calypso* had sailed on the first tide that morning.

'Can you check the passenger manifest?'

'I haven't got it in front of me, but if you give me a minute, I can make a call. What name are you looking for?'

Betancourt stood in silence, watching the telephone until it rang. Owen confirmed that a Miss M Ridpath was on the list.

Chapter Thirty-Four

A few weeks later, he received a call from Evelyn.

'I'm fine. There's really no need to check up on me.'

'Who said I was checking up on you? I provide emergency services. Nothing more. You're big enough to look after yourself, now.'

'In that case, what's this about?'

'I just wanted to see you. I have something to show you.' There was a small silence. 'And something to tell you.' She sounded apprehensive. If she needed his help, then he had to give it. No question.

'Where are you?'

'At work. I've got about another hour's worth to do here. How about we meet for tea? Say, four o'clock? There's a place on the corner of Ord Street and River Valley Road. *La Pâtisserie*, it's called. French. It's all the rage, apparently.'

'I know it,' he assured her. 'Four o'clock.'

The proprietrix recognised him and treated him with more deference than she had during his previous visit. She showed them to a quiet table near the window.

'I'm impressed,' Evelyn said. 'Are you a regular?'

'Hardly. I came here once with Molly Ridpath.'

The same pinafored waitress who had served him last time deposited cakes and a pot of tea on the table, and, when she had left, Evelyn drew a brown envelope from her handbag.

'Do you read the *Times*?'

'The *Straits Times*?'

'No, the *Times* from London.'

'Of course not. Why would I?'

'Because you might learn things about the big wide world outside Singapore.'

He shrugged. 'Why would I want to do that?'

'This, for instance.' Evelyn opened the envelope, took out a newspaper clipping, and handed it to him. Wiping his hands on his trousers to remove the accumulated crumbs, he unfolded the article. It contained a photograph of Molly Ridpath, dressed in what he guessed was the latest in smart fashion, beaming out at the camera. She was holding some sort of certificate. At her shoulder, a step behind, stood another woman, older, sharing the joy of the occasion. So alike were their features, she could only have been Molly's mother. He read the caption below.

Miss Molly Ridpath with her mother, Mrs Mary Ridpath, daughter and wife respectively of the late renowned archaeologist, Dr Donald Ridpath, receiving the Farquhar Prize for Excellence in Archaeology for Dr Ridpath's work on the origins of Singapore.

He'd thought that Molly Ridpath might have kept a lower profile, but then, why should she? He wasn't sure himself exactly what crime she'd committed. If he'd been hard-pressed, he could probably have thought of something, but seeing as how, between them, Bonham, Callan, Melrose, and Garfield, the American, had drawn a discreet veil over the whole thing, there was no one pushing him for anything.

He refolded the clipping and handed it back. 'She's still a fugitive.'

'To qualify as a fugitive, don't you have to have someone pursuing you? What have you done to bring this *fugitive* to justice?'

He didn't answer.

'Exactly. Nothing. All she did was recover what was rightfully hers.'

Evelyn was probably correct, but he didn't feel like admitting it, so he gave a non-committal grunt.

They talked some more about how things would be a lot better if more women felt able to do what was the right thing for them and not for the men they followed. At least, Evelyn talked and Betancourt half-listened.

After a while, he noticed there was something about her voice that seemed different, unusual. A falsely heightened level of energy. A lack of circumspection. Evelyn, who was normally so sure of what she thought and believed that she rarely had to rely on hyperbole to make a point, seemed to be convincing herself about what she was saying, as much as trying to persuade him.

'What did you want to tell me?'

'What?'

'On the phone: you said you had something to show me. You've shown me the clipping. Then you said you had something to tell me, too.'

She fidgeted with a piece of banana cake, tearing fragments off it and dropping them onto her plate. Her eyes darted around the room, not stopping anywhere in particular, and he noticed her neck had reddened, a sure sign she was flustered.

'Evelyn?'

'It's Alistair.'

Grey had got himself into some sort of difficulty and now

Evelyn was looking for his help in untangling the mess. He forced himself to suppress a satisfied smile.

'Go on then. What has he done?'

She threw down the remains of the cake and glared. 'He's asked me to marry him. You know, be his wife, to have and to hold, happily ever after, from this day forth. That is what he's done.'

He found himself briefly speechless. Then he let out a guffaw. 'He did what? Poor chap. I almost feel sorry for him. I hope you let him down gently.'

Evelyn's eyes flashed, but she said nothing, and Betancourt was gripped with a sudden rush of numbing panic. He dropped his cup and a brown stain radiated across the tablecloth.

'For God's sake, you can't be serious?'

'Why not?' she demanded. 'He's a good man. He'd be there for me when I needed him. And what's more—' She stopped herself.

'Go on. What *is* more?'

She sat silently for a moment, and when she continued, all the anger had drained from her voice.

'I think it's time we both moved on. But you...'

He sat silent. What did she want him to say? Eventually, the words came out unbidden.

'I can't stop looking. I wouldn't know how to.'

'Ah,' she said.

And then she gathered her things and left.

Note from the author

The Betancourt Mysteries are works of fiction. I have, however, tried to represent Singapore as it was in 1940 as truthfully and realistically as I could. The street names and other place names are as accurate as my research allowed, and for that I'm grateful to OneMap, a website produced by the Singapore Land Authority, and to the National Archives of Singapore for making available their wealth of historical material. There are a few exceptions to this approach. There was no morgue named the Crypt under the Singapore River. Nor were there a Royal Edinburgh & Imperial Bank, a *Straits Tribune*, a St Seraphima's School for Girls, or an Excelsior Hotel (though there is one now, I believe).

Conversely, the characters are all products of my imagination, the only exception being a reference to René Onraet, a former Inspector-General of the Straits Settlement Police.

Glossary

Aiyah – An expression of dismay, exasperation, or surprise. (Chiefly amongst Chinese dialect speakers.)

Amok – Malay word meaning a violently raging, wild, or frenzied state. Also, as a noun: a person in such a state.

Baju melayu – traditional garment worn by Malay men, comprising a tunic with a stiff upright collar, trousers, and, typically, a contrasting skirt.

Bee hoon – fried noodle dish made from rice vermicelli with the addition of meats, seafood, vegetables, and condiments.

Bintang Emas – Malay for gold star.

Cacak – cheaper, less potent drug, made from opium adulterated with burnt sugar, lemon juice, and *jijing* (the remains of burnt opium).

Chandu – opium that has been prepared for smoking. From Malay.

Chettiars – subgroup of the Tamil community who originated from Chettinad in Tamil Nadu, India. In Singapore, they became established as bankers and financiers.

Durian – highly prized large, oval, tropical fruit with a hard skin covered in sharp points, and containing yellow, orange, or red flesh. The fruit has a distinctive, pungent smell that many find overpowering. From the Malay *duri*, meaning thorn.

Godown – sea or riverside warehouse, used for storing cargo.

Hoon – Chinese weight used to measure opium for retail sale. Equivalent to 1/10 of a chee, or 1/100 of a tahil, or 0.376 grams.

Istana – palace or other official grand residence

Jaga – watchman or guard.

Jijing – opium dross (the remains of burnt opium), used to adulterate *chandu*, and occasionally sold as a low-quality substitute for opium.

Karung guni – rag and bone collector.

Kelong – offshore platform, usually built from bamboo and wood, from which fish can be caught.

Kopi tiam – coffee shop, which may also sell simple meals.

Kratom – tropical tree (Mitragyna speciosa) native to Southeast Asia, with leaves containing compounds that can have psychotropic effects.

Long drop – simple toilet comprising a hole in the floor.

Mandore – stable foreman.

Mat salleh – colloquial Malay term for white people. Sometimes pejorative.

Mem – Malay honorific for a woman.

Monkey blood – mercurochrome: a red-coloured topical antiseptic for minor cuts and scrapes.

Pipa tsai – female singers and musicians, especially those who play the pipa – a traditional stringed instrument. Usually employed by clubs to entertain male clientele.

Roti paratha – flatbread made from flour and ghee, sold by street vendors.

Samsui women – female immigrants who came to Singapore in the early part of the twentieth century in search of work. Typically employed as general labourers in the construction industry.

Glossary

Serani – Eurasian (of people) (from the Malay approximation of *Nazarene*, meaning Christian).

Sinseh – practitioner of traditional Chinese medicine.

Songkok – brimless cap, usually made of black or embroidered felt, cotton or velvet, worn by Malay men as part of their formal dress.

Suteretsu – Japanese red-light district (pronounced *suh-tret-suh, an Amakusa dialect transliteration of the English word 'streets'*).

Syce – stable groom. Also, a driver (chauffeur).

Toddy – distilled palm wine.

Tongkang – wooden boat used to ferry cargo from ships offshore to the docks or river.

Tuan – Malay honorific for a man.

Vibhuti – sacred ash made of burnt dried wood, burnt cow dung, and/or cremated bodies.

Acknowledgments

My heartfelt thanks to everyone who has helped and supported me during the writing of *Chasing the Dragon*. In particular, thank you to:

My agent, Euan Thorneycroft, and all the team at AM Heath for their support and encouragement.

My publishers, Rebecca Collins and Adrian Hobart, at Hobeck Books for believing in the book and for delivering it into the world.

Sue Davison, editor extraordinaire, for spotting everything I missed. I don't know how you do it.

Jem Butcher, for another superb cover design.

My brilliant beta readers, Lori Sheirich and Roe Lane, for your inspired suggestions. This book would have been all the poorer without you.

Jeff Leong and Marcus Ng of the Singapore History Group for helping me locate the exact site of the former opium preparation plant at Telok Blangah (the now-empty plot next to Marang Road, near the Harbourfront MRT station, in case you're wondering.)

Fellow writers and Waffle Press-ers, Natalie Marlow, Denise Beardon, and the above-mentioned Roe for their unconditional support (not to mention the many laughs along the way).

My wife, Lillian, for her eagle-eyed proof-reading, but most of all for her love, support, and encouragement.

Finally, the island nation of Singapore – you are a never-ending source of entrancing stories.

Waking the Tiger

Shortlisted for a Crime Writers' Association John Creasey (New Blood) Dagger 2022.
Finalist for the Ngaio Marsh Awards Best First Novel 2022.
Longlisted for the Bloody Scotland McIlvanney Prize for Scottish Crime Book of the Year 2021 and shortlisted for the Scottish Crime Debut of the Year 2021.

'Intricately plotted, thoroughly authentic and in Betancourt, a world-weary but witty and appealing protagonist, Waking the Tiger is a wonderfully accomplished debut. I felt transported back to the Singapore of the 1940s and I can't wait for the next one. Wightman is a writer we can expect great things of.'
Abir Mukherjee

'A splendidly evoked 1930s Singapore, a determined and engaging detective and a dark and twisting tale - *Waking the Tiger* is historical crime fiction at its best.' **William Ryan, author of the Captain Korolev series and winner of Guardian Novel of the Year**

Mark Wightman's *Waking the Tiger* was the winner of the Pitch Perfect event at the Bloody Scotland Crime Festival in 2017. Mark was also selected to be one of the seventeen UNESCO City of Literature Story Shop emerging writers at the 2017 Edinburgh International Book Festival.

A young Japanese woman is found dead on the dockside, her throat slashed

Inspector Maximo Betancourt is working a new beat, one he didn't ask for. Following the disappearance of his wife, his life and career have fallen apart.

A distinctive tiger tattoo is the only clue to her identity

Once a rising star of Singapore CID, Betancourt has been relegated to the Marine Division, with tedious dockyard disputes and goods inspections among his new duties.

Who is she? And why are the authorities turning a blind eye?

But when a beautiful, unidentified Japanese woman is found murdered in the shadow of a warehouse owned by one of Singapore's most powerful families, Betancourt defies orders and pursues those responsible. What he discovers will bring him into conflict with powerful enemies, and force him to face his personal demons.

About the Author

Mark Wightman was born in Edinburgh before growing up in the Far East, first in Hong Kong and then in Singapore.

His debut novel was *Waking the Tiger*, which was shortlisted for the Crime Writers' Association John Creasey (New Blood) Dagger, the Ngaio Marsh Awards Best First Novel, and the Scottish Crime Debut of the Year. It was also longlisted for the McIlvanney Prize for Scottish Crime Book of the Year.

Chasing the Dragon is his second novel.

To find out more about Mark and his writing please visit his website or follow him on social media:

Website: www.markwightmanauthor.com

Facebook: www.facebook.com/mark.wightman.18

Twitter: @mark_wightman

Hobeck Books - the home of great stories

Hobeck Books is an independent publisher of crime, thrillers and suspense fiction and we have one aim – to bring you the books you want to read.

For more details about our books, our authors, including Mark Wightman and our plans, plus the chance to download free novellas, sign up for our newsletter at **www.hobeck.net**.

You can also find us on Twitter **@hobeckbooks** or on Facebook **www.facebook.com/hobeckbooks10**.

Hobeck Books also presents a weekly podcast, the Hobcast, where founders Adrian Hobart and Rebecca Collins discuss all things book related, key issues from each week, including the ups and downs of running a creative business. Each episode includes an interview with one of the people who make Hobeck possible: the editors, the authors, the cover designers. These are the people who help Hobeck bring great stories to life. Without them, Hobeck wouldn't exist. The Hobcast can be listened to from all the usual platforms but it can also be found on the Hobeck website: **www.hobeck. net/hobcast**.

Finally, if you enjoyed this book, please also leave a review on the site you bought it from and spread the word. Reviews are hugely important to writers and they help other readers also.